It's a Long Way to Oregon

THE WESTWARD SAGA OF
THE KEIZUR (KEIZER) FAMILY

An Historical Novel by

JERRY MᶜGEE

ESJAY PRESS
KEIZER, OREGON

CREDITS AND ACKNOWLEDGMENTS

Evelyn Hoxsey—cover painting

Norma Benson—Editor/technical advisor

Ron Sacchi—back cover photo

James Taylor—technical advisor

Esjay Press
1030 Ridgepoint Street NE
Keizer, Oregon

ISBN10: 0-9672772-4-8
ISBN13: 978-0-9672772-4-0

Book design and layout by Gorham Printing

Printed in 12pt. Garamond

DEDICATED TO

My sister Norma McGee Benson
In appreciation for her support and encouragement

Follow the Keizurs West

1 Thomas and Mary Keizur born on the same day in 1793 in N. Carolina
2 Married 1813
3 Left N. Carolina for Tennessee 1827
4 Left Tennessee for Arkansas 1833
5 Left Arkansas for Missouri 1842
6 Left Independence, Missouri for Oregon May 18, 1843
7 Kansas River crossing
8 First child born on what was to become The Oregon Trail. Reeda Keizur Ford gave birth to a son (Tilman Ford) June 5,1843
9 Division of the Oregon Emigration Co. into two divisions, i.e. The Cow Column and The Light Column. The Keizurs were part of the Cow Column led by Jesse Applegate June 9
10 Forced march to the Platte River June 17
11 Buffalo country
12 Banishment of Kenny O'Regan June 24
13 South Fork crossing July 1
14 Dr. Marcus Whitman arrives
15 Cathedral Rock (Court House Rock)
16 Scott's Bluff
17 Fort Laramie
18 First death July 17 (Joel Hembree six years old)
19 Willow Springs
20 South Pass August 8
21 Pacific Springs (where the water runs west)August 11
22 Fort Bridger August 14
23 Fort Hall August 27
24 The California Cutoff
25 Snake River Three Island crossing September 12
26 Fort Boise September 18
27 Dr. Whitman leaves the Column October 2
28 Blue Mountain crossing October 3-8
29 Whitman Mission October 11
30 The Columbia River
31 The Dalles October 25
32 Fort Vancouver October 30
33 Oregon City November 6
34 Willamette River
35 Keizur Bottoms-Keizur Rapids November 15
36 The end of the trail

INTRODUCTION

There is the impression that the stories of the emigrants over the Oregon Trail begin at Independence or Westport, Missouri. Independence was the most popular "jump-off" site, however, most of the emigrants had already traveled many miles just to get to Independence. They came from the Ohio Valley, Indiana, Illinois, and even from Europe. Missouri and Arkansas were probably the greatest contributors.

The family, on which this story is based, actually started their journey in North Carolina in 1827. They traveled over 900 miles by wagon and foot before they ever got to their jump-off destination of Independence, Missouri, by 1843. Once at Independence they began an additional march of 2,000 miles to reach their destination of Oregon. They traveled over what was to be known as the Oregon Trail.

Many of the pioneers kept diaries or "logs". Most of these written accounts started as they left Independence, thus giving the impression that their stories began there. Women kept most of the written records. The exception was the emigrant train of 1843. For some unexplained reason, no diary has ever surfaced written by a woman in the 1843 emigration. This is just one of many, of those little bits of trivia, that makes this story unique. However, James Nesmith, a young man in the "Great Migration" of 1843, left a detailed account from his perspective, much to the delight of modern day researchers.

Every soul that traversed this treacherous route was courageous. No one has ever refuted that. However, they were not all saints or heroes. There were scam artists, deserters, murderers, and ne'er do wells, all in their midst.

However, the vast majority were truly heroes. They came from all walks of life, but most of them had an agricultural background i.e. farmers.

The wagon train of 1843 is of special interest, since it was the largest ever, and the first to take wagons all the way to Oregon. For over half the distance they had no trail to follow. Many of the now famous landmarks along the trail had not, as yet, been named. Naming the landmarks remained for later pioneers. So in reality, the wagon train of 1843 did not go over the "Oregon Trail". There *was* no Oregon Trail. They blazed the Oregon Trail for tens of thousands to follow.

It is also important to remember that the so-called Oregon Territory, was not as yet part of the United States. This vast area was under a nervous joint occupancy agreement between England and the United States. Both countries had a legal claim to Oregon, at least from their perspective. The American claim was based on the "right of discovery", by virtue of the American sea Captain Robert Gray who discovered the Columbia River, and claiming the river "and all it drains", for America. In addition, we had treaties and purchases from Spain and France.

England also claimed, "the right of discovery", based on the explorations of sea Captains George Vancouver, Sir Francis Drake, and others. England also had a treaty with Russia, but, "the right of occupancy", usually makes the stronger case. In other words, who had the most folks in the area of question. In this regard, England had the much stronger claim. The Hudson's Bay Company, a British fur monopoly, controlled all this vast area with their string of forts, outposts, and stations.

Americans had made several attempts to get a piece of the fur trade, with the efforts of the Astorians and others, but in every case, the Hudson's Bay Company either bought them out, or scared the Americans off with tough trading practices. The British case for "occupancy" far exceeded that of the United States.

But the young nation of the United States, barely 50 years old, had several things going for it. First, they had two very determined U.S. Senators, i.e. Linn and Benton, working very hard to pass a free land program.

The Donation Land Act would grant public land to pioneers willing to go to Oregon to settle. If successful, this plan would counter England's numeric superiority. In other words, America would have more boots on the ground.

In addition, the general population and the emigrants specifically, were passionately patriotic. Many really did believe in the concept of "Manifest Destiny", that is to say, that America had a destiny ordained by God, to span the continent "from sea to shining sea", and nothing could stop them. Presidential candidate James K. Polk campaigned on the slogan, "54 forty or fight", making reference to a willingness to go to war for all of the Oregon Territory, plus some.

What England did not know was that President Polk did not care that much, one way or the other, about the Oregon Territory. It was Texas he wanted. Polk certainly did not want a two front war, with Mexico on the south and west, and England on the west and north.

And what the American leaders did not know was that England was not interested in going to war over Oregon either. England had its hands full, with war clouds gathering over Europe. And besides, the fur trade, which was the economic attraction for England, was in its final years. Silk from China had replaced beaver from Oregon. The fashionable men of London, New York, and Paris, were buying silk top hats, not beaver top hats. Consequently, Oregon had gone down in value in the minds of English politicians.

Neither nation really wanted a war over Oregon. So, a treaty was rather quickly struck with the 49th parallel set as the border. To put this all in perspective, it may be interesting to note of what the Oregon Territory consisted. The borders of the Oregon Territory were generally thought to range from the crest of "the great Stony Mountains" (The Rockies) to the east, to the shores of the Pacific Ocean on the west, and from Spanish America on the south (the border of the present states of California and Oregon) to the southern tip of the Queen Charlotte Islands on the north. This is a lot of real estate.

This then is the backdrop, as the "Great Emigration" of 1843, crossed the stage of American history.

CONTENTS

CHAPTER 1

Early Years in North Carolina

I was born in Cabarrus County, North Carolina November, 1793. I was the youngest of eight children born to George and Mary Kiser. They named me, Thomas Dove Keizur. My middle name was my mother's maiden name.

In 1764 my grandfather Peter bought 101 acres of land that extended on both sides of Rocky River in Mecklenburg County in the Province of North Carolina. He paid ten pounds and two shillings for his land. I really have no idea, how much ten pounds represented in American currency. He bought his land from Arthur Dobbs, Captain General, Governor Commander In Chief, in and over, the Province of North Carolina. You will note that this was over a decade before the American Revolution, which separated us from the Crown of England. Grandfather Peter Kiser resented the four shillings per 100 acres, that the King of England taxed him. For this, and other reasons, he was a rabid supporter of the Revolution.

We are Germans. Our family emigrated to the new world from Alsace-Lorraine, which at that time, and up until 1789, was part of Germany. In 1789, France overran the area. Grandpa Peter could read and write German and French and had a passing ability to speak English. However, on deeds and other legal papers, he signed with just a "*P.*"

I am not sure how Grandpa Kiser got to Mecklenburg County. The name Mecklenburg may have attracted him. He knew there would be other stout and honest German settlers there. After all, Mecklenburg was a well-known German state on the Baltic Sea in northern Germany. And indeed, he found such familiar family names, as the Letringers, Clingermans, Misenhimers, and Neusmans, already farming there.

And speaking of names, I am sure you have observed, that the spelling of our family name was changed. My grandfather spelled his last name Kiser, my father changed it to Kisor, and sometimes to Kyser. When I was born they spelled my name Keizur. I am not sure why it was changed so many times, but I always thought it was their attempt to Americanize the name. After all Kaiser, means King, or ruler, to Germans, and that didn't set well with old flag-waving Peter. I have seen the name spelled fifteen, (yes, fifteen) different ways. On one property deed that I signed as a witness, the name was spelled four different ways. But to me, it is Keizur, and Keizur it will remain.

Over time, my grandfather and my father, added other pieces of land to their Rocky River holdings. One such purchase, of sixty acres, included one-fourth interest in a gold and silver mine.

I was about eight years old when my Grandfather Peter died. His will caused quite a stir. It was the Old World custom, for the oldest son to inherit all the land. In some cases, other sons would get a token amount, but the widow and any daughters received nothing.

So, no one would have been surprised, if my Uncle Peter had inherited all the land, since he was not only the oldest son, but also grandpa's namesake. However, Grandfather's will stated that his widow was to receive one third of the "moveable estate, including Grandmother Fanning's spinning wheel." The land was to be divided into eight equal parcels, and deeded to his three sons and five daughters. He thought that was the American way, "Share and share alike".

And, there were other provisions that really got people's attention. His will freed the four slaves he owned. That was not too unique. It was not uncommon to free loyal and faithful slaves on the death of the master, but grandpa went even further. He willed each slave five acres of land that ran contiguous. In other words he gave a block of twenty acres to the four freed slaves .He was quoted as saying, "To be 'free' without land, is not free at all." There were "wags" who, said, "The slaves were old. They wouldn't bring much at auction anyway." That may have been true, but it did not explain his gift of the land.

As it turned out, my Uncle Peter was neither surprised nor disappointed in his father's will. He had fully discussed the will with my dying Grandfather. At first, some of the siblings thought that my grandmother should have received some of the land. But it had already been established, that she was to live the rest of her life with my Uncle Peter and his family.

Uncle Peter had already divided the land into eight parcels, as equal and practical as possible, using tributaries of the Rocky River as natural dividing borders. He numbered the pieces of land and put eight numbers in a hat for each sibling to draw.

The intended consequence of my grandfather's will was to bring his family closer together, rather than torn apart, which is so often the case where there is an estate involved.

My first fifteen years was as a carefree farm boy. I hunted and rode my horse for miles over the rugged Rocky River terrain. I was intimate with every tributary to the Rocky River.

On one of these horseback rides, I crossed over onto the George Gorman farm, following the track of a deer. As I came out of the ring of trees and brush that surrounded one of the Gorman cotton patches, I heard a commotion. One of the Gorman boys was whipping a Negro buck with his horsewhip. The slave had fallen to the ground but Gorman continued to whip him. I had no idea, of what infraction the slave was guilty, but Gorman was going to whip him to death. Long slash marks were oozing blood across the Black's bare back. An owner certainly had the right to discipline a slave, but it was obvious to me that Gorman was going too far.

The Gorman boy was so intent on the whipping, that he did not hear me, until I had galloped directly up to him. Gorman paused, and then raised the whip to deliver yet another blow to the defenseless Negro.

"If you lay that whip on one more time, I will put a bullet in your knee," I declared.

"You are interfering with my God given responsibilities," Gorman said, "You better mind your own business."

"If you hit that Boy one more time, you will limp the rest of your mean life," and I lowered my gun to within eight inches of his right knee.

Gorman violently spurred his horse and shouted, "You have just made a bad mistake. You haven't heard the last of this." And he galloped away spurring his horse at every stride.

I extended my hand to the bleeding Negro, and pulled him up behind me. I headed at once for the river, which was only about a quarter of a mile away. I sat him down on a rock where he could put his bare feet in the cold water. Gorman's horse had stepped on one of his feet, and I suspected the bones were crushed. I swabbed his bleeding back with my wet neckerchief. He never said a word or flinched, as I washed the rips in his skin, although the pain must have been extreme.

"Can you get home from here?" I asked. He nodded that he could.

"What is your name?" I asked.

"Bob, Suh. My name is Bob."

That was all the words he spoke.

"Well, Bob, you better hightail it for home, and have your mammy put some bag balm on those cuts."

I left him then soaking his injured foot in the cold river water. Our paths would cross again as I will detail later.

I learned to milk at about the age of ten. Up until that time Mom did the milking. She hated it. Milking was the only thing I can remember my mother complaining about.

She refused to teach my older sisters, Polly and Ester, how to milk. She reasoned, that no future husband could insist that they milk the cows, if they could honestly say they didn't know how.

Our cow was an old Guernsey that we called Molly Moo Cow. Molly's third calf was a little heifer that my Dad gave me to raise. I called her Penny. Penny was the beginning of a small herd of cattle that I eventually raised.

The only thing about my cows that I didn't like was taking them to my Uncle Fredrick's place, when the cows came in heat. Uncle Fredrick had a fine bull. I didn't mind the walk of three miles to get there and it was no problem leading the cows to the bull, but coming back home, was always a task. My cows were too sociable, I think. They always wanted to linger awhile.

I saw Mary Girley for the first time, at the Rocky River church. It was an all day trip to go to church, and my family only went from May to October, and not every Sunday even then. But I liked to go when the weather was nice. We all wore our shoes and our special shirts that we saved for special days, such as funerals and weddings.

After church everyone gathered in the oak grove for a community dinner, before we all headed back to our own farms. I saw Mary. I didn't talk to her, but I was totally smitten by her. She was the prettiest girl I had ever seen.

The next time I saw her was again after church. It was the second Sunday in June. Mrs. Girley had made a huge strawberry shortcake in honor of her daughter's fifteenth birthday. As I passed by Mary, who was serving the shortcake, I said, "Happy birthday, Miss Girley."

"This isn't really my actual birthday, but thank you, Thomas."

How she knew my name, I couldn't imagine.

"My birthday was actually in November," she said, "November 19 to be exact."

"That is my birthday too. I was born November 19, 1793," I said.

"And so was I," Mary said. "We are exactly the same age. Isn't that a wonder?"

"Then why are you having a birthday party in June?" I asked.

"You can't have strawberry shortcake in November."

I was holding up the shortcake line, so we couldn't talk more at that time, but later when we chose up sides to play, "pump-pump pull away", Mary was chosen as a captain, because it was her birthday party. And she selected me as her first choice to be on her team. I ran from base to base like a deer. No one could catch me and we eventually won the game.

Several months later at a basket social, I was about to be outbid for Mary's basket by Old Man Spikerman. I only had seventy-five cents then Mrs. Girley, Mary's mother, slipped me a silver dollar. I suppose that was the beginning of our courtship. We were married November 13, 1813. We moved into a 20 foot by 20 foot log cabin that my brothers helped me build, on a 100 acre tract that my father had inherited on Cribbs Creek. This union was destined to last for 40 years and ended only when Mary passed away in 1853 at the age of sixty.

As a wedding gift to her new husband, Mary presented me with a pair of socks. She had picked the cotton, spun the yarn, and knitted the socks herself. I wore these same socks on very special occasions. As the family moved westward, the socks went westward also. My sons, a grandson, and a great grandson, all wore the same socks on the occasion of their respective weddings. (The socks are now part of the Oregon Historical Society's collection-catalog number 1462)

Our first child, Mary Louise, was born on President Washington's birthday, February 22, 1817. About a year later, Sarah Lucinda was born. Matilda Caroline was born in 1821 and our first son, John Brooks, was born in 1824, followed a year later with our fourth daughter, Beede Ann.

Gold was discovered by chance, in Cabarrus County in 1799. It was discovered on the farm of John Reed, a local farmer. Reed had been a Hessian soldier, and one of many who received a land grant, by virtue of their laying down their arms and deserting the British Army in the Revolutionary War.

In 1799, Reed found a large nugget in a canyon on his farm. He did not recognize it for what it was and used it as a doorstop for three years, until someone identified the heavy rock as *gold*. Farmer Reed's doorstop was a seventeen pound gold nugget.

Within a short time, other nuggets weighing as much as 28 pounds each, were found on the Reed farm. Eventually more than ten million dollars in gold was taken from the Reed property alone. Ten million is a lot of wealth any time, but in 1799 it would really get your attention.

Soon, gold was discovered in Anson, Burke, Mecklenburg, and other North Carolina Counties. By 1839 all the gold mined in the United States was mined in North Carolina. All the gold coins minted at the New Philadelphia mint were minted with North Carolina gold.

A local newspaper touted North Carolina as the "Golden State", because of the great lumps of precious metal found there.

In the beginning it was strictly placer mining, not hard rock mining. Gold had been deposited in the canyons and gulches for untold centuries by flash floods cutting gold embedded in white quartz in the nearby hills. All that was really needed to find gold was a shovel and running water and hard work. A gold pan wasn't even necessary, but they were used. At first, farmers picked through the gravel by hand in the many creeks. Many nuggets were found in freshly plowed fields after rainstorms. "Long Toms", or sluice boxes, were soon developed. But, the effort to obtain gold soon became too labor intensive for the white gentry, and slaves were brought in from the cotton fields. The corn, wheat, and cotton fields, soon lay fallow, without the slaves to work and harvest the crops.

Gold was found on some Keizur land. In fact my father, George Kiser developed two mine sites, but no gold was found on my land. I looked some, but as I told Mary, "I'm a farmer. I want to raise corn, and grain, and raise cattle, and breed fine horses, but not cotton. Cotton takes slaves, and we can't afford slaves."

"We can't afford slaves, and we shouldn't have them for other reasons," Mary said.

"The only reason I would mine seriously would be to buy more land to work," I said. But, buying more land to expand our farm was totally out of the question, because the land speculation caused by the gold rush placed land beyond our reach. The flourmill had closed and all the workers from the mill were at the creeks. Without the mill, we had no way to grind our wheat and corn. Agriculture was no longer the main endeavor in the County, and we were becoming disenchanted.

I had discussed with Mary going west to Tennessee. Land was being opened, as a result of the Indians being forced to move further west, after the treaty with the Chickasaws in 1805, which was over twenty years ago.

"Uncle Fredrick went to Tennessee three years ago, and he hasn't come back. Maybe its time for us to go west too," I mused.

"How soon can we go?" Mary asked. "Perhaps we could look up your uncle Fredrick when we get to Tennessee."

"When we get the crops in, we will talk about Tennessee," I promised.

It all came to a head in late September of 1827. I had taken a wagon full of fine wheat, all sacked and tied, to the gristmill to have the wheat ground into flour. I would sell most of the flour to the mill, keeping some for our own use. I left at daybreak for the nine mile trip to the gristmill. When I got there, a sign on the mill said, "CLOSED". I inquired about the next mill, which was another ten miles away. The information I received did nothing to assure me, that it was still open.

I got home at dusk. Mary and all the children came racing out to greet me and to examine the sacks of flour. "The mill has closed. They have diverted the water to a sluice box up in the canyon," I explained to a bewildered family. "I sold the wheat to Mr. Schnedly for hog food."

"Hog food? Oh Thomas, all your beautiful wheat? What did it bring?"

"$3.50 and that's not the end of it, Mary. Why would we shuck the corn? It will never be ground into meal for us to sell. There is no reason to pick the corn. I will turn the cattle into the corn field in the morning."

"How far is Tennessee?" Mary asked. "Let's go to Tennessee as soon as possible. If we leave soon our next child will be born in Tennessee."

"Mary, I can't feed our five children now. This is not the time to be thinking about another baby," I admonished.

"It's a little late, Mr. Keizur to debate the matter." Mary smiled.

"Mary, Mary, if you're with child again, you can't go to Tennessee in a bouncing, jerking wagon."

"Then I guess I will walk, if you walk with me. How far did you say it is to Tennessee?"

"I have no idea," I replied.

"Then we need to be finding that out, Thomas. Children, we are going west to Tennessee."

The next week was spent packing and repacking our wagon. "All I need to take is the children's clothing, our blankets, my spinning wheel, and a few cooking utensils, and the family Bible, of course," Mary said.

"We will take a half a sack of seed potatoes, a sack of seed corn, and the new plow. We can tie a shovel and axe to the side of the wagon," I added.

"If there is room in the wagon, Thomas, I would sorely like to take some remembrance of our little home on the Rocky," Mary said.

"What did you have in mind? A remembrance is good, since it is not likely we will ever return."

"I would like to take five cuttings of my pretty little pink rose bush."

"I see no problem with that. What can a rose cutting weigh? But why five cuttings?"

"One for each of our children," Mary explained.

"We should go to the Rocky River church this Sunday to say good bye to our friends and neighbors," Mary said.

"Will you have an auction?" a neighbor asked.

"What little we own would not make a good auction," I said. "We will give most of it away except for the pigs and chickens. We would like to sell them." I replied.

"What about your land? You border me on the west," another neighbor asked.

"Are you interested?"

"I could be, but I don't talk business on the Sabbath. I'll ride over on Wednesday and we can talk."

It was a quiet wagon ride home on a warm September evening. The children may not have realized it, but we did, that we would probably never see these good friends again. No one mentioned that. All the neighbors talked and acted like they would see us the next Sunday.

But the events of this day were far from over.

As we turned into our lane and started up the knoll to our cabin a huge black man stepped out of the shadows and stood in the middle of the lane. I handed the reins to Mary and told her to wait in the wagon. As I started to slide down from the wagon to the ground the black man limped over to my side of the wagon.

"Do you remember me, Suh? Aus Bob. They's call me Big Bob. Aus don't mean you no harm. Aus jest wants to talk."

"I do remember you, Bob, you belong to Mr. Gorman, I believe."

"Yaz Suh. And that's what Ize wants to talk about. Ifn you can spare the time".

"Mary, take the children to the cabin. Perhaps Bob will help me put the team and wagon away, and we need to get some hay down for the team, and water them. Are you alone Bob?"

"Oh yaz, Suh. There ain't nobody knows Ize here."

"Bob, this is my wife, Mary and these are my children. Children, this is, Mr. Bob."

Bob removed a dirty felt hat and bowed from his waist nearly to the ground. "Yaz Suh, Yaz Suh."

"Shall I put a pot of tea on the table? You will have tea with us, Mr. Bob?" Mary asked.

"Oh no, M'm. Ize shouldn't do that."

"Nonsense, there will be candlelight inside and I like to see the face of the person I'm talking with," I said.

Big Bob sat on the very edge of his chair with his hat still grasped in his hands.

"Now what is it you want to talk to me about?" I asked.

Bob turned to Mary; "Your man saved my life once. Ize do believe young Master Gorman would have beaten me to death. As it was my foot never healed right. Oh, was Master George mad."

"Because his son beat you within an inch of your life?" Mary asked.

"Oh, no Missus. That was no never mind, but he now had a gimpy slave. I lost value."

"Go on with your story," I said.

"Well, Suh, Master George is dying that's for sure. My Missus is his house girl and she heard them going over Old Master George's will. Young Gorman gets most all including us slaves. Near the end of the will he talks about me right out. Myrna, that's my Missus, memorized each word. Now I have it set in my memory."

"What does the will say?"

"It sez, 'if my Negro Bob does not appear to be a faithful and dutiful slave, I order my Executor to hire him out for such a certain term as they shall see cause, and if he appears to be a dutiful Boy, he may return to his family, but should he appear the least bit unruly, I order that he be sold to the most severe master, not less than 200 miles from this place'. It goes on, but that's the part about me. Suh, you knows, as does Ize knows that Ize a dead Nigger. But what's to become of my Missus and my little ones?"

"You have children?" Mary asked.

"My Missus has bore me three beautiful young'uns and one is a fine strapping young Buck. They's all know the Lord, and they's can say the Lord's Prayer, every word." This brought a broad smile of pride to the otherwise somber Bob.

Mary turned away so that the moisture swelling in her eyes would not be seen.

"Bob, I can't believe that you walked eight miles just to recite Gorman's will, as repugnant as it may be. What is on your mind?"

"No, Suh, I didn't come to tell you that. To put it right out. Ize come to ask you if you could see your way to buy me, before Old Master George dies."

"You want me to buy you? I have never owned a slave. I guess we have never been big enough to own slaves."

"Or small enough," Mary interrupted.

"Anyway, we have very little cash, and what I do have and hope to get out of the sale of our land, we will need when we get to Tennessee. Even if I wanted to buy you, which I'm not saying I do, I couldn't afford you even if you are sold cheap, because of your bad foot. I can see your predicament, but I have no money to buy a slave I can't afford, nor need. I just can't help you, Bob, I am so sorry."

"Ize knows you can't afford no slave, but ifins Ize gave you the money would you buy me?"

"Money? Do you have money?" I asked incredulously.

"Gold! Ize got gold!" With that he reached into a pocket of his bib overalls and produced a leather pouch. Bob untied the drawstrings and dumped the contents on to the kitchen table. In the shimmering candlelight, shone well over a hundred gold nuggets, each about the size of a marble.

"This is stolen gold. No slave has this sort of wealth," I declared.

"Ize picked them all up my own self. Ize picked them up only where the Master never looked, and only after he tells us to 'hurry up and move on'. Ize don't feel the Master owns all the deer, or all the trout, or all the gold. Ize don't rightly feel I stole it."

"But how did you manage to get away with this? I've been down in the ravines where the slaves have been shoveling gravel. I know they strip you in the morning and give you bib overalls to work in, and then recover the overalls at night before the slaves return to their shacks. And I know they beat slaves who high grade gold."

"Beat? No one has tried to do any high grading, since they hung Thomas Jefferson Brown last year. We all had to watch him hang," Bob said.

"Then how did you smuggle this much gold out?" I wanted to know.

"I swallered it. One or two nuggets at a time. Then my missus separated the nuggets from my droppings the next day."

Mary who had been counting and holding up each nugget suddenly dropped her hands to her apron and wiped them.

"You have taken a severe risk in showing us this gold," I said.

"Suh, how much risk should a man take for his family? Suh, I'm not talking freedom here, Ize talking about being rid of oppression."

"Why not talk about freedom?" Mary interrupted. "Thomas, you know how I feel about slavery. Take this man's gold, stolen or not, buy him and his family, and give them their freedom. Gorman will get his gold back when you pay for Bob and we won't keep a pebble of it. Your Grandfather Peter signed the 'freeman's papers' for his slaves, but he said that a man without land is never really free. So, sell Bob some land. We could sell him this cabin and a little land. Then they would truly be free."

"Whoa, Mary. One step at a time. I want to sell this place to our good neighbors. He may want the cabin and he may not buy the rest of the land if a free Black is his neighbor."

"Try it, Thomas! The Lord will guide you."

This conversation had been ensuing between Mary and me, as if Big Bob wasn't in the room. But as he began to comprehend the meaning of what he was hearing, he dropped to his knees and began to weep uncontrollably. Mary knelt by his side, also weeping, and put her arm around the big Black man's shoulders.

I walked out into the bright September moonlight with a feeling of great spirituality, such as I had never experienced before.

After awhile Bob came out of the cabin. "Ize got to go. Ize don't run fast no more and Ize gots to be back by daybreak. We go to the ravines before daylight and if Ize missing, there will be a heap of trouble."

I glanced at the position of the moon. "You will never make the eight miles by daybreak. Take our mare. Turn her loose when you get to the top of the last ridge. Spank her on the butt and she will come home."

Mary was in bed when I came in, but I knew she was not asleep.

"Our departure may be delayed a few days," I whispered. "I have some business to attend to."

"Our travel west will go just fine for us. Wherever we go in this great land, we can walk in freedom. We may fail, or we may succeed, but we are free. Isn't that why our grandfathers fought in the war? I am very proud of you, Thomas."

"Let's get some sleep. The morning will come too soon, and there is much to do, and I'm proud of you too."

CHAPTER 2

Leaving North Carolina

"Mr. Gorman, my name is…"

"I know who you are. You're one of George Kiser's Boys. Never liked George much. What can I do for you?"

"Dad doesn't like you much either. I'm going to Tennessee. I hope to start a stud farm, and I want to buy a slave or two, if you can spare any."

"I just bought four more at auction. Very expensive, I might add."

"Well, I don't have time to go to the auction and anyway, I don't want your best Buck. I have noticed one who works in the ravines. Seems kind of slow. He has a gimp foot or something. But he would be all right to exercise the brood mares and things like that. Do you know the Black I mean?"

"Certainly, that would be Big Bob. But that foot is nothing. He's my best Boy. Very docile and faithful. Some of these slaves are unruly and hard to handle, but Bob has had all the steam taken out of him. I would have to get top dollar for a slave like that."

"How much is 'top dollar'?"

"Oh, I would need two hundred in Philadelphia dollars. I won't take paper notes, only hard money."

Just then Myrna, Bob's wife, entered the room with a dust cloth. "Is she a house girl?" I asked.

"Very good one too."

"My wife is expecting our sixth child and she will need help. Throw her in, and I will pay the two hundred dollars. If her teeth are sound." I added.

"Come here, Girl. This gentleman needs to see your teeth. She is solid. Go ahead and feel her."

I walked over to where Myrna was standing in the doorway. I whispered to her, "Just endure this a little longer, Myrna." She nodded, that she understood. I ran my fingers over the back of her teeth and peered into her mouth. I turned her around and felt her buttock then pinched the calves of her legs.

"She seems solid enough," I reported. "Does she eat much?"

"Just left-overs. Oh, another thing, she has some pickaninnies, take them too."

"No, I don't need to buy any distractions. How many are we talking about?"

"I don't know, but I know she has one Buck Nigger. It is hard to say if he will live to manhood or not, but if he does, you could get some return for your money."

"The problem with that is, a person may have to feed him for several years, before he is worth anything. I can't pay that kind of money for a gimp field hand, and a house girl, with God knows how many kids. But I have $190 dollars in hard currency with me right now, if you will throw in the whole sad lot of them, and if you can draw up a bill of sale today, before I have time to change my mind, I will take them all. I will send a wagon over for them and their belongings in the morning. Can you have them ready?"

"There better not be much in the way of belongings, but they will be ready to go."

Mary drove the wagon over to the Gormans the next day to gather up our new holdings. Big Bob, Myrna, and the three little children sat downcast with sad expressions on their faces pretending they hated to leave. They waved slowly to some old black ladies as we passed. But as

27

the wagon crested the last ridge that put the Gorman farm out of sight, Bob and his little family, popped out of the wagon and started hopping around in circles in total jubilation.

We sold most of our land to Nathan Green our neighbor to the east, who happens to be my brother-in-law. Nathan and my older sister Polly were married fifteen years ago and so selling them the land was keeping it in the family. The land he bought was on the west side of Rocky River. It consisted of approximately 230 acres. We sold it for $805, five hundred now, and the rest to come later.

We sold the land bordering Cribbs Creek, a tributary to Rocky River, to Asa Traywick , for $75. It was about 100 acres that Mary had inherited. This left twenty acres lying on the east side of Rocky River. The border between this tract and the Green property was the mid line of the river. Our little cabin was on this piece of land. I offered this land to Bob for $200, which was top dollar, but it did have the cabin. This left Bob with about $500 in gold. Nathan Green said it did not matter to him to have a Free Black as a neighbor, as long as he didn't go hunting beyond the Rocky River Ridge.

All deeds, quit claims, and other papers, were notarized and filed, at the Cabarrus County Court House. The papers making Bob and Myrna "freemen" said, "Bob and Myrna Gorman and all their issue". Bob and Myrna made their marks, since neither could write.

We learned much later that Bob and Myrna had many more children, all becoming well-known citizens in the region. Their second son was named Thomas Keizur Gorman, and became a lawyer. Another son became a minister of sorts.

When we finally pulled out for Tennessee a light mist was falling and a hint of fall was in the air. We were all in a good mood, and yet a bit sad, as we headed northwest toward Statesville. We rode silently for hours. We had said our goodbyes to our parents and siblings the night before. The older girls knew full well, that they would never see their cousins again, but the hardest for them was hugging their grandparents for the last time, and, as was often the case, we never saw our people again. We learned many years later that my father had included me in his will. It said, "Share and share alike, assuming son, Thomas Dove, is still alive."

From Statesville we went southwest about one hundred miles to the Asheville area, and then down the eastside of the Great Smoky Mountains to Ducktown, and from there to Chattanooga, and finally to north of Lookout Mountain to Pulaski, Tennessee, the County seat of Giles County. This was a total of about 375 miles, we estimated. The only difficult leg of the trip was down the Great Smokies where the trail was little used. We made the journey in 32 days and that was with laying over in Ducktown for two days and not traveling on Sundays. We didn't know it then, but this journey from North Carolina to Tennessee, was the first of several moves that would better prepare us for a more dramatic move that would take us to a place called Oregon.

Tennessee was somewhat of a disappointment to us. The choice land had already been occupied and the price of available land was beyond our means. Therefore, we leased land to begin our stud farm. We arrived in Tennessee with a fine team of Morgans, two mares and a good stud horse. We also brought our old friend Molly Moo Cow and her latest offspring, a fine heifer, and two very protective wolf hounds. Our cash resources were $1,180 in Philadelphia dollars.

Our second son, Pleasant Cicero Keizur, was born in 1828, in Giles County, Tennessee. Francis Marion, our third son, and seventh child, was also born in Tennessee, in 1830. Pleasant, was always the brunt of friendly jokes, due to his mother naming him "Pleasant". "Pleasant" was the popular name given to boys, for a short while during these years, and Mary just liked the sound.

We were beginning to have some reservations about Tennessee and when the landlord doubled the price of our lease, we knew we would be moving on. But we signed the lease for another three years. We did quite well in buying broken down horses from settlers coming west. We would rehabilitate the horses by resting and feeding them, and then sell them to people headed further west or down to Texas. One of the keys to our success was in matching teams up, and spending the time to train them to work together. The economy was generally poor, and no one had cash for stud fees, so we often traded stud fees for more cattle. But our stud services did not materialize like we had hoped.

There was a general uneasiness throughout the land, primarily over the question of slavery. The neighbor to our west was an abolitionist, to the point of being a zealot, and our neighbor on our east owned slaves. There was always friction in the air. Fourteen years earlier a law had been passed called the "Missouri Compromise". At that time, there were eleven slave states and eleven "free" states. Maine wanted to join the Union and everyone knew that Maine would come in as a "free" state. This would give the abolitionists of the north two more Senators and at least one more Representative, upsetting the voting balance in Congress. The compromise was to bring Missouri in as a state at the same time, only it would be a slave state. Thus the balance was maintained, which meant that nothing would be done regarding the slave issues. Missouri was admitted to the Union in 1821 as the 24th star in our beloved flag.

Mary and I tried to stay aloof of the slavery question. We could not afford slaves and we didn't like the concept too much anyway. Mary had much stronger views on the subject than I. She was very close to being an abolitionist.

I joined the new political party called Democrats. I did so primarily because our own Andy Jackson had been nominated for president. Andy was from Tennessee, and that was a good enough reason to support him as a nominee as our sixth president. General Andy Jackson came into national prominence several years earlier for his victory at the Battle of New Orleans, where Jackson with his Tennessee Volunteers and Kentucky long rifles, along with a few pirates, defeated a major British army. On the strength of this event, Jackson was elected senator from Tennessee. We learned later that the treaty ending the war of 1812, between Britain and the United States, had been signed two weeks before the Battle of New

Orleans, making the battle unnecessary. You would think by listening to men talk, that everyone in Tennessee had served with Jackson.

Andy didn't win the presidency in 1825. Some fellow by the name of John Q. Adams won.

The election had ended in a tie, so the House of Representatives selected the president. Andy was out maneuvered and lost the tie. However, four years later he did win the presidency and was inaugurated in 1829. However, Andy started putting on heirs once he got to Washington and another Tennessean caught our imagination. His name was Davy Crockett.

The frontier produced a number of legendary figures, but none more popular than Davy Crockett. Crockett was a member of the Whig party, which was in opposition to Jackson. I switched to the Whig party in 1833, to support Davy Crockett.

CHAPTER 3

Mary Louise

Up to this point, this has been a story related by my Dad, Thomas Dove Keizur, known to his friends simply as TD. But now it is my turn to add my perspective, as a small girl saw the events of the time.

I am the first born of Mary and Thomas Keizur. I was named Mary Louise after my mother. I was born on President Washington's birthday in 1817, in our North Carolina cabin on Rocky River. I think being born on February 22 is what influenced me to be so patriotic.

I was ten years old when we left North Carolina to try to find my great uncle Fredrick, who had gone to Tennessee. The year was 1827.

I remember walking for miles day after day, but my folks say I rode in the wagon with my two sisters Sarah Lucinda and Matilda Caroline and my brother John Brooks and the baby Beede Ann.

We were on the trail from late summer until early fall, but the weather was fine for the most part. According to Dad, we covered 375 miles in a little over a month. Dad did not push our team of Morgans and gave them plenty of time to graze grass. We saw only two riders between Asheville and Ducktown. They camped with us one night. The men talked politics around the campfire and mother let us children listen. They felt that the Abolitionists were stirring up trouble with the Blacks, and there was bound to be more slave revolts. That evening was the first time I had heard the term "Manifest Destiny".

When our guests carefully explained this term, I was greatly pleased to know that God was on the side of America, and that our nation had a destiny to expand from ocean to ocean.

The young men rode with us as we skirted the Great Smokies, which was the most difficult stretch of the trail. They were headed west, perhaps going as far as St. Louis, Missouri. They knew they would have adventure and make a fortune in the west.

I was sorry to see them go. It was as if we had known them forever.

We settled outside of Pulaski raising horses and cattle. I became my father's "helper". I went with him to the auctions and saw his skill at picking out animals of good breeding, but ones that were just run down. He explained his auction strategy to me: "You never lose money by dropping out early, only by staying in too long."

My father taught me to ride like a man, none of this side-saddle lady style, but like a man. He taught me how to swing an axe, and how to pull, "don't push", on a two man cross-cut saw, and he taught me how to shoot.

I saw how other men sought his advice, and I was proud that he was considered a leader. One Sunday at a Whig rally in Pulaski, our Tennessee hero, Indian fighter and frontiersman, Davy Crockett, was the speaker. He was introduced as "half horse and half alligator". My father stood up and shouted, "Half horse, half alligator with a touch of snapping turtle". This brought the house down. Davy from that day on introduced himself as "half horse, half alligator" then he would pause and say, "with a touch of snapping turtle".

The thing my dad admired about Davy was his straight talk. When he was sent to Washington, D.C., he still wore his fringed buckskin clothes. He never tried to be something he was not. Whereas, Andrew Jackson tried to be more sophisticated and dressed like a New York lawyer, Davy was a backwoodsman and proud of it.

As everyone knows Davy went south to Texas, although Dad had talked to him about going to the far west instead. Davy was one of the 200

Texans who died to the man, at the Alamo. The Alamo gave the Texans their battle cry, but it also delayed General Antonio Lopez de Santa Anna and his army of 3,000, long enough for General Sam Houston to form his army to defeat Santa Anna.

We had already moved to Arkansas in 1836, at the time of the Alamo. My father wept like a baby at the word of Davy Crockett's death. Dad was already thinking Oregon at this early date, and he often wondered aloud, "What would have been the outcome of history had Davy gone west instead of south". Most of the horses we sold were going to Texas.

We had been in Tennessee for six years and I could tell my Dad was losing interest in leasing land for our horse raising business. With my mother's full support, the decision was made to migrate another 275 miles west to the Little Rock, Arkansas area in Van Buren County. Arkansas was not a state yet, but we knew it would be a state someday and if we could obtain land at a reasonable price, it would go up in value once statehood was achieved. And again, the rumor was that land was still cheap in Arkansas.

Our family now consisted of seven children, four girls and three boys and mother was pregnant with her eighth. At the time we left Tennessee for Arkansas, I was seventeen years old; Sarah Lucinda was sixteen; Matilda Caroline was thirteen; John Brooks ten; Beede Ann was nine; Pleasant Cicero was six; and Francis Marion was only four.

We pulled two wagons, and drove 43 horses and three cows out of Tennessee to Jacksonville, Arkansas. The first 100 miles took us to Bolivar, then 75 miles to Memphis, where we crossed the Missippippi River by flat boat. It took us three days to complete the crossing. We then turned southwest 100 miles to Jacksonville, which is just east of Little Rock, Arkansas.

Dad drove one team and Mother drove the other. In the back of Mother's wagon wrapped in burlap, were eight pink rose cuttings, one for each of us children.

My job was to herd the livestock. My job was very important, but easy because we had good grass and water, plus I had the good fortune of having our faithful "bell mare". The herd followed the bell mare without hesitation. The bell around the mare's neck had a clear tinkling sound that seemed to say, "Follow me". The mare produced different bell sounds by various motions of her head. I loved this little horse.

Sarah Lucinda had the more difficult job, I believe. She had to ride herd over our other five siblings. John Brooks was ten now, and was milking one cow. Dad milked the other two. It just took John Brooks too long to milk more than one cow. We never called John by his first name only. It was always "John Brooks". Some of his friends thought "Brooks" was his last name.

The total trip of 275 miles took us a month, although we were on the trail only twenty-four days. But with the three days crossing the Missippippi River, and a three-day layover near Bolivar while we waited out a major storm, it was a full month for the trip.

Jacksonville had a one-room school, which was only three miles from our new ranch, which Dad leased. I was too old to start school, but all the other children down to Pleasant, attended from November to March. The school Master was Mr. McCabe. Mr. McCabe had lost his right leg below the knee at the battle of San Jancinto. He had been an officer under General Sam Houston, but had returned to his home in Arkansas after his injury.

Mr. McCabe stayed with different families in the area as partial payment for his services as a teacher. The month that he stayed with our family was a highlight of the year. All my siblings were on their best behavior for that month and I always thought we ate a little better that month.

For some reason, Mr. McCabe became attracted to me and asked my father if he could "call" on me. Dad gave his permission. Dad loved to talk politics with Mr. McCabe and I always thought this was why he so willingly granted Mr. McCabe the privilege of "calling". I was flattered and wondered if this meant I didn't have to call him Mr., anymore.

Mr. McCabe rode his skinny horse to our ranch nearly every Sunday. He came early for dinner and stayed late for supper. He taught me to read, and always had time to play games with the children, and to talk politics with Dad. He had obtained excerpts from the Lewis and Clark Journals, which he read to the entire family holding my Dad and Mother spellbound.

One Sunday evening, he asked me if I would consider being his wife. I was eighteen and I knew I should already be married, but I really had no romantic inclination for Mr. McCabe. I told him, "While I admire you greatly as the gentleman you are, I am not ready to marry."

"Is it because of my leg?" he asked.

"In all honesty, that may be part of it," I replied.

"Thank you for being so candid. In time, you would probably overlook that, but I do appreciate your honesty."

Mr. McCabe left within a few days for Texas where, as we learned later, he was elected to the new Republic's Legislature.

In the meantime I became attracted to a young man five years my senior by the name of Joseph Hess. Joe Hess raced horses and worked at his father's still. He had the reputation as being a hard-drinking roughneck, but he did know horses. No one could see what I saw in him. My folks were polite, but not pleased, I could tell.

We were married October 22, 1836, in Van Buren County, Arkansas. Our first child, a boy was born in 1837. We named him Tillman. We had our second child Mary, named after my mother and me, in 1839. And then in 1840, less than a year later, we had Sarah, named after my sister. Virginia arrived in 1842, and our second son was born in 1843. We named him William Harrison. William was born just before we left to go to Oregon. I had eight more children after we reached Oregon for a total of 13, but this is getting way ahead of our story. And for now I will turn the story back to my Dad.

CHAPTER 4

Further West

By 1838 we had survived four years in Arkansas, but barely. Inflation was rampant across the nation. The "panic" began two years earlier, in May of 1837, with all the major banks folding in New York and other eastern states. It was the first total collapse of the financial institutions in the young nation. The panic spread rapidly westward. Hard currency was in short supply, and what few Philadelphia dollars appeared, was quickly hoarded. Land speculation in Arkansas was rampant. We knew that once Arkansas came into the Union, prices for land would skyrocket, but we were not prepared in June, 1836, for land to triple and then triple again in the asking prices. Arkansas became the 25th state in June of 1836.

I was still a member of the Whig Party and supported William Henry Harrison for President. Harrison may have won it, except for the splitting of the party by Daniel Webster, representing the North, and Hugh White representing the Southern wing of the party. Little Martin Van Buren was elected president.

The political division between North and South was becoming quite rigid. We had hoped that our Vice Presidential candidate had sufficient votes for a victory. But for the first time, and I believe only time, the Senate had to choose the Vice President and they chose Richard M. Johnson of Kentucky, whoever he was.

To some extent the farmers were able to survive the severe economic times because they had crops with which to barter. But it became apparent to Mary and me that we would never be able to buy our own piece of land, and leasing land as we were doing was a downward spiral to eventual ruin. Although we hung on for four more difficult years, we knew we would be moving again. Texas was an option, but we were not excited about taking the family south to a lawless land. There was always the concern about the issue of slavery, which many of us felt would be settled only by warfare, or possibly by a slave revolt, such as had occurred in North Carolina.

Mary and I were each 45 years old. If we were still in out teens Texas would be a possibility, but not for middle-aged farmer and horse trader with nine children, and incredibly, Mary was pregnant with our tenth child. Texas was not a good option for the Keizurs.

By mid July the hay was all cut and shocked and our twenty acres of corn was doing fine. The corn was six feet high and was beginning to tassel. The corn crop was very important to us. It would provide meal for our bread, forage for the cattle and feed to fatten the hogs, and if there was any surplus, which I was certain there would be, the local stills would buy any corn that was available. Thus corn was an important cash crop. There were four stills locally including the Hess still operated by Joe Hess and his father. In brief, we needed a good corn crop to make it another year and it looked like we would have it.

Gabriel McGee, known to us as "Old Gabe", lived by himself about two miles away. Gabe often hired out to us for a few days of work. On those occasions he ate with us and slept over in the barn. He said he would work for nothing just to have a piece of Mary's apple pie. Gabe liked the children and kept them entertained for hours with his tales of the Santa Fe Trail, and of his years as a Mountain Man in the fur trade. He had been as far west as Fort Hall on the Snake River.

This July morning Gabe came riding down our lane. He always rode erect in the saddle, but this morning he was even more rigid, and he wore a uniform, but there was something else. Besides his Kentucky long rifle, he wore a holstered new revolver. I had been aware of Colt's invention for several years, but I had never seen a Colt revolver.

"Gabe, have you joined the Federal Army? You look absolutely dashing in that uniform," Mary exclaimed.

"Not exactly, Ma'am," Gabe replied. "I will explain all of this a little later. Thomas, do you have time to harness up the buggy and drive you and Mary over to your corn field?"

"I suppose, but why?" I asked. "I was just over there three days ago."

"If you can spare the time, I think you and Mary should go take a look," Gabe said.

I admit he had my curiosity up, and it was only a twenty-minute ride from our ranch house to the cornfield. "We will meet you there," I said.

As we breasted the knoll, overlooking our cornfield, a sight unfolded for which we were unprepared. The corn stalks were flattened to the ground, or they were not there at all. I was dumbfounded. Someone had removed the fence rails and had driven a herd of cattle and horses into our cornfield. Mary gasped, "The corn crop is ruined. Who would do such a thing?"

Someone had turned a sizable herd into our field to graze on the tender corn stalks, and what had not been eaten, had been trampled into the ground.

"If someone needed fodder for their cattle, why didn't they cut three or four rows and take it. We would gladly give some to a needy group of emigrants migrating through. But by turning their herd into the field, the cattle trampled more than they ate," I lamented.

"Can we replant?" Mary asked.

"It's too late in the year. The corn would never mature if, in fact, the seeds germinated at all," Gabe offered.

"To make matters worse we will not have seed for next year. I had planned to save seed from this year's crop. Now we will have to buy more seed for next year," I said.

Gabe had remained silent while this disaster sunk in.

"I will say again, who would have done this to my family? And why?" Mary cried.

"There appears to be about forty to fifty in this group," Gabe observed. "Some of them may have been your neighbors. They are Mormons."

"Mormons? Who the hell are Mormons?" I demanded.

"Mormonism is a new religion," Mary explained. "It is a Christian sect. The ladies were talking about them after church last Sunday."

"Well, what they have done to my cornfield is not very Christian like," I pointed out.

"Let me explain their thinking as best I can, as told to me by my friends in Missouri," Gabe volunteered.

"The misdirection of these people, seems to have arisen from their practicing certain 'rules of action'. The basis of these 'rules', is the assumption that they are the 'Saints' to whom the Lord promised the 'inheritance of the earth'; and as such, they feel they have the right to take possession of whatever they may desire. Any means are justified to restore to them, 'The Children of God', what God has ordained is rightfully theirs. They refer to your crops and cattle and land as the 'Lord's store'. So you see in their eyes they are not stealing your corn. How can you steal something that is already yours?"

"It *is* stealing! They are taking the food from my children. They are taking our livelihood," I stammered.

"Not through their eyes, is all I'm saying," Gabe explained. "However, I must say in all their cases the 'Saints' showed a kind regard for the happiness of you who are not so understanding of their faith. They have avoided exciting the ungodly, by not allowing themselves to be seen in the act. In order for peace to reign as long as possible they do their 'restoring', at night.

"There are bands of such believers going through Arkansas and Missouri on their way to gather at a new city called 'Far West'. There they have laid out grounds for their new temple and 'The Lord's Store' and they plan a permanent establishment of their community. They first located near Independence, Missouri but they found the Missourians there to be quite 'obnoxious', and so they crossed the Missouri River and founded this new town of Far West."

Mary interrupted, "I left two apple pies cooling on the kitchen counter. I made them with the finest gravenstein apples in Arkansas. Come back to the house and explain your fancy uniform. I know your story, whatever it is, will hold the children spellbound."

"Mrs. Keizur, I have much work to do this week, but I am never so pressed, that I wouldn't have time to eat a piece of your pie."

Somewhere between the first and second piece of apple pie, Gabe said, "It would be rude of me not to ask for seconds". The boys clamored to have Gabe explain his uniform. John Brooks was twelve and Pleasant, ten. Just the right age to hear another story about fighting the Comanche on the Santa Fe Trail.

"I have been commissioned at the rank of Captain by the Adjutant General of the Missouri Militia. He rode with me on the Santa Fe Trail. The Governor of the state of Missouri has called out the Militia to drive the Mormons out of their new city of Far West and out of the state. I have been authorized to raise a platoon of Arkansawers to join them."

"Does this mean bloodshed?" Mary asked.

"It could. But our orders of engagement do not call for aggressive action yet. The platoon of Arkansawers is to bracket the bands as they move through Arkansas. We are not to engage them in Arkansas. There are some technical reasons for this, something about the Missouri Militia being in Arkansas, sort of dilemma. We are to warn the farmers to watch their cattle and crops, but we are to let the 'Saints' know we are watching, but we are to fire only to defend ourselves. I rode over here today to ask you to join me."

"I'm not a soldier, I'm a farmer, and while I can't condone the actions of these people, I don't believe it to be a capital offense," I said.

"Neither do I. This is America, a man can believe what he wants to and go peacefully in that belief, wherever he wants, but there are hot heads and vigilante groups that are forming. We are needed to protect the farmers and their crops, and just as importantly, we will be needed to protect the women and children of the Mormons, from the farmers. I need clear thinking leaders who the younger men will follow and listen to. That is why I am recruiting you. You are a recognized leader of men."

"How long would Thomas be gone?" Mary inquired.

"It is an enlistment for three months. So, you would be back for the fall harvesting, not that you have much left to harvest." Gabe said.

At this point Mary, not Thomas, made the decision. "Thomas, you must go, it's your duty. We will be all right until you get back."

"It is settled then. I will ride with you, Gabe. I believe it *is* my duty. Is there anything else I should know?"

"You haven't asked about the pay."

"I never thought there would be pay for doing your duty," I declared.

"On being mustered out, you will get $20 dollars in gold coin and ten dollars in script. The script is probably worthless, but you will be allowed to keep your Militia side arm, which is a Colt .44, and you will be given 20 rounds of ammunition. Bring a second saddle horse, a blanket, your long rifle, and a week's supply of grub.

"We leave at four in the morning from the Jacksonville square. Oh, yes, your son-in-law, Joe Hess has signed up. He is bringing your daughter and their family to stay here at the ranch for the duration. In fact they are not too far behind me."

"That is good," Mary said.

"Oh, another thing. We have absolutely no authority until we reach the Missouri line. You will be sworn in to the Missouri Militia there and given a uniform."

"Didn't I hear someplace that soldiers captured out of uniform are shot as spies?" I jokingly asked.

"Something like that I guess. I must be going. I will see you in the morning. There will be no sleep for me tonight. I will be looking forward to another piece of pie in October, Mrs. Keizur." With a tip of his hat to

Mary he was off down the lane with John Brooks and Pleasant running after him, until he broke into a trot and left the boys behind.

We caught up with the Mormon Band after two hard days of riding. Gabe sent me in to their camp unarmed and under a white flag. I explained our two purposes i.e. to prevent their destruction of any property and to protect them from any aggression against them by residents of the area. They instructed me to, "Tell your Captain we don't need his protection. The Tribe of Dan is our protector against whatever you call 'laws.'"

The Prophet Joe recruited a military wing of the Mormon faithful, which he called The Tribe of Dan. We knew it would be these men we would face in case of combat. In fact, the Mormons had already dubbed their adventure as the "Mormon War."

When the Arkansas men took their oath to the Missouri Militia, Gabe McGee was promoted to the rank of Colonel by "executive order", but the men elected the other ranks. They elected me as their Captain.

The Governor of Missouri ordered the State Militia, "To fight and subdue the Mormons at Far West, and to take from them the property, which the Tribe of Dan had deposited in their brick storehouse."

Acting on that order, we surrounded this "citadel of Zion" and demanded their surrender. However, we were informed that the Prophet Joe had revealed to him that a great "Angelic Host" would appear on the day of the battle and would give power and victory to the Saints. Believing that they were invulnerable, the Mormons threw up a weak breastwork made of one-inch pine planks around their camp. One-inch pine planks would be no match for our six-pounder. Colonel Gabe repeatedly called for their peaceful surrender. Each time we were rebuffed.

Once again Colonel Gabe McGee called on me as his chief negotiator and asked me to try one more time to bring the issue to a peaceful solution. This time I took four troopers with me and we retained our side arms. They would not let me parley with the Prophet Joe Smith, but I explained that the attack would begin at noon the next day. Our artillery, which consisted of six and ten pounders, would demolish their flimsy breastwork and many women and children would be in harms way. I suggested to them, that if the Tribe of Dan wanted a fight, they would have one; but we were willing to give the women and children safe passage out of the camp. Otherwise many would be killed or injured, because a cannon ball cannot discriminate warrior from non-warrior. If they resisted, they would be subdued by cannon barrage followed by a bayonet charge. If however, they surrendered, they would be allowed to leave Missouri unmolested, but the stores in their brick warehouse could not be removed, because the stores were stolen property.

They had from that hour (10:AM), until noon the next day to decide. I insisted that they set their watches exactly with mine so that there would be no confusion. Their reply was immediate. "The Tribe of Dan will accept the Militia's unconditional surrender if the Militia surrenders at once, but once the heavenly host arrives it would be in God's hands and accepting your surrender then may not be possible."

"Are you seriously asking the Missouri Militia to lay down its arms?" I inquired.

"Yes, and to do it at once."

"I will inform our Commander of your demands," I said and whirled in a trot.

Gabe considered that the "heavenly host" they were expecting might be in the form of more units of the Tribe of Dan, which our scouts had reported were massing across the Missouri River only three miles away. "If we are not watchful we could sustain a charge to our rear," Gabe mused.

Colonel Gabe ordered me to take fifty mounted troopers with two six pounders and two teams of artillerymen and establish a rear guard on the bluffs overlooking the most likely fording site on the river. My orders were specifically, "to fire into their boats as they approached mid stream and to send runners back at the first sign of a mass crossing."

We were dug in on the heights by midnight and carefully spaced to avoid any concentration of their fire. The artillery teams carefully estimated the range. We noted huge bonfires on the opposite shore, but no attempt was made to cross over. I reasoned that, if a fording were to be attempted, they would do so at first light. We also knew that we had been scouted and our strength was probably known. I sent Joe Hess, who I had taken with me, to report that we were in position. Joe left at 2:AM.

So, I did not actually witness the surrender of Far West, which occurred about ten the next morning. If the story as told and retold, is true, it was indeed a bizarre ending to the so-called "Mormon War".

As told to us, a sturdy Missourian growing impatient with all this "Arm funteral" approached the brick storehouse with a pickaxe in hand, determined, "to lay a blow on it." A "sister" dressed in a long white robe came forward, and made it known that, "The Lord of the faithful has revealed to the Prophet Joseph, that every hand raised against the holy structure will instantly wither away."

The Missourian hesitated but replied, "Well, Ol Gal, I'll go it on me one hand anyhow." The blow was struck, and lo and behold the hand did not wither away. "I doubles up now," the Missourian announced, and with both hands, delivered a heavy blow upon a corner brick crumbling it to dust. The entire building quickly fell under the blows of many vigorous arms swinging pick axes.

The confidence of the "Saints" in their Prophet waned and surrender followed without a shot fired.

The Colonel took a few principal leaders into custody, but true to his word the main body was permitted to leave to go to their next new home of Quincy, Illinois.

The Arkansas Boys were mustered out the next week. Since we had only served five weeks, rather than the three months' enlistment period, the Governor paid each man ten dollars in gold and twenty dollars in script, which was just the opposite of what he had promised. But we did get to keep our Colt Revolvers and forty rounds. We didn't complain. Some of the Boys did some target shooting and used up some of their ammunition, but Joe Hess and I had all forty rounds remaining.

I was anxious to see Mary and the children so Joe and I left almost at once for home. Gabe did not come home with us. "I didn't leave anything in Arkansas. I was never meant to be a farmer anyway," he explained.

"Will you be staying in the St.Louis area?" I asked.

"No, I think I will head further west to Independence. I have some friends there to look up from my days on the Santa Fe Trail. If you ever get to Independence, look me up."

"I will do that," I promised. "It has been a good experience serving under you."

We shook hands all around, and Joe and I headed south. I kept my militia tunic and my Captain bars to show the boys. My time in the Missouri Militia was a good experience as it turned out. I learned a great deal that would be useful in our future adventures.

CHAPTER 5

Trail to Missouri

The family was glad to see Joe and I, and we were glad to be home. Joe and I told and retold the stories we had heard and things we had experienced. But the stories kept coming back to a place called Oregon. Everyone was talking about the possibility of free land and brewing trouble with Great Britain over this vast region.

I had purchased a little reading track for twenty-five cents. A Bostonian schoolteacher named Hall Kelley wrote it. It seems that Mr. Kelley had organized a group called The American Society for Encouraging the Settlement of the Oregon Territory. The title was longer than the book. But the pamphlet described the region in glowing terms. He said in the little book, "Oregon is brimming with salmon, beaver, timber, and with farmlands so rich that the production of vegetables, grain and cattle will require comparatively but little labor."

It made for exciting reading, but Hall Kelley lost a great deal of credibility with the Keizurs by writing, "Even the trip from Boston to the Pacific Coast would be no more taxing than a pleasant summer outing. The settlers would move overland in comfortable wagons…" He went on to say, "Congress would underwrite most of the expenses, and the costs would be negligible—ranging from $50 for adults to $5 for children under two."

"Comfortable wagons? A comfortable wagon has never been invented," Mary laughed. "He is talking to a family who has migrated from North Carolina to Tennessee to Arkansas in wagons. Comfortable? My eye."

"They say that this Hall Kelley fellow, invented the classroom blackboard. Perhaps, he should concentrate more on being a school teacher," I commented. In spite of our skepticism over his flowery descriptions, we read and reread Hall Kelley's booklet.

A far more compelling story circulated among the Protestant churches from St. Louis to Boston, and even to our little church in Arkansas.

The story was first printed in an 1833 issue of *The Christian Advocate and Journal* and was repeated from every Methodist pulpit in the land. The story told of four Indian chiefs, three Nez Perce, and one Flathead, who were sent by their tribes to bring back the white man's book showing the true mode of worshipping the Great Spirit. As they called it, "the book of directions."

The Nez Perce remembered, "the red haired chief," William Clark, of Lewis and Clark fame, and sought him out in St. Louis where Clark had become the Superintendent of Indian Affairs. Tragically, two of the Indians died from starvation and exhaustion almost upon arrival in St. Louis. Soon after, the third Chief died and the fourth died on a Missouri River boat, while trying to return to his people.

Obviously, all four were "Martyrs in pursuit of the True God." Since the four noble Indians were willing to travel over 3,000 miles in search of the Bible, the very least the devout of Arkansas could do was to continue to give a little money for the likes of such great evangelist missionaries as Jason Lee and his nephew Daniel Lee and to Dr. Marcus Whitman and his beautiful wife, Narcissa.

At least these missionaries had actually been to Oregon, unlike Hall Kelley who had only dreamed of Oregon. Jason Lee led his party to Oregon in 1834, and established a mission on the banks of a river called Willamette. Every minister seemed to pronounce this river differently. Lee spelled it out phonetically in one of his many letters to the east. He said the river is pronounced, "Wil-lam- met." It is easy enough to say, if you don't think how it is spelled.

Lee's many letters and appeals to the Mission Board to send reinforcements to "this land of bounty" was answered by thirteen men, women, and children, who sailed around the Horn arriving in 1837. The letters describing Oregon in glowing terms was the general topic of discussion in many farm homes, as it certainly was in the Keizur home.

"What do you make of this land called Oregon?" I asked Mary.

"I think, *it's a long way to Oregon.*"

In 1836, a young medical doctor by the name of Marcus Whitman took his new bride, Narcissa and traveled as far as Fort Hall by wagon, converted to a cart, proving that a white woman, a pregnant one at that, could travel overland to Oregon, and proving that a wagon could go a great part of the way. "What do you think of that?" I asked Mary.

She replied, "I think, *it's a long way to Oregon.*"

Narcissa Whitman wrote long interesting letters to her mother who published many of them. So the nation was becoming well acquainted with the Whitmans. On Narcissa's 29th birthday, March 14, 1837, she gave birth to Alice Clarissa Whitman, perhaps the first white child born in the Oregon Territory. The entire newspaper reading public on the eastern seaboard rejoiced, even though the news took six months in arriving and even longer to reach St. Louis, Independence, and Jacksonville, Arkansas.

The sad news of little Alice drowning in the Walla Walla River, when she was barely two years old, stunned the nation.

The entire congregation of our little church wept, as the preacher offered a prayer for the soul of little Alice Whitman.

Beede Ann wondered aloud, why Narcissa always referred to Marcus Whitman as "my husband" rather than by his name. In her letters, Narcissa would say, "my husband did this," or "my husband did that," but never Marcus, did this or that.

"It sounds so strange to me," Beede said.

But strange or not, America rejoiced at their victories and cried at their losses. Everyone was talking about, and thinking of Oregon, and many called this "The Oregon fever."

In early 1843, Thomas J. Farnham published his account of his journey to the Willamette Valley, Oregon Territory. Farnham was hired by Horace Greeley, the great newspaper publisher, to make a trip to Oregon, and, "relate his experiences to those interested in moving west."

And the Keizurs were indeed interested. Exactly when we made our decision to go to Oregon, it is hard to say. It was not done by a vote of the family, or any specific decision point in time. But from 1840 on, we knew we were going.

So, it was in April,1842 we started for Oregon. Our goal was to join the Dr. Elijah White Party that was to leave Independence, Missouri in the middle of May. We knew of the Birdwell/Bartleson Party that left in 1841, but they were California bound and we were going to Oregon. From what we had heard, we felt that the Birdwell party was too small, although they had hired Tom Fitzpatrick as their pilot. Fitzpatrick was a well-known mountain man and an experienced guide.

The White Party was expected to have over a hundred immigrants in it, which would provide safety in numbers, and they were definitely Oregon bound.

The Keizur Party consisted of Mary and me of course, and Mary Louise and her family consisting of her husband, Joe Hess and their four children Tillman, Mary Jane, Sarah E., and Virginia with their ages from one to five, and Mary Louise was expecting their fifth child.

Sarah Lucinda, our second daughter, had married Levi Corzine at the age of sixteen. Levi died suddenly just before their first child was born in 1841. So their little daughter named Mary Ann never knew her father. When Levi died so suddenly Sarah Lucinda and little Mary Ann moved in with us. So it was natural they would go to Oregon with us. Mary Ann was not yet three, when we left for Independence.

Our next girl is Matilda Caroline. She also married at sixteen. She married a good farm boy named Samuel Penter. Samuel was seven years her senior. They had one boy Thomas, named after me, who was four, when we started for Independence.

Our first son, John Brooks, would be nineteen in December and he was full-grown.

Beede Ann married John Ford at the age of seventeen in June of 1842, less than a year before we were to leave. Beede was pregnant with their first child at the time we left for Independence. Beede's husband had an older brother, named Nimrod Ford, and he was a welcomed addition to our Party.

Pleasant, our second son, was about fifteen and nearly full-grown. Francis, our third son, was thirteen and was usually a lot of help. Elizabeth Jane, was only eight and our fourth son and tenth child, was William Henry Harrison, only four.

So all together, there were twenty-three souls in our Party and we were expecting our twenty-fourth and twenty-fifth. To be more correct, Beede and Matilda Caroline were doing the "expecting."

There were no bands playing or flags waving when we pulled out for Independence. Our goodbyes were much easier for us, compared to when we left North Carolina. The Ford boys and Joe Hess had families they were leaving behind. In Joe's case his "goodbye" to his father only served to delay a batch of moonshine coming off the still. Joe never got along well with his father and neither shed any tears at their parting.

But saying goodbye for John and Nimrod Ford was very difficult. Their parents were not young and the boys were their only children. Everyone realistically knew they would never see each other again. Mrs. Ford kept a stiff upper lip but their father wept.

Mr. And Mrs. Ford were soon to be grandparents for the first time, but they knew they would never see their grandchild. The Ford boys promised to send them word when we had all reached Oregon safely. But, *it's a long way to Oregon.*

So, we pulled out of Jacksonville under threatening skies. We were pulling four wagons and a buggy, all loaded to the gunnels. Mary Louise took over driving the herd of loose cattle and extra horses, just as she had done when we left Tennessee. She was actually elated to be back riding a horse and was glad to turn her brood over to her sister, Sarah Lucinda. Although Mary Louise was pregnant with her fifth child, riding horse-back was easier on her than riding in a bouncing jerking wagon. There was ample grass and water for the livestock and with our trusty bell mare, plus four wolfhounds that had been trained to herd cattle, Mary Louise had little difficulty in driving the herd. The wolfhounds had been trained to nip at the heels of any lagging or straying critter. I say trained, because wolfhounds by nature go for the head of an animal, and that's not the way to herd cattle. They must be taught to nip heels. They quickly learn to avoid the kicks by the animals on their own.

We were taking a herd of forty fine horses, all broken, plus a double team of Morgan draft horses for each wagon. A single Morgan pulled the buggy. In addition we were taking five milk cows. The milk cows were either daughters or granddaughters of Old Molly Moo Cow. Our main food supply consisted of barrels of oatmeal, corn meal and pickled pork.

And in the back of a wagon wrapped in burlap, Mary had placed ten cuttings from her pretty pink rose bush.

"If you don't mind, Mary, I think I had better count those rose cuttings. I don't want any surprises," I said.

We studied two routes to Independence. The shortest route was to go almost due north to Jefferson City, Missouri, then turn due west to Independence. A longer route by about 75 miles was to follow the Arkansas River to Alma, Arkansas and then turn north to Independence. We chose the longer route because we thought it would provide better grass for the livestock. Taking this route proved to have been a serious error. We had not accounted for the additional creek crossings and the many steep gulches and ravines. The total route would be about 400 miles.

We estimated that we could average about fifteen miles a day and, therefore, we would be at the jump-off site in plenty of time. Unfortunately, we did not make fifteen miles on any single day, let alone an average of fifteen. But the thing that really slowed us down was sickness in the family.

On the third day out, a sudden thunderstorm whipped up and drenched us to the skin. It continued to rain for the next seven days. The wind was severe and kept blowing our tents down at night. Consequently, we all slept wet and chilled night after night. One by one the entire family became very ill with congestive lungs and uncontrollable diarrhea. We took ginger powder to curb the "runs" just as you would give ginger to a calf that had the scours. It may have helped some. We were all so sick that we made the decision to lay over at Russellville for five days. We were not off to an auspicious start, and when we discovered that our barrels of oatmeal had all been soaked and had begun to mildew, our spirits sank. For some reason, the corn meal did not get wet, and that is what we lived on for the rest of the trip to Independence. The livestock was glad to get the moldy oats since they had grazed the grass to the bare ground around our impromptu camp. We knew we would need to restore our provisions at Independence and we knew the prices would be very high.

Mary and I had $890 dollars. The Hesses had $250. The Fords had nothing, but Levi Corzine had left Sarah Lucinda $300 when he died. So all together our cash resources were less than $1,500 dollars. We pooled what we collectively had, and put Mary in charge of the cash. She put the money in a box under the wooden seat of the wagon she was driving. The joke of the family was "Mom is sitting on our money", and quite literally she was.

As we became sick one by one Beede, or Reeda as she preferred to be called, was the nurse and the doctor all in one. She made "rounds" at every hour of the night. Her candlelight shone through the dark nights like an angel's beacon. She placed cool wet cloths on our foreheads trying to break our fever. She taught the children how to twirl the wet cloths in the air to make them cooler while they waited for Reeda's next visit.

Even as a small girl, it was Reeda who nursed the runt piglets after the sow abandoned them. It was Reeda that the hounds would go to, to have a thorn removed from a paw. She had successfully set the broken leg of a trampled lamb. When her little brother Francis, fell from the apple tree and broke his arm and it was clear that the arm was not going to mend straight at the elbow, she devised a leather sack filled with sand, to pull the arm straight. The arm ended up nearly straight. We nicknamed Reeda, "Dr. Reeda" a title she proudly carried the rest of her life.

I don't know how she managed to take care of us all. She was just as sick as the rest of us. But night after night with the rain rolling off her cloak, she would appear, feel our foreheads, replace the cool cloths and adjust our blankets. If her patient was awake, she would whisper words of encouragement, "It will be light soon. You will feel better then. You need to take a little drink or you will dry out," and so forth.

Late one night as the tent wall dripped water down on our already sodden blankets Mary whispered to me, "Thomas, how many of our family will meet their Maker on this trip to Oregon?"

"None, Mary, none of our family will die on this trip. I promise you. We will all make it. In fact our family will even increase when Dr. Reeda has her little one and Mary Louise has hers."

"I pray that you are right," Mary whispered.

CHAPTER 6

Independence, Missouri

We finally rolled to within two miles of Independence on the last day of May and set up camp on a little knoll. Early the next morning John Ford and I rode into town to get some fresh commodities and to reconnoiter the area in search of Dr. White's Party. We soon learned to our dismay, that the White Party had left Independence on May 14, with eighteen wagons and a total of 112 people.

They were two weeks ahead of us. "Can we catch up?" John Brooks asked. We debated the pros and cons into the evening. If we stood any chance of catching the White Party, we would have to leave very early in the morning and then push each day from dawn to dark. This would be quite an effort, even if we were well, which we were not. In truth, we were exhausted, starved, and weak. However, "If we don't push on, what do we do?" Returning to Arkansas was not a good option and staying here was even worse.

The campfire had been lit and the pot of black beans, that was to be our supper, was boiling, when the wolfhounds alerted us that we would soon have company. A single rider was approaching.

"Take the dogs by their collars, but be ready to turn them loose," Joe Hess ordered, "there may be more of them out there." The women and children slowly, and without being told, started moving toward the nearest wagon.

The rider stopped beyond the ring of light from our fire. "Asking permission to enter camp," the man shouted.

"Enter then. Permission granted, but ride slowly with your hands in sight stranger," I yelled back.

"Hang on to those hounds! It's only me, Gabe McGee."

"What a sight for sore eyes to see!" Mary exclaimed, rushing forward to hug Old Gabe.

"If that's beans I smell, I got a slab of thick bacon that would go right smart in the pot. I don't suppose you have any apple pie do you ,Mary?"

"No, unfortunately, but if we did you could have the largest piece."

Just Gabe's arrival was a tremendous lift to everyone's spirits, and about that time they needed a lift.

"How did you find us?" I asked.

"Some folks in town said a bunch of Arkies had squatted on Burke's Hill. So I thought it could be the Keizurs, or if not, perhaps the folks would know of you."

"We're not Arkies. We're North Carolinians, Sir," John Brooks reminded us all.

"I know that must be true, because an Arkie would never call me, Sir," and we all laughed.

Immediately the discussion turned to whether he thought we could, or even should, try to catch the White Party.

Gabe was on his second bowl of black beans and bacon before he offered an opinion.

"If you ask me, trying to catch the White Party would be a recipe for disaster," Gabe bluntly said. "For one thing, the prairie grass is late this year. What forage there was, the White Party has taken to the bare ground. And forgive me for saying it, but you folks are in no shape for a forced march. You would have to go twice as fast as the White Party to catch them. If they were traveling ten miles a day, you would have to go twenty, to catch them in a month, if you ever would catch them. Your women and little ones are tired now. They need rest, Thomas."

"We are just coming out of a sick spell, but we will be at full strength in a short while." I explained.

"You won't come out of a 'sick spell' on a forced march, I can tell you that," Gabe replied.

"What would you suggest, Colonel?" Joe Hess inquired.

"Well, you have two options as I see it. You can turn around and go back to Arkansas, or some point in between, or you can winter over here and catch the next wagon train in the spring. There will be a major emigration in '43, as I hear it. But let's sleep on it. I have some ideas you may want to think on, that we can talk about tomorrow."

"Colonel, would you be interested in a cup of good spirits?" Joe Hess asked.

Mary looked at Thomas and Thomas looked at Mary Louise, who looked at Joe in surprise and disgust.

"When we were carefully selecting things to bring, it did not include any of your father's corn whiskey," Mary Louise declared with a frown.

"Don't mind if I do," Gabe said, unmindful of the tension around the issue.

The rest of the family settled in for the night, but Gabe and Joe Hess sat around the dying campfire drinking and telling tall tales and laughing over more than one cup of fine Arkansas corn whiskey.

In the morning Gabe inspected our gear. "The wagons may be good farm wagons but they will never hold up for 2,000 miles. They will fall apart. We will build stronger ones."

"Can we do that?" Joe asked.

"Absolutely," Gabe answered.

"If we had the materials, I can build anything," Samuel Penter added. Sam was the only one of our Party who had carpenter experience other than what any farmer might have.

"Here's my proposition," Gabe went on. "I have a place out on Sugar Creek about two miles north of Independence. There is a large log house, sort of rambling, but solid. The place has a big barn and long hay shed. There is a three-acre corral that needs some fence repair, but once fixed up, it will be adequate for your livestock.

"I bought this run down spread for the oak that is on it. I have a standing contract with the riverboat companies for $2 a cord for all I can deliver to their docks, that is delivered and stacked.

"I will pay you and your clan $1.50 a cord. I'll sit back, and look and watch, and exploit my friends. We will take this summer and winter getting *really* prepared for the trip next spring. Every ounce of preparation done now will save us time, if not our lives, because I can tell you, *it's a long way to Oregon*".

"Save *us* time? Are you going to Oregon too?" Mary asked.

"Not to Oregon. Oregon is for farmers and married folks who want to colonize the territory. I'm not made out to be a farmer and I'm too old to get married. I will trail with you to Ft. Hall and then head south for California. What do you say Thomas? Come winter with me."

"Now, Gabe, you are not too old to marry." Sarah said.

"Spoken like a frustrated widow," brother John sniped.

"Gabe, your offer is a Godsend, but frankly we can't pay much," I warned.

"If Mary will agree to be the chief cook, and if you and your boys cut lots of cord wood, I'll make 50 cents a cord and you will get all the calluses. Is it a deal?"

"It's a deal", I said. And we shook hands all around.

Within the week we had the corral repaired to hold the livestock. The barn was big enough to hold all four of our wagons. We stripped the wagons down to just the bed and running gear for wood hauling. The log house had a tremendous cast iron stove to Mary's delight.

Our woodcutting and hauling crew consisted of Joe Hess, the two Ford boys, Sam Penter, John Brooks, Pleasant, and me of course. Young Thomas age thirteen, and Francis age ten, took over the milking of the cows morning and night, rotating the cattle pastures, and keeping the wood box full for their mother. They both wanted to be with the "men" in the woods, and they did come out to help load the wagons on occasion, but Mary explained to her sons, that she needed and wanted them near to help, and "protect" the women and younger children.

Mary Louise came to the wood lot when she felt able, much to her mother's concern. It was too bad in this case that she was pregnant, because her output in chopping and sawing was equal to any of the men.

Mary reminded us, that at a church fundraiser for the Reverend Jason Lee back in Jacksonville, Jason Lee was described as "a robust man who could chop two cords of wood an hour."

"I would like to see him do that," I said. "I hope he preaches as good as he chops wood." Our output for the seven of us, was between ten and twelve cords, for a ten-hour day. That included hauling the wood two miles to the docks and stacking it.

"How much wood is a cord?" John Brooks inquired.

"The official measurement is 4 ft x 4 ft x 8 ft. or 128 cubic feet," Samuel Penter explained. "Or, whatever it is sold as," he said with a laugh. We cut and split the wood in four-foot lengths, which made measuring it easy, and it was the length the steamboat captains desired.

The fifteen dollars to eighteen dollars a day, began to add up, and kept us from dipping into our cash reserves that Mary still sat on, figuratively speaking.

"Those are fine teams of Morgans you have, though they will break down on a long haul. They will make excellent trading material for the animals you need," Gabe advised.

"What draft animal would you suggest?" I asked.

"Either mules or oxen," Gabe replied. "We used mules on the Santa Fe Trail. Our wagons were huge and it was not uncommon to have forty mules to a wagon."

"I've never liked mules," Joe said.

"Well, they have their place. They are faster, more nimble, and the Indians seldom steal a mule, except to eat. But the Santa Fe Trail is relatively flat ground and the mules would do better there than they would in the mountains. But for a trip like we are contemplating I would go with oxen. Again, the Indians are not interested in oxen. However, oxen are loyal and faithful. They are easily trained, and when well matched, they form a powerful team and you don't need forty of them to pull a wagon, perhaps only four to six.

"But the greatest advantage to the oxen is often overlooked. And that is their cloven hoofs. A horse's hoof, or mule's hoof, is solid, as you know, but the oxen have a split hoof like two big toes. They can spread their toes in mud or snow or on river bottoms to gain traction, whereas a horse just flounders in mud. There are other smaller considerations as well. Such as yoking up a team of oxen is not nearly the problem of harnessing up a team of mules or horses. Remember there are no reins or leather straps to worry about. With oxen the drover walks beside the animal. You don't drive oxen, you lead them. And another important consideration is the fact that oxen will eat anything and seemingly thrive. I have seen them, when the ground was covered with snow, eat the bark off fence posts."

We all nodded our heads in understanding. "It would appear that we need to do some trading for oxen," I said.

We found out in short order that the Morgans were excellent trading stock. Gabe introduced me to the finer points in selecting oxen. "Make sure they are well matched as to size, particularly their height at the shoulders. Make sure they have been properly castrated. A half castrated ox is still a bull at heart. You don't need a bull with romantic inclinations pulling your wagons."

Mary Louise accompanied me often to the auctions. "Just like the old days, Dad," she said. Mary Louise quickly picked up an eye for good oxen. We looked for run down, tired beasts, recently from their journey from Illinois, or Indiana, or other points east.

We paid fifteen to twenty five dollars a head for oxen, but we could sell a matched team of Morgans for $150 to $200 dollars, and we had sixteen matched pairs of Morgans.

We reluctantly realized, that four wagons would be too many, so we settled on two wagons. Therefore, we needed three yokes of oxen per wagon, and a spare yoke of oxen for each wagon. Our plan was to rotate the oxen to where they would be relieved every fourth day. So all told we needed sixteen oxen.

The wood operation was the perfect environment to train the oxen. Like a fine athlete preparing for a contest, the oxen needed to be brought into top physical condition. And with the oxen, we were able to haul wood deep into the winter, due to their cloven hoofs, whereas with the horses we would have been done hauling wood shortly after the first mud developed in the woods.

"The hoofs of the oxen is an advantage, but we have to take care of them," Gabe advised. "It will begin by our shoeing the oxen. Don't think of a solid shoe such, as you would put on a horse. An ox requires two smaller shoes per hoof, one for each toe if you will.

"Because the hoof is split on the oxen, they are subject to gravel, dirt, and sharp grass stubble, getting imbedded between the split in their hoofs. As they continue to walk, the rocks and so forth are shoved deeper and deeper in this area of their hoofs, causing the ox to go lame, as they favor their sore hoof. We don't need a lame ox half way to Oregon."

"Is there a solution or someway we can prevent this from happening?" John Ford inquired.

"I think so," Reeda offered. "If the boys had dirt between their toes we would clean it out. We should do the same for the oxen. Let me sleep on this challenge."

By the next evening Reeda had fashioned a wooden tool shaped like a colander plunger, that would be used in making pear butter, or the like. It was a tapered stick, tapering down to about a quarter of an inch, with a rounded point. "A digging stick, if you will," she said.

Reeda chose a huge ox named Ben on which to experiment. After a few trials she had Ben picking up one hoof at a time and bending it backward like you would in shoeing a horse, to allow Reeda to dig away. To everyone's amazement Big Ben spread his toes to assist in the procedure. The big ox enjoyed it, and why not, if you think about it. Before the week was out Reeda had every oxen looking forward to their evening toe dig. It required only a few minutes per animal and it lead significantly to the taming of these huge animals.

I instructed everyone, that I never wanted to see a whip put to the oxen. Each drover had a cane they carried, and by placing the cane across the oxen's back, or on its rump, or across his neck, he would willingly go, where ever we wanted him to go, although slowly.

Reeda told us, "Oxen are faithful and dutiful. They want to please their masters. Each one has its own personality just like we do, and each one should have their own name, just like the rest of the family. The names should be short. Ben, not Benjamin." Almost every one named his own oxen. "Wasn't that fun?" she laughed.

Samuel made wooden currycombs for us to curry the animals after a heavy rain. The advantage to currying an animal is the rain will quickly run off and they do not get chilled. The oxen soon learned to expect a little currying after a hard rainstorm. The smaller children loved to do the currying, and it took only a few minutes.

The teams of oxen were taught five verbal commands. Gee, for right; haw, for left; whoa, to stop; gid dup, to start; and whoa back, to step back. They were trained to react to both male and female voices. Even the children could drive the oxen. How well the oxen responded depended a lot on the authority in the voice of the drover.

The Keizur Family

(Age at the time the Keizurs left Independence, Missouri for Oregon)

Thomas Dove Keizur (50) Mary Girley Keizur (50)

Mary Louise Keizur Hess (26) Joseph Hess (31)

    Tillman Cullwell Hess (6)

    Mary Jane Hess (4)

    Sarah E. Hess (3)

    Virginia Rowley Hess (1)

    William H. Hess (3 months)

Sarah Lucinda Keizur Corzine (25) Widow of Levi Corzine

    Mary Ann Corzine (2)

Matilda Caroline Keizur Penter (22) Samuel Penter (29)

    Thomas H. Penter (4)

    S. Monroe Penter (2 months)

John Brooks Keizur (19)

Beede Ann (Reeda) Keizur Ford (18) John Ford (25)

    Tilman Ford (born on the Trail to Oregon)

Pleasant Cicero Keizur (15)

Francis Marion Keizur (13)

Thomas Cullwell Keizur (10)

Elizabeth Jane Keizur (8)

William Henry Harrison Keizur (4)

(Not related but traveled with the Keizurs)

Nimrod Ford (26) (brother of John Ford)

Kenneth Darius O'Regan (17)

Col. Gabriel McGee (65 ?)

CHAPTER 7

Kenneth O'Regan

One day in October, we were all cutting wood as usual when one of the wolfhounds alerted us that we were about to have a visitor. Over the brow of the hill came a red haired skinny boy about fifteen or sixteen years old. He was analyzing us all the way, as he came directly toward us, just as we were all looking him over.

Without speaking a word he took the axe out of Pleasant's hand. Pleasant had been chopping on a four inch oak limb. With two whacks, the redhead had the limb cut in half and quickly moved up the limb, where it was about five inches thick and dispatched it in three swings of the axe.

"It is all day I can be doing that," he announced, "and it is work I am looking after."

"Well, that's a fine show, Lad, but we aren't hiring any woodcutters," I said.

"I would expect to be paid only for what I cut. And I can out cut any Mon here, when it comes to axe swinging."

"Where are you from, Son?" I asked

"From the east of here," the boy said.

"East? That's not very specific," Gabe said.

"Irish, I'm Irish by way of Boston."

"How did you get to Missouri? Where's your horse."

"It's walking I've been doing, No horse do I have."

"He talks funny," Pleasant remarked.

"I am on my way to join my Clan somewhere to the west. I can't stay long. But I could use a little work at the moment."

"Do you have a name?" Gabe asked.

"My name is Kenneth Darius O'Regan. The O'Regans have land somewhere to the west. Somewhere," he added. Kenneth pulled a yellowed torn flyer from the inside of his shirt. "See? It's O'Regan I am going."

The tattered flyer said, "*WANTED: Brave men to go to Oregon*".

"That says Oregon. Can't you read?" Pleasant laughed. "We're going to Oregon too".

The young man was totally crushed and didn't understand his mistake.

"You talk too much Pleasant," Joe Hess admonished. Then Joe turned to me. "Why not let the kid work. We could pay him a dollar a cord and still pocket 50 cents for us."

"That would neither be honest, nor fair," I said. "If he cuts a cord, he gets paid for a cord. You have a job, young Irishman."

Kenneth O'Regan made the chips fly. Not only was he strong, but also he knew how to use an axe. As the sun set and we had finished loading the day's efforts, I asked Kenneth, "Will we see you tomorrow?"

"That you will, Sir."

"Where is your camp and your gear?"

"I'm wearing all I own. But I stayed last night in the glen by the little creek."

"Come home with us. You can sleep in the hay barn with us boys," Pleasant said. "Dad, could he?"

"We can try it for a spell and see how it goes."

"I don't much like the kid," Joe Hess murmured. "I think he's a Papist. See the silver cross he wears around his neck?"

"Catholics aren't the only ones to wear a cross and I don't think the lad will spend much time trying to convert you," Gabe observed.

Within a week Kenneth, or Kenny as he preferred to be called, had been taught to milk by Francis and little Thomas. He got up early to help the smaller boys with the milking and cleaning the barn, but we did not get in from the woods in time for him to help with the evening milking. But Kenny helped in other ways whenever he could, no matter how tired he must have been. And he was soon as much a part of our family as anyone. Before winter fell it was taken for granted that Kenneth Darius O'Regan was going to Oregon with the Keizurs, and Mary Keizur had one more son.

As fall and winter began to meet in late October, and the daylight hours were reduced, we went from ten-hour days to eight hours. We rigged lanterns in the barn and worked after supper on constructing our two new wagons. Sam Penter was put in charge of the design and construction of the wagons. Our wagons were designed after the "Yankee wagon" with a few variations. "The Conestoga wagon seems too big and heavy to me," Sam said.

Gabe agreed, "Conestoga wagons are fine for the Santa Fe trade but the Studebaker brothers don't know how to build them light and strong."

Samuel had many good ideas and seemed to relish his assignment and the responsibility it incurred.

"We will build our wagons strong enough so they won't break down under a 2,500 pound load. We will make the box of well-cured oak. But the sides will be of pine. Pine is strong, but much lighter than oak. We will use iron very sparingly because of its weight but we will use iron for the wheel rims and to reinforce parts that will receive the greatest strain such as the axles and hounds.

"The boxes will be four feet wide, and ten feet long, giving us forty square feet of floor space. The sides will be four feet high with the top six inches slanting out. So when it rains the water will drip or run off without getting our belongings wet inside. We will use flattened hickory bows to support the cover. The bows should give us over five feet of headroom in the wagons.

"The tongue, which is a critical part of the running gear, will be made of close grained oak. I will select that wood myself. But the most critical part of the running gear, is the wheels. We will fashion our wheels with two and half inch iron rims one half inch thick. The spokes should be made of Osage orange, but we don't have any in this area, so we will use white oak. We want to minimize the shrinkage. The hubs are another matter. They need to be four inches thick. The reinforcing stakes on the bed will be cut to the rough dimensions of the spokes. So if we break a spoke, which we surely will, sooner or later, we will use the stakes for the spoke replacements. The tongue will be jointed, so it will not break under a sudden jolt going over a rock, or into a hole."

The oak planks that formed the box had to fit very tightly. Sam inspected each joint by placing a thin piece of hemp between the planks. If he could pull the hemp out it wasn't tight enough for him. It was easy enough to plane the high spots, but where there was a "wow", or low spot the entire length of the plank would have to be planed down. The drawknife was the best tool to use in this case.

Sam insisted that we use no nails as fasteners. "We will use rivets, pegs, or bolts but no nails." Sam ordered.

While the wagons were laboriously being built, the women were busy treating and sewing the sail canvas we bought for the wagon covers. They strung the heavy canvas by rope across one end of the barn. Both sides of the canvas were painted with linseed oil until the covers would not absorb any more. Then grommets were installed every foot, or ten on a side. Finally every seam was covered with bee's wax. The grommets were stretched to slide over wood pegs, which had a slight slant to them. The cover could quickly be removed in case of a sudden stiff wind. This would reduce the danger of the wagons being overturned. Or just one side could be unhooked and rolled back for easy packing and unpacking.

In December Mary Louise and Joe Hess had their fifth child, a boy, who they named William Henry Harrison Hess, after President Harrison who died in 1841, after only one month in office. Reeda served as her sister's midwife.

At last the wagons were finished and tested. With the oxen trained and in very good condition we turned our attention seriously to what we would be taking on the 2,000-mile trip to the Willamette Valley in Oregon.

Gabe's stated position was, "If it's not something to eat, or wear, or a tool to be used, leave it."

Mary pointed out, "The family Bible may not be viewed by Gabe, as food, or clothing, or as a tool, but I consider the Bible all of that and more. And the family Bible *is* going. That is the end of that discussion."

But Gabe made the mistake of trying one more time. "The Bible must weigh five to seven pounds. Those pounds could be of rolled oats or cornmeal which could be a day's ration for a starving family."

"If our survival comes down to five pounds of oatmeal, we have no business even starting. The Bible goes where I go. And while I'm at it, I have wrapped ten pink rose starts to take. I hope one of the ten will make it to Oregon. The Bible, and the pink rose starts are going. That is the end of that discussion."

CHAPTER 8

Preparations

Our challenge was to provide provisions for fifteen adults, or near adults, six children, five infants under the age of three and two babies yet to be born. Early on Gabe said his plans were to drive a buggy by horse and that he would be responsible for his own provisions.

We all gave Gabe a bad time for indicating he was taking a horse to pull his buggy, after all the effort he took to sell us on oxen. "My load will be different," he said. "I will be taking needles, thread, thimbles, and perhaps leather boots, to sell in California. My load will be light. I will trail two other horses to rotate into the harness. By rotating every day the horses should hold up. But if one goes lame I'll butcher it for meat."

"You can't be serious," John said. "You can't eat a horse. No one would eat a horse."

"Remember, I was a Mountain Man. Mountain Men do not harbor meaningless taboos. We will eat horse or mule, when we get hungry enough."

"Not me, I would rather starve."

"Let's hope it doesn't come to that, but if it does you will eat horse meat. Of course those four wolfhounds will go first. They will be so skinny by then, that they won't make a decent meal."

For some unexplained reason, the four hounds began to howl and we all laughed until tears came.

Even with Gabe off our list to plan for, it was going to be a challenge to plan for five or six months of trail life. Our staples will be rolled oats, cornmeal, and wheat flour. With those basics, coupled with adequate cooking lard and saleratus, or baking soda, a family could survive. In addition and for variety we planned to take dry beans, dry peas, rice, and dried fruit.

We studied all the "guides" that were available. Gabe was very skeptical of the guides, having been written for the most part by "authorities", who had never crossed the Missouri River. For example, one popular guidebook suggested 200 pounds of flour and 45 pounds of bacon, per adult. For our party of fifteen adult eaters and six children, we would have to pack 4,410 pounds of these items alone, and we had designed our Yankee wagons to carry only 5,000 pounds between the two wagons.

"That's ridiculous," I said, "that would leave capacity for everything else, at less than 600 pounds."

"In regard to taking bacon, you better plan on eating it all in the first three weeks. If you don't, you can put it alongside the wagons and it will be crawling with enough worms to keep pace with us, if you can get all the worms going in the same direction," Gabe offered. Mary didn't think that was funny.

"Or look at this suggestion," Mary said referring to the guidebook. "It is recommended that we include 50 pounds of lard per adult. That's 700 pounds of lard."

"What will we do with 700 pounds of lard?" Samuel Penter asked.

"The lard is used for cooking wheat flour cakes and so forth," Matilda answered.

"I have a better idea," Reeda offered. "Why not cook with butter? If we skim the cream off the milk each morning and night and put it in a churn, after lurching and bouncing all day it will be butter, and we would also have buttermilk to drink. Cooking with butter is healthier for us than cooking with lard. Particularly when the lard becomes rancid, as it surely will. I just saved us 700 pounds of weight. Let the cows carry the cooking grease."

We will take five cows with us, with all of them bred back, with at least two due to freshen while we are on the trail. With three cows producing, it should give everyone a cup of milk in the morning and another one at night, plus all the butter we will need plus the buttermilk.

"Aunt Reeda is due to freshen on the trail too. Will that help?" Six year old Tillman Hess wondered aloud. He didn't understand the roar of laughter from the adults.

"I suggest another approach," John Ford interjected. "Let's determine what must go in the way of tools, seed, rope, spare oxen shoes, spare parts for the running gear, clothing, and so forth and then estimate that weight and fill the remainder of our capacity with food staples."

"That's a good plan," Gabe said.

So, the winter months were spent in determining and arguing the merits of each non-food item and gathering the materials into piles.

We had brought two iron clad plows from Arkansas. We reduced that to one plow. We had one axe and one crosscut saw per wagon, but we left the ripsaw. We took one shovel and one spade, but also a second blade for each, minus the handles. We bought two coils of braided hemp rope for each wagon. Each coil was 100 feet long with eyes braided into the end of each rope. This gave us a total of 400 feet of rope.

For the small tools we finally agreed upon a carpenter's claw hammer, a six-pound sledgehammer, two hardwood wedges, a brace with four bits, and a whetting stone.

Next came the cooking and eating utensils. We decided on two kettles with six-inch legs, a tin plate and tin cup for each person, plus a spoon and fork, two butcher knives, a very large cast iron frying pan, a mess pan to mix bread in, and a baking pan.

The cooking gear was stored in a pine box with rope handles. We took two tin buckets for milking, but we used "gutta percha" for our water pails. Gutta percha is a substance painted on canvas to waterproof the canvas. Gutta percha pails are much lighter than tin buckets.

Sleeping arrangements were still another worry, but once again Samuel Penter came up with the solution. "The 'Old folks', that would be Mary and Thomas, should sleep in one wagon using a buffalo robe as a mattress and wool blankets for cover. There is room on top of the supplies for their bed and it would be quite cozy. The other married couples, that is John and Reeda, Mary Louise and Joe, and Matilda and I will rotate turns in the other wagon. So each couple could get a good night's sleep every third night. For the rest, it will be tents with sleeping tarps on the ground and a buffalo robe for cover."

The tents were the only source of cross words on our trip from Arkansas. Setting them up, taking them down wet, blowing over in the night, always when we were tired, and on and on. Once again, Sam, with his innovative mind, determined that with a little thought there must be a better way. His solution was clever and simple. He installed wooden hooks half way up the wagon cover hoops and he had the women sew grommets into canvas to match the hooks. He then took a ten-foot long pole and attached the canvas to that. He had reinforced pockets sewed in the corners of the canvas. He cut lightweight tent stakes, about four feet long, with a rail screwed on to pound on, to set the stakes. When we stopped at night the canvas was rolled out, the stakes set, and our tents were set up. Each piece of canvas extended twelve feet wide. Each wagon had this arrangement on each side of the wagons. So in effect, this gave us four tents, with about ten x ten foot useable space for each tent. The tents could be set up in about fifteen minutes and taken down in ten minutes. If the tents were wet, they would dry out on the next day's march. The beauty of it all was everyone could set up the tents, even the smaller children. Once the tents were rolled out, ground oilskins were laid down and a trench was dug around the perimeter of the tents. The smaller children often liked to sleep under the wagons rather than the side tents. When they did, it added four more feet to our sleeping area per wagon. We had the women sew side curtains that could be attached if we wanted them. We used the side curtains when it was raining hard otherwise the cool breeze blowing under the canvas tents was quite welcomed. The only draw back to this arrangement, was at a time of high winds, the side tents acted as a sail, and jeopardized the wagon being tipped over. We would have to deal with that if the need arose.

Sam Penter was justifiably pleased with his creation, "But what are the Keizur girls going to argue about if they don't have the conflicts over the tents with which to deal?" Sam wondered aloud.

"Don't you worry about that, Sam. We can always find something," Matilda said.

Even the wolfhounds found this arrangement to their liking. They slept two to each side, at the head and foot of each tent. "It would be a pretty dumb Indian to try to sneak in on us," little Tillman observed.

CHAPTER 9

Outfitting

Our trip into Independence, to buy our "trail" clothes, was like a holiday for us. Independence, Missouri had been established only seven years earlier. It was the out-fitting center and headquarters for the lucrative trade being carried over the Santa Fe Trail. St Louis was the fur trading capital and home base for the Mountain Men, but Independence 250 miles to the west, was the terminal for the Santa Fe trade.

The Independence town site covered 250 acres and was laid out in 1827, and included in that area, were sixteen springs producing pure water. By 1843, a rough railroad ran from the bustling village to the docks on the river. The place where the riverboats actually docked was known as Independence Landing, or sometimes called Wagon City.

On the streets of Independence and in the surrounding countryside emigrants were already gathering by late February. They were coming from points east and south. Fortunately, there was an ample supply of wood and brush for their campfires, which flickered at night, from all the nearby hillsides. In the evenings a blue haze of wood smoke hung over the town.

At any one time, on the streets of Independence, you could hear French, Spanish, English (with many dialects), and a multitude of Indian languages. For the children, it was all very exciting to see and hear the hustle and bustle of the "big" city.

There was a constant hammering and banging coming from the dozen blacksmith shops. At this time, there were more blacksmith shops, than grog houses, but this was destined to soon change.

As we trooped into town, and down the muddy main street, we passed within an arms length of the three "houses of comfort", which were near the city square, and where the new courthouse was scheduled to be built. It was mid day, and apparently, it was the custom of "the ladies of the night" to sit on benches in the sun watching the activities of the milling crowd and alerting potential customers of their presence.

All the Keizur men stared straight ahead and the Keizur women looked the other way, but stole glances at the "fallen angels".

Elizabeth Jane, our eight year old said, "Mommy, look at the ladies in the pretty dresses."

"Elizabeth, don't stare, it isn't proper."

"But look at the lady in the pretty red dress," she whispered back.

All the Keizur ladies turned as one, to also glance at the lady in the red velvet dress.

Our first stop was at a shop with a hand painted sign saying, "Missouri Millinery".

"We will start at our heads and go to our toes," Mary announced.

"I don't want a hat. I will wear my bonnet," declared Matilda. "So will I," added Sarah. "Hats look too masculine, and we will make bonnets for all the little girls."

In the window display were black and brown wide-rimmed hats made of felt or pressed fur. Each had a woven leather chinstrap with a bolo fastener. Mary and I went into the shop. There just wasn't room for everybody to go in.

"Are the new felt hats waterproof?" Mary asked the proprietor.

"Indeed they are, Madam."

"Do you have different sizes?"

"Indeed we do, Madam. We have two sizes, too large and too small."

Mary ignored the attempt at humor. "I need eleven large black hats, three small black hats, and three large brown ones. How much are they?"

"That's seventeen hats, if I counted right." The man was all business now. "With that number I could let you have them at 75 cents a hat."

Mary looked forlorn and started to leave, but she reached into her skirt pocket and took out a shiny ten-dollar gold piece. "This is all I have, and we so wanted the hats."

The shopkeeper took the ten dollar gold piece and bit it with his eye-teeth. "It's a deal," he announced.

Outside there was a flurry of trying on new hats and sliding the bolo up and down.

"Who gets the brown hats, Mary?" I asked.

"Brown is for the women who want to wear them and black is for the men. I want to be able to tell the men from the women when we have dust all over us."

Around the corner we went to the bootery. Again Mary did the talking, "Sir, you have some very fine looking boots in the window. How much are the ones that are calf high."

"The boots are the finest on the frontier. They have been made of Mexican steer hides, a year in the tanning process," the little stooped over boot maker said.

"How much?"

"Are we talking one pair, or two?"

"We need two pairs each, for twenty two people."

"It will take me two weeks to make that many and it will cost you a dollar a pair."

"I will give you two ten dollar gold pieces now and two more when we pick the boots up," Mary said.

"But lady that is only forty dollars. I said a dollar a pair so that makes it forty four dollars."

"Do we have a deal or not?" Mary asked.

"Let me get down some butcher paper and let's start tracing feet," he said. "You line them up so I can trace and number the patterns."

"Take your shoes off and line up from the oldest to the youngest. You first Gabe. And when you get to this young man (tapping John Brooks on the shoulder), and from there on down the line, make the second pair a half size larger."

"I fully understand."

The children were all giggles and twitters. "It tickles" Francis Marion laughed.

As we left, the old man lowered a sack over the sign in the window and put up another one that said, "Temporarily closed."

"We will see you in two weeks," Mary said.

"The boots will be ready," the little old man replied.

There were three clothing outfitters and we pretty much absorbed their stocks. Mary once again did the negotiations, only this time she played one store against the other to get her price. We purchased duck cloth pants with belt loops and suspenders, wool long handled underwear, wool shirts, and long wool scarves, Most of the women and girls split their long skirts and sewed them up the middle to make pantaloons,

"Really, quite fashionable for the times," Reeda pointed out. Mary and Sarah Lucinda preferred their long skirts.

"I want all those lonesome bachelors to know I'm a woman," Sarah quipped.

John Brooks was going to say something clever but thought better of it.

"This was better than any Christmas we ever had," Elizabeth said. And we all agreed.

"I have never had a new pair of boots, or a new shirt, in me life," Kenny O'Regan stated.

We trailed home nearly $400 dollars lighter than when we left in the morning. We were almost ready and excitement was running high for young and old.

"I think I could have gotten the hats for less," Mary lamented.

A few final arrangements needed to be made and it was already the first of April. We felt that the grass would be high enough on the plains by mid May. Several emigrant trains had already rolled into Independence and we heard that there were more en route.

CHAPTER 10

Reeda's Medicine Bag

Reeda insisted that her husband build a wooden box to hold all her "remedies". He argued about the extra weight, but to no avail. "The witch must have her brew," he chided her.

We were frankly quite proud of Reeda's self-taught medical knowledge. If the children did not feel well, they knew that Dr. Reeda would help them feel better. Reeda described the contents of her medicine chest: "There is ground up cascara bark to make you "go", there is ginger powder to make you stop "going", or red oak bark if ginger did not work, powdered rhubarb root for arthritis, ginseng leaves for asthma (and Little William often had trouble breathing), pine resin to use after bleeding a person, sassafras root to make tea, lady's slipper leaves to build blood, powdered quinine for colds, eucalyptus leaves for congestion, blue gum leaves, soda, ginseng root, catnip, a plug of tobacco for stings and bites, peppermint tea for upset stomachs, vanilla and bluestone for toothaches, sulphur for lifting warts, and asafetida bags. And a host of other things for this and that. And while I'm at it, Joe Hess, I want whatever is left of that jug of Arkansas whiskey, that you have hidden."

"What whiskey?" Joe whined.

"Mary Louise, I want Joe's whiskey, and I want it now, so I can pack it before he gets a chance to drink more of it."

"I think she means business, Joe. I think you better go get it now," Mary Louise said.

"But there is over half a jug. Certainly you won't want that much" Joe said in near panic.

"Get it now," Reeda and Mary Louise said in unison.

"O.K., O.K. I'll get it."

"What does that mean? What does O.K. mean? It sounds vulgar," Mary Louise said.

"What does O.K. mean? It means all right. Everybody in town says it now. It's a new term."

"Well it sounds vulgar and please don't use the term around me," Mary Louise replied.

Soon every one was using the term O.K. but it had not been used prior to 1842.

Finally, Reeda had the children gather rose hips or rose buds. She planned to prescribe these bitter little morsels to everyone on a daily basis. "This will prevent trail scurvy. Without fresh fruits and vegetables for weeks on end, we could get scurvy just like the sailors do on the high seas. Rose hips will help prevent this. We will just take one or two with our evening meal."

To complete her kit she had her husband, John, grind a knife down to a rounded edge. "It's sharp as a razor, just perfect for bleeding," she explained.

We had confidence in our "Doctor Reeda", and confidence goes a long way in healing.

We still had more last minute chores before we were "ready". Mary gave the little ones the chore of greasing the new boots, with bear grease. The boys, Tillman, Little Thomas, Thomas Cullwell, and William Harrison, who is only four, all loved to get their hands in the grease pot, but the girls, Mary Jane and Elizabeth Jane, thought the grease was "icky," but, they did a commendable job, including wiping the excess grease off with rags.

We all broke our new boots in. Everyone but the very smallest would be walking. If we all rode, the oxen would have over a ton of extra weight to pull. The small children were expected to walk until the noon stop, then they could ride and nap in the afternoon if they wanted to. Reeda and Mary Louise could ride whenever they got tired. Mary Louise had not fully regained her strength after the birth of little William. Virginia, only one, and Mary Ann, only two, would ride most of the time, with whichever older girl was riding at the time, to watch over them.

I asked Mary Louise to help me "cut out" 21 of our finest mares and one good stallion that we would take to Oregon. She picked three and four year olds, all saddle broken. This left us with 23 horses, mostly Morgans, which we had driven from Arkansas. Gabe selected three from that group to rotate pulling his buggy. His buggy loaded, weighed only about six hundred pounds. His horses would certainly not be over stressed. Gabe had purchased a multitude of small service items to take, enough to start a small store in California.

CHAPTER 11

Final Preparations

Every guidebook suggested that every man of fighting age should carry a rifle. In our case, all the males down to, and including Francis Marion at ten years old, had his own rifle, and all the Keizur women had rifles too, and they knew how to use them.

Gabe, Joe Hess and I still had our Missouri Militia revolvers. Counting Gabe and Kenneth, the Keizurs could muster 15 rifles, three revolvers and one shotgun. We were a virtual army.

Every Saturday afternoon, for the final two months of our stay on Sugar Creek, we walked to a back area to practice shooting. Gabe was in charge of the training, because of his military experience. He spent most of the time showing us how to shoot from a kneeling position and a prone position. He taught us how to shoot into the sun. "Indians will usually charge with their backs to the sun so the sun will be in your eyes," he informed us. He taught us how to gauge range uphill. "In most cases the Indians will have the high ground and shooting up hill takes a little getting used to," he explained. He taught us to aim at the mid section of a man and at the center of the horse if the enemy is mounted. We didn't much like the thought of shooting horses, yet we could understand his reasoning.

Of our rifles, three were Kentucky long rifles with an accuracy range of 100 yards, whereas the rest were effective at about 50-60 yards. He advised us against "volley" shooting. "These aren't Red Coats marching in a line. These are seasoned and brave warriors fighting for their land and their way of life," he explained, "so staggered shooting is what we want, with the Kentucky rifles firing first, while the rest hold."

"The Comanche soon caught on to the 'volley shooting'. They taunted us just ten yards beyond our range. When we fired, they charged for sixty seconds, hell bent for election. They had learned that it took a good rifleman 60 seconds to reload and fire, although there are liars that claim they can do it in ten seconds. An Indian can put seven arrows on target at 60 yards, and closing within that distance, while the whites are reloading. This is hardly a challenge for a 'Brave'. In a charge, the Chief will lead. The Kentucky rifles should concentrate on that man.

"Anyway, I don't expect any pitched battles with our Red Brothers. They would be crazy to pull a frontal attack on a train of wagons as large as I see gathering. However, this training will come in handy when you fight the British in Oregon and I predict you surely will have to fight them. But as you take on the Red Coats, think of me, because I will be fighting the Spanish in California. I have no personal animosity toward the Spanish, but I would really like one more crack at the Queen's Men."

One drill all the younger boys enjoyed, consisted of sending three or four of the boys beyond the hill to play the part of the Indians. Their job was to whoop and holler and charge to a mark 150 yards away, stop and taunt us, being allowed to call the adults every derogatory name of which they could think. The rest of the Keizurs waited with unloaded guns. Gabe's voice boomed, "Steady! Steady! Kentucky rifles ready! As the boys approached the 100 yard mark Gabe shouted, "Kentucky rifles, fire! Even numbers, ready, aim, fire! Odd numbers, ready, aim, fire!" And as the boys dashed down the hill, "Fire at will!"

We had to explain to Little Will Harrison, that when we "fire at will" we didn't mean at him.

"Now, Mary, you are in command. You direct the fire and give the orders."

Mary Keizur in a calm deliberate voice called out the orders.

Gabe was adamant about carrying a rifle correctly, and woe be to the poor soul that pointed a gun, loaded or not, in the direction of another person.

"Thomas, it is my advice to you to have your Clan rack their guns until, or unless, there is a clear and impending danger of attack, or unless they are on night guard duty. There will be more pioneers killed by their own guns than at the hands of the pesky Redskins. I would bet my poke on that. Besides carrying a rifle all day long is wasted energy. A rifle gets very heavy after a few miles and *it's a long way to Oregon.*"

We followed the old soldier's good advice and had gun racks built and attached to the inside of the hoops supporting the canvas tops. The first person into the wagon, man or woman, passed the rifles out the back of the wagons. The only exception to our "racking the guns", was Joe, Gabe and me, with our revolvers, which we always had on us.

We had used very little cash while wintering over. With what we had upon arrival and the pay from the wood hauling, plus the Morgans that we sold, Mary had nearly $9000 in gold coin, most of it in 20 dollar gold pieces. This was a substantial fortune. The Keizurs were not going to Oregon destitute, but that amount was a worry to Mary. She had Samuel build two small false bottom receptacles in the floor of the wagons. She divided the gold between the two wagons. "In case we lose a wagon in a river crossing, we won't lose everything, unless we lose both wagons some way." To counter even that unlikely occurrence, she called everyone together, down to the four year olds, and gave everyone a 20 dollar gold piece to put in his pocket, seventeen gold pieces distributed in pockets. "Watch after these coins and don't lose them. When we get to Oregon, I will collect them all from you. If worse comes to absolute worse, we will still have a little money to begin our new life."

CHAPTER 12

Departure for Oregon

It was now approaching the middle of May, 1843. We decided we were as ready as we could be. The wagons were packed and repacked. Our oxen were well trained and powerful from the long hauls of cordwood from Sugar Creek to the docks. The oxen seemed to sense that a special task was awaiting them.

But most importantly, we Keizurs were all in excellent condition, including Reeda, the pregnant member of our party. Reeda was due in early June, only weeks away.

We gathered for our last supper in the United States. Usually we sat at four tables, but tonight we arranged them in an el shape, so we would all be together. Gabe, Mary and I were at the head table. In all, twenty-seven members of the Keizur Party including Kenny O'Regan, sat in silence while John Brooks offered the invocation. It was his standard "Grace". I was a little disappointed, because here was a perfect chance to wax poetic, but I never said anything. This could very well be the last time we all sat together at one time.

We had a leg of lamb, dandelion salad, winter squash, corn bread with honey and all the trimmings. Joe Hess had managed to obtain a gallon of currant wine for the adults and the children had warm buttermilk, with chunks of butter still floating in it.

When the supper was finally over, and the second glass of currant wine was poured, Gabe stood up and struck his glass a few times to get everyone's attention.

"I want to make a speech," he announced.

"But before you do, Colonel McGee, I have something I want to say," Mary said. The room quieted, to hear what the matron of the Clan had to say. Somewhat reluctantly, Gabe surrendered the floor and sat back down in his chair.

"My family owes you an eternal debt of gratitude, Gabe. You gave us honest advice a year ago, when we were thinking about trying to catch Dr. White's Party, already three weeks ahead of us on the trail. We were in poor health, as you could see, we had poorly equipped wagons, and we had Morgans to pull them, rather than oxen. The Morgans are a gallant breed, but they would have broken down on the long trail.

"Gabe, I believe you may have saved the lives of all I hold dear, with your sound advice. Had we gone on then, I don't think all of us would have lived to see the promise land called Oregon. We weren't prepared. Now, it is quite possible that some of us won't make it to Oregon anyway. *It's a long way to Oregon* but your help has given us a fighting chance. And our thanks do not end with your sage advice. You gave us all a dry and safe place to winter over, plus employment for the menfolk."

Mary turned to the children who had been listening to every word their mother and grandmother was saying. "You children should give thanks every night in your prayers to God, for lending us Gabe." The children all nodded their understanding. "That's what I had to say, and it needed to be said." Everyone clapped and cheered as Mary sat down. "Now I believe you wanted to say something, Gabe," Mary said.

"I can't remember exactly," Gabe was speechless.

"Then perhaps a poor Irish Lad can have his say," Kenny O'Regan said, getting to his feet. "I never had a family. I never knew my father, and me mither had to give me away so there would be enough for the others to eat. You have allowed me to be part of your family. I now *have* a father, who I can follow and respect. I now *have* a mother, who worries about me. I have brothers and sisters and soon, I think, I will have one more. I have grown four inches in height and I weigh 30 pounds more than when I arrived on Sugar Creek, thanks to the best cook in Missouri and I have two pairs of good boots and a twenty dollar gold piece in me pocket.

"But the most important thing, I spent years being afraid. I'm not sure you all know what a terrible thing it is to be always afraid. For the last ten months, with this family, I haven't been afraid. I go to sleep now, because I'm not afraid.

"All the praise you gave Mr. McGee was well deserved, but the glue that holds you all together is the love and respect you have for Mr. Keizur. Thomas Dove Keizur will get us all to Oregon, of that I am sure." The family sat in silence thinking of what this stray boy had articulated.

"I remember what I was going to say now," Gabe interrupted their thoughts. "Before we leave in the morning, will you boys be sure the wood box is left full?" We roared with laughter.

"Very profound, Gabe. Very profound." I exclaimed.

"And a little kindling too," Gabe added.

In the morning Gabe tacked a sign on the door. It said, "Stranger, you are welcome to stay awhile. When you leave, fill the wood box. Col. Gabriel McGee".

"Gabe, you could easily sell this spread," I said.

"I suppose I could, but I may want to come back here someday when I get old," Gabe laughed.

We were scheduled to leave at daybreak, but Gabe had one more "lesson" for the Keizurs. "Gather around. I want to show everybody something. You too, Thomas. Gather around."

Gabe took an oak limb about four inches in diameter and placed it in front of the wheel of the lead wagon. "Gid dup! Gid dup!" he commanded the oxen. The loaded wagon pulled over the oak limb breaking it with a loud snap.

"The point of this little demonstration is to impress upon you all, that the iron rim on that wheel doesn't know the difference between that oak limb and your ankle or foot. If you get under the wheel, you will lose something. Don't blame the oxen for a sudden jerk of the wagon, be expecting it. Don't blame the oxen if the wagon rolls backward six inches, be expecting it. School is over let's get this outfit on its way."

We planned to pay passage to cross the Missouri River by flat boat. It required nearly three full days to get our Party ferried across. The flat boat could safely take just one wagon at a time or six head of livestock. Besides the twelve oxen we were taking, we had five milk cows, twenty-two saddle horses, ten Morgans that we had not had time to sell, and four excited wolfhounds. And oh, yes, twenty-five Keizurs.

We rolled about three miles down the well-worn Santa Fe Trail and set up our camp. Wagons of every type and description were rolling in with more people than I could imagine. There was a holiday atmosphere to the entire arena.

The spring had been unusually dry, and the prairie grass had not grown adequately to sustain the grazing of so many oxen and other cattle. A delay was necessary, which caused a great deal of anxiety among the emigrants.

"If we don't get started soon, you Oregon bound folks will never get through the dreaded Blue Mountains before the snow falls," Gabe predicted.

On May 15· a wagon train Party of remarkable size, moved passed us. There were over a dozen wagons and a herd of cattle we guessed to be one to two thousand head in number. This emigrant band moved a mile beyond the Keizurs to set up their temporary camp. That evening a single rider approached from the direction of the newcomers' huge encampment.

"Permission to enter your camp," the rider called out.

"By all means," I replied. "You're welcome to our camp."

The stranger dismounted and extended his hand. My name is Applegate. Jesse Applegate. I'm the Captain of the Applegate Party, but perhaps you have heard of us. Where are you from and are you going to Oregon?"

"We come from the other side of Independence, a short way and yes, we are going to Oregon, God willing," I said.

"We are neighbors and family from near St. Louis that formed a company to go to Oregon," Jesse Applegate explained. "We have been on the trail twelve days just to reach Independence and nearly that many days to get our Party across the Missouri River," Jesse Applegate said.

"Are we supposed to be impressed?" Joe Hess mumbled under his breath.

"My two older brothers Lindsay and Charles and their families are with us too. Altogether the Applegates number twenty-two people, but with us are about eight Burnetts, seven Beagles, two Beales just to name a few and then we have hired a number of bull whackers and cattle drovers. I guess there are about forty-five or so of us all told. You have quite a group of your own I see. Are all these folks family?"

"All but two are related, but they are all family. We're the Keizur Party. My name is Thomas Keizur."

"I'm pleased to meet you all and I'm looking forward to getting better acquainted. I have sent riders out to all the camps that we can reach with this flyer, saying for all who are going to Oregon to meet tomorrow at the Old Fitzhugh Mill for the purpose of organizing The Oregon Emigration Company. Women folk are welcome, but only male leaders of each family will have a say."

"What if the leader of a family happens to be a woman?" Mary Louise asked. Jesse Applegate shrugged his shoulders.

"We understand and we will see you at Fitzhugh's Mill," I said.

"Oh, yes, by the way," Jesse said, "If we select a Captain at Fitzhugh's I would be willing to serve."

'We will keep that in mind." I replied.

After Jesse Applegate rode off Mary asked, "What do you make of him?"

"Rather aggressive if you ask me," Gabe volunteered.

"He definitely views himself as the leader," I said. "Time will tell. However, someone needs to step forward to organize this train. I heard today that there are 120 wagons more or less and between 800 and a thousand souls driving over 4,000 head of cattle. It is truly 'a great migration'. If we are not organized in some fashion we will be just a rabble. We don't want a leader that is a shrinking violet. Jesse Applegate is not a shrinking violet."

"I think you should be the Captain," Joe Hess said.

"I *am* the Captain of my family. No elected person can change that and we will be good followers, unless the leadership endangers my family."

"Hear! Hear!" Gabe said. "A good leader must have good followers or he is not a leader. Every Army must have its 'chain of command' and this train is very much like an Army going to Oregon or California."

CHAPTER 13

Fitzhugh's Mill

The meeting at Fitzhugh's Mill was on the 18th of May, and was very well attended. The meeting was convened at noon, with Jesse Applegate pounding on the table with a half brick, to get order. Committees were formed to draw the "rules for the journey". Every male over the age of sixteen could have a vote in all matters. And every man with a vote would be expected to take his turn at guard duty.

They decided, nearly unanimously, not to schedule the election of officers until we reached the Kansas River crossing, approximately 85 miles distant. "This will give everyone a good shake down opportunity to test our animals and gear and will give the emigrants a chance to get better acquainted, before we elect our officers," Jesse said. Everyone agreed that it was a good idea to wait a short period of time.

Jesse was directed to draw up the final written agreement, with the stated purpose of, "keeping good order and promoting civil and military discipline."

A man called Peter Burnett, of the Applegate Party, was asked to lead a small delegation to find, and hire, a competent pilot, or guide, and to negotiate fair compensation. Several had heard of a man named John Gantt, an ex army officer with the rank of Captain. The delegation was to return to Independence and try to locate John Gantt. A young man, only 23, served as the recording secretary. His name was Jim Nesmith. He was also asked to be the Orderly Sergeant, with the primary duty of scheduling the rotation of the night guards. This was a major responsibility for one so young.

I reluctantly accepted the assignment of "readiness officer". It would be my duty to go down the line of emigrants and attest to their "ability and ableness" to proceed over the trail to Oregon, without their wagons and gear being a liability to the entire Company.

Gabe and I started at once on our task. Most of the outfits were not as well equipped as we were. But I would not say they would be a liability to anyone else. So we made a few suggestions that seemed to be well received. For example many of them did not have their grease bucket covered. The grease bucket usually hung on the back of the wagon and was used to grease the running gear such as the hubs. With their grease buckets uncovered, dust would collect in the grease and when used, would cause undue wear on the running gear, just the opposite of what the grease was intended to do.

We came to a wagon with a large oak pump organ strapped to the back of the wagon. "I advise you to leave the pump organ," I told them.

"Can't do that Pilgrim," the emigrant stated. "That's the only way my wife would consent to go to Oregon, is to take the organ."

"I don't suppose you would consider leaving both your wife and her pump organ," Gabe asked.

"If you insist upon bringing the oak organ, promise me you will jettison it before your animals break down, afterward is too late," I said.

"I promise, but we must start with it."

About a mile further on, we heard a high-pitched squeaking and squawking sound like a bunch of wildcats in a bag. Over a knoll, slowly rolled five, two wheeled carts. The wheels were made by sawing off the ends of large logs about four inches thick, with a hole drilled in the center of each "round" with a timber shoved through the hole to form the axel. The squeaking and screeching sound was made by the axle turning in the hole in the center of the wheel. A single mule pulled each cart. The mules were in very poor condition. In each cart were women and children, also undernourished and not in good condition, with obvious signs of fatigue, and we had barely begun the trip. There was no chance that this group could make it to Oregon.

Only one of the Party could speak English. "Who are you? And where are you from?"

The lightest skinned man, and the one who could speak English said, "We are Me`tis from near Fort Garry, Canada by way of Pembina, Minnesota by way of the Red River Valley."

"Me`tis? I have never heard of you."

"We are half breeds, Sioux, Cree, and French. We have traveled far and for many months. There will be much bloodshed in our land soon. The big fur companies like Hudson's Bay Company and the Nor'westers are choosing right now who will live and who will die. Joseph Rolette, an Astor agent, contracted us to bring pelts to St.Paul. Astor offered a fair price, which the Company did not. But the Hudson's Bay Company put a pox on us. If the Company men don't kill us, the Red Coats will. So if we must fight the Red Coats, we will do it in Oregon, where at least there is a promise of a better life for our families."

"I would be derelict in my duties to let you join our Company. You can't make it equipped as you are. You will perish on the trail and frankly you will slow us down. But this is still America, although barely. I can't tell you, that you can't go to Oregon equipped in any fashion, but I do have the authority to deny you the safety of the Oregon Emigration Company. My advice to you is to take your women and children back to where you came from and fight for your rights there."

The spokesman translated my message to the others in French and in Cree. As the meaning began to seep in, the men began to weep openly and the women and children tried to console them.

"That is a classic example of cultural role reversal," Gabe observed. "Well I can't take much more of this." He tapped the weeping spokesman on the shoulder to get his attention. "I have a better idea," he said. "You take your families and your squeaking contraptions back to the Missouri River and get across someway. When you are across, ask someone how to get to Sugar Creek. It's not far. Go up the creek about a mile and a half and you will find a big old rambling log house with a barn that still has loose hay in it. Take the sign off the door and go in and build yourself a big fire. This is my place. Stay there as long as you like, and until your people are healthy. Winter over and follow us next spring, or go home. But when you leave fill the wood box and put the sign back on the door."

After several attempts, the interpreter got the meaning of Gabe's message across to the rest of the Me'tis and when it finally sunk in, the men all rushed over to embrace Gabe kissing him on both cheeks.

"My God! This is enough to make me change my mind."

We watched, as they slowly turned their mule carts around to head back, and we could hear the wheels squeaking long after they were out of sight.

"Gabe, you old rascal you are all heart. That was a kind thing you did there."

"To tell you the truth, they reminded me too much of another family coming in from Arkansas about a year ago." Gabe said.

"I never did properly kiss you on the cheek, Gabe."

"And if you try now, you will never sing bass in the church choir again."

On the ride back to our camp after completing our inspection tour, we talked about the Me'tis people. Gabe commented, "If they make it to Oregon someday, they will make loyal American citizens; and if you have to fight the British in Oregon, which I think is a foregone conclusion, you will be glad to have them on your side."

On Saturday May 20, 1843, the Oregon Emigration Company was officially formed. Jesse Applegate's "rules" included a method to "recall" any elected officer. His rules stated that it required one third of the members to call such a special election, but simple majority would decide it. The rules also called for the election of a "Council" of nine, to serve as judge, jury, and arbitrator of all disputes. The decision of the Council was final, with no appeal rights.

Jesse's rules would be our constitution for the next five to six months and to give the man full credit, he wrote these rules in just two day's time.

The team of representatives sent to recruit a pilot came back without success. This was a grave matter. No one in the entire Company had ever been to Oregon. No one knew the way, and what maps were available were not reliable, or worse. We could start Monday, May 22, because the trail began by following the well-established Santa Fe Trail, but before long a guide would be needed.

Daniel Matheny and William Martin were instructed to return to Independence and "try harder". We needed a pilot, or this Company was headed for disaster.

The search was more successful this time. The Committee was able to employ fifty-three year old, John Gantt. Gantt had served in the Army and had risen to the rank of Captain. Since leaving the Army in 1829, he had spent the next fourteen years in various capacities in the fur trade. He had made several trips over the route as far as Fort Hall. He had never been a bona fide Mountain Man, because he served more in the management aspects of the fur trade, as opposed to actually trapping, or securing pelts. However, he had in those years been involved in numerous Indian scrimmages, and the subsequent negotiations to bring peace, even if the peace was temporary.

Jesse Applegate introduced John Gantt, "as a borderer, who has passed his life on the verge of civilization, and has been chosen to this post of leader from his knowledge of the savage and his experience in travel through roadless wastes."

The Captain agreed to guide the Company as far as Fort Hall, for one dollar a person. Martin and Matheny were enthusiastically congratulated for having concluded such a favorable deal for our Pilot. Martin was reported as having answered, "It helped to have the man unemployed and in a serious need for a job."

"But wait a moment," Old man Zackery whined, "What happens after Fort Hall?"

William Martin then gave the Oregon Emigration Company the best news yet. "Dr. Marcus Whitman, known by reputation to most of you, will be joining us en route. He is returning to his mission on the Walla Walla River, which is a tributary to the Columbia River. He has agreed to guide us from Fort Hall to the Columbia River. He knows the route."

"How much will he charge?" old Zackery wanted to know.

"It would be contrary to his Christian ideals to charge us anything except for the small amount of food taken from around our camp fires at supper time," Martin explained.

The Dr. Marcus Whitman news was good news, really good news. Reeda was ecstatic. "I hope I can meet him in person. A real trained doctor of medicine. Wouldn't it be something if he arrived in time to deliver my baby?"

"Then from Fort Hall, will we have two pilots? And which one will be held accountable for our safety?" Once again old man Zackery was the skeptic.

"This old wet blanket is getting on my nerves," Joe Hess whispered to his wife, Mary Louise.

William Martin replied to Zackery, "Captain Gantt's personal plans are to turn off at Fort Hall to go to California. Marcus will be our only guide from that point on."

Dr. Marcus Whitman was returning to Oregon after a mid winter ride from his mission on the Walla Walla to the east coast. The Mission Board was about to pull the financial plug on his missionary efforts. The "ride" will go down in history as one of the great feats of courage. The Mission Board felt that he was spending too much time and resources in an agricultural adventure, rather than saving the souls of Indians. Whitman had modeled his endeavors after the successful enterprises of Jason and Daniel Lee in the Willamette Valley. The main difference that Whitman did not take into consideration was that most of the Native population had already vanished due to disease in the Willamette Valley. So the Lees went to agriculture and schools for the children of whites and "half breeds" because there were so few members of the Calapooya tribe remaining. There were few Indians to "save". Contrast this to the mid-Columbia Natives, where Marcus Whitman located, who had strong organized tribal communities such as the Cayuse, Walla Walla, Umatilla, and Yakima.

Whitman was, however, a very convincing orator before his Mission Board, and rescued his Mission. While he was on the east coast in the winter and spring of 1843 he made the "rounds" of the New York, Boston, and Washington, D.C. politicians and influential leaders of the time. Every speech and contact he made, he extolled the beauty and wealth of the Oregon country. He felt that the United States should try to gain control of Oregon from England and their surrogate, The Hudson's Bay Company. First, by negotiations, but if that didn't work, then he felt America should fight for Oregon.

He had a personal audience with President Tyler, and by all accounts won him over, to the importance of Oregon.

He spent time with Senators Linn and Benton, both from Missouri, and strong advocates for the U.S. taking control of the Oregon Territory. Many felt that Whitman's winter ride from Oregon to the east coast saved Oregon for America. This may have been a bit of an overstatement, but his trip did raise the awareness of Oregon. But perhaps the most important thing he accomplished was to convince immigrants that it was possible to take wagons all the way to Oregon, although Marcus and Narcissa had taken a wagon only as far as Fort Hall. Whitman and the other Oregon advocates knew that it was absolutely necessary to establish a land bridge to the west. England saw the importance of a land connection and tried to colonize Oregon by bringing people from the Red River region of Canada. Perhaps one reason for the Red River program to flounder and the Americans to succeed, was the fact that the American immigrant efforts were individually inspired, whereas the Red River adventure was government sponsored and inspired, if not ordered. Not, that the U.S. government was not involved. They were, and with Linn and Benton introducing legislation for the government to grant "free" land to the emigrants, they would become much more involved.

Most emigrants, including the Keizurs, felt that in time there would be some sort of land grants for settling in the Oregon Territory, and it was this prospect of free public land that was the main motivator for the emigrants. It is fair to say that some emigrants went to Oregon for other reasons than the hope of free land. For example, some went to Oregon for their health, others just for the adventure, but for Thomas D. Keizur and the Applegates, it was for *LAND*.

To have Marcus Whitman join our Company was a great morale booster, not to mention the assurance of having a trained medical doctor in our midst.

By the second day most of the wagons had reached the Elm Grove campsite a distance of some 35 miles from Independence, Missouri. This route followed the old Santa Fe Trail. The trail was well marked and the going was easy. The Elm Grove consisted of two nearly dead elm trees which had been hacked apart for firewood. Mary Keizur commented, "Two nearly dead trees does not make a grove. I hope this isn't the harbinger of the other place names along this trip."

On the 24th of May, we reached a stream called the Wakarusa. Some of the emigrants had experience in fording streams since bridges were few and far between, but, for others this would be their first major crossing.

Peter Burnett led the train to the nearest point on the stream for the crossing. The banks on both sides were steep and the bottom of the river was sandy, which would make the crossing difficult. John Brooks reported to his father, that he had scouted up stream and found a much better place for fording.

"You are probably right, John, but let's go with the leaders for now," I said.

While we were camped the evening of the 24th, a lone rider came upon us. It was Captain Gantt our recently hired pilot. "Maybe Gantt will not like the crossing place," said John.

"Remember, the role of the pilot is to be our compass, not our mother," Gabe interjected.

CHAPTER 14

Kansas River Crossing

Only a day later, the Company was facing a major test, crossing the Kansas River. The Kansas River was usually fairly docile, but at this time it was running bank to bank with the spring runoff.

"Fording is out," I declared, and Peter and others agreed. A Frenchman by the name of Papin had been running a raft with the help of several Kaw, or Kansas Indians. Jesse Applegate, Peter Burnett and William Martin tried to hire Papin and his raft, but the Frenchman demanded an outlandish price

"Our options are to wait until the river goes down which may take three weeks, or we can build our own raft," Jesse Applegate declared. The decision was not difficult. The weather was pleasant and the trees were plentiful and the raft building commenced at once and went quite well.

Morton McCarver oversaw the construction of the raft. He had been a flatboat operator on the Mississippi River to New Orleans and understood the bindings and the buoyancy needed for the loads. We Keizur men did what we had been doing all winter and made the chips fly. By noon with everyone doing their part, we had completed the raft and had lines ready to pull our raft across and one rope attached to pull it back. John Brooks swam our cattle across with our bell mare leading the way. Soon the other cattle followed.

Alexander Zackery, who had already proven to be a bit obnoxious, felt the process was going too slow and agreed to the Frenchman's price. Zackery obviously had the resources that many did not. Zackery,cutting a side deal with Papin, angered many of the other immigrants, who were working together for a common cause.

Zackery overloaded Papin's raft against Papin's pleas not to do so. At the last moment Zackery placed three of his women folk, and Marth, their fourteen year old slave girl and her infant child on top of the load.

The overloaded raft tipped over in the middle of the boiling current. Two large Caw Braves immediately threw off their blankets and dove into the water, as the rest of us watched helplessly. The Indians were powerful swimmers and saved all four of the women including Marth and her baby. In fact, the Indians saved Marth first, which enraged Old Zackery. Zackery raised his buggy whip to strike the black girl, as though she was responsible some way for Zackery's problems. Walter Matney grabbed the whip from behind and broke the whip over his knee and handed Zackery the two pieces.

Walter Matney was a hired teamster with Zackery's outfit. Zackery never forgave Matney for "interfering with his property". This entire episode, played out right in front of all of us, and we all formed a very negative impression of Alexander Zackery.

But the Zackery episode did not end there. Alex Zackery marched up to the two Caw Indians and ordered them back into the water to retrieve some boxes of Zackery's gear, which had hung up on some brush. Another emigrant was about to intercede, when the Caws indicated they had saved the women for free, but to save the boxes would cost Zackery a 20 dollar gold piece, which incidentally, was the price that Papin had charged to cross the stream.

One of the Indians put the gold coin in his mouth and they both dove back into the cold water and retrieved the boxes. Reeda brought two cups of steaming hot coffee for the young swimmers, and she attempted to hug the nearest of the young men, but he quickly backed away. Gabe pounded the swimmers on their shoulders in a gesture of appreciation, which they responded to with grins.

"I will remember that a slap on the shoulder is well understood, where a hug from a very pregnant white woman, may not be." Reeda said.

There was another unusual occurrence at the Kansas River crossing. A young teamster by the name of William Vaughn, who had been hired by Peter Stuart, another emigrant, to drive one of Peter's wagons to Oregon for his food, was swimming their stock across the river, when he was seized with severe cramps. James Nesmith saw that Vaughn was in trouble and with no hesitation dove in to rescue William. However, William panicked and fought James, endangering them both. Peter Stewart dove in to come to James's assistance. Together they were able to subdue William Vaughn and drag him ashore. But William Vaughn was unconscious. Edward Lenox the sixteen-year-old son of Daniel Lenox quickly ran to their wagon and got a barrel. The young men draped William over the barrel and started pumping his arms. Someone ran to get Reeda, who was already recognized as the unofficial doctor. Reeda hurried as fast as her enlarged body would allow. The boys were about to give up their efforts as being futile, when Reeda screamed, "Don't stop! Don't stop!" Her screaming startled the boys who both began pumping Williams's arms more vigorously. William groaned and emitted enough water, "to raise the Kansas River six inches." Vaughn spent the next day sleeping in the wagon "on the doctor's orders" but returned to full duty the next day.

Peter Burnett made an interesting observation. "We escaped several tragedies in this crossing. We will have many more crossings to come between here and Oregon. *It's a long way to Oregon.* I doubt if anyone who witnessed these events will be casual about any future crossing. It will make us all realize this is dangerous business."

It took six days to get the entire Company across the Kansas River. The early crossers set up camp, which they dubbed "Camp Delay".

It was at the Kansas River crossing that we caught up with a group of Catholic Missionaries. Father Peter Devos, Father Adrian Hoecken and several lay brothers had left a week earlier. They had two wheeled carts, each pulled by a single mule. They were headed for Flathead country.

It had been decided at Fitzhugh's Mill that we would have election of permanent officers once we had crossed the Kansas River. Each male sixteen or over would have a vote. So in the Keizur's Party, our eligible voters would be myself, Gabe, Joe Hess, John and Nimrod Ford, John Brooks, and Kenny O'Regan. Pleasant was not eligible to vote at fifteen. Several neighbors asked me if I would be a candidate for the Captain's office and Gabe was openly promoting me. "I appreciate your remarks. They are very flattering, however, I am the Captain of my Clan and that is enough responsibility for one man. I am not a candidate for any office."

CHAPTER 15

Sir William Stewart

While we were at Camp Delay, a most interesting Party joined us, led by Sir William Drumond Stewart, a Scottish nobleman. Gabe had encountered him twice before; once when he was at a Rocky Mountain Rendezvous in 1833, and once in Old Santa Fe.

"Sir William has been on the western frontier at least ten years and this is at least his third trip to the far west. It is my opinion he is a British spy," Gabe said.

Captain Gantt joined us. "What do you know about the Stewart Party?"

"I remember him quite well. He is a highly educated, high class Britisher. He fought in the Napoleonic Wars. In fact he was decorated at Waterloo. He still receives half pay as a Captain in the Queen's Army. If I understand the Queen of England, she wouldn't continue to pay without some returns. He poses as a hunter and his Party is made up of a few rich Americans, who are out here just for sport."

"It looks like a Party of about sixty or perhaps more. I jotted down some names that I thought you may have heard before." Captain Gantt said.

"It's not likely. I have never traveled with a rich crowd." Gabe said.

"Their guide is William Sublette and they are waiting to be joined by another Sublette brother."

"That would be Solomon Sublette. Old Bill and Solomon Sublette are the best guides money can buy. Who else do they have?"

"There are several members of a Choteau family and several members of a Menard family."

"Don't know them."

"There are several reporters who are supposedly writing books or journals. They asked a lot of questions about us. Their names are Mathieu Field and Richard Graham."

"Graham is a spy for sure. I would like to see what he is writing." Gabe commented.

"There is a German botanist named Leuder, goes by the initials of E.J. There is a Richard Rowland who I think is an American. He appears quite wealthy, and another American who wears a U.S. Army pin on his coat. He said he was on a six month leave from the Army."

"Was his name Sid Smith?" Gabe smiled.

"I believe his name was Sidney Smith. Do you know him?"

"Sid is an American spy spying on the British spies. I feel a little better now. Uncle Sam will know all that the Queen learns, only faster." Gabe laughed.

"Their outfit consists of eight carts, one wagon, and a small barouche."

"What is a barouche?" I asked.

"A barouche is a small four-wheeled wagon with a low body. It is a pleasure vehicle with a folding top and two inside seats that face each other and an outside upper seat for the driver. Real fancy," Captain Gantt explained. "In addition they have camp cooks, hired drovers, and several servants. It is a real "pleasure" outfit. Oh, yes, there are two cartographers, whatever that is."

"They are map makers sometimes posing as artists. Sir William will return with an analysis of every river crossing, mountain pass, and alternate route all sketched out by the 'artist'".

"Are they any threat to us?" I asked.

"No, in fact they could be of great assistance if we should encounter hostiles. The threat, if there is one, is in the packet sent east by a rider every third day or so. Someone in the east already knows our strength, our destination and many other facts. If they determine we are headed for California, they will see it as a problem for the Spanish; but if they see our destination as Oregon, then they will have an interest." Gabe said.

"I can't imagine the Queen of England having a spy watch us," I said.

"Why not? We sent out Captains Lewis and Clark. They were a military organization, and Captain Bonneville didn't fool Dr. John McLaughlin, or anybody else. And what about Lieutenant Fremont? He isn't out here just for his health. We will see Fremont before long with his party of English hating French-Canadians. They are not far behind us."

"Speaking of French Canadians, there was one with them, a guide I believe, and his name was Batiste Charbonneau."

"He would be about forty years old now. That's Sacagawea's son born while she was with Lewis and Clark. Batiste is well educated and spent time in Europe. So he is back on the frontier again. Tell me, is Sir William riding a big white stallion? That was always Sir William's trademark."

"Yes, he is, as a matter of fact," Captain Gantt said.

"I must ride over and drink rum with them. They will have plenty of rum," Gabe said.

We had crossed the Kansas River and so it was time to elect permanent officers. The entire Company met June first at noon on the only little knoll in the area. Sir William Stewart and the troupe of "hunters" came over "to watch American democracy at work".

Peter Burnett convened the meeting. He laboriously went over all the rules on voting. The women and children sat attentively. There were four announced candidates for the leadership position of "Captain". They were Peter Burnett, Jesse Applegate, William Martin and the biggest surprise, Alex Zackery.

Peter began the process by asking if any of the candidates wanted to give a speech. But none did. Then Peter raised his hand over the head of Jesse Applegate. "All those in favor of Mr. Applegate say 'Aye'." A good scattering of "Ayes" was shouted out then a few more from the opposite side of the throng.

"This ain't going to work." Peter declared.

"Division! I call for the division of the house," shouted Lindsay Applegate.

"What does he mean?" Kenneth O'Regan asked John Brooks. "What is a division of the house?"

"That means that it is impossible to elect a winner by a voice vote."

Peter was not flustered in the least. He had expected this turn of events. "Gentlemen, it is impractical to prepare a written ballot and even a show of hands would be hard to count. But I have a suggestion if you all agree to it." Peter Burnett had everyone's attention and he did not have to speak above his usual voice level.

"The four men who are vying for the Captaincy should stand about ten feet apart with their backs to the crowd. Then the four should start walking away into the open prairie. Any man who supports me will fall in behind me in single file, or if you support Mr. Martin, or another, just file in behind your man, as he walks away. Do you all understand?"

An Aide De Camp to Sir William Stewart said under his breath, "How on earth did this American rabble ever defeat His Majesty's Armies?"

Sir William answered him, "And these will be the same men and their women who will wrest Oregon from our grasp. There is nothing in the world that can stop them."

As the four would be captains began to walk outward, the seriousness of the moment vanished and a holiday spirit began. The four men began walking faster and a little faster. Finally Jesse broke into a jog, and William Martin began to run, and soon all but Old Man Zackery was running pell mell toward the horizon. About a quarter of a mile out Jesse looked back at his line of running men. He had good support, but he could see he did not have enough to win a simple majority. By this time every man was running at his top speed. Suddenly Jesse pointed at Peter Burnett, and shouted "Applegates merge! Applegates merge!" and he swung his line into Peter Burnett's line. William Martin saw what Jesse had done and he too pointed toward Peter Burnett and his line meshed into the Burnett supporters. Now there was one long line tripping, shoving and laughing curving back and forth, in one long serpentine. The choice had been made. It was nearly unanimous, except for Old Zackery and the two hired teamsters, who walked behind him, probably out of fear of losing their jobs.

The Aide De Camp to Sir William exclaimed, "My God, they're not even civilized. They can't even conduct a proper election".

Sir William turned to one of his journalists, "Write this down. I want a full written report of what we witnessed here today."

The newsman submitted his report to Sir William and then to an eastern newspaper which, as we learned much later, said in part:

Here was a congregation of rough, bold, and adventurous men, gathered from distant and opposite points of the Union, just forming an acquaintance with each other, to last, in all probability, through good or ill fortune, through the rest of their days. Few of them expected, or thought of ever returning to the states again.

They had with them their wives and children, and aged, depending relatives. They were going with stout and determined hearts to traverse a wild and desolate region, and take possession of a far corner of their country destined to prove a new and strong arm of a mighty nation. These men were running about the Prairie, in long strings; the leaders—in sport and for the purpose of puzzling the judges, doubling and winding in the drollest fashion; so that the all-important business of forming a government seemed very much like the merry schoolboy game of 'snapping the whip'. 'Running for office' is certainly performed in more literal fashion on the prairie than we see the same sort of business performed in town,"

Twenty-three year old James Nesmith was selected to continue his role as "Orderly Sergeant". He was strong and had shown his bravery during the Kansas River crossing incident when he saved Vaughn's life. Also, he was single and totally unattached, which was thought would make his decisions completely unbiased.

Peter Burnett, now Captain Burnett and the "Council" wasted no time in adjusting some of the rules. The most significant change had to do with the "loose cattle". The old rule was that no emigrant could have more than three head of loose cattle per man, sixteen or older. The Applegates had over 2,000 head of loose cattle and several other emigrants had 100 or more.

With our herd of horses, extra oxen, and our five milk cows, this rule had caught us. But this rule was completely thrown out. This change in rules brought ripples of discontent and grumbling. It didn't help, when it was pointed out, that this rule change favored seven of the nine members on "the Council".

It wasn't just that the non-cattle emigrants were expected to help guard another man's cattle, but it was already perceived that the loose cattle were slowing the entire Company. A nasty rumor persisted that the "have-not" emigrants were not guarding the cattle with any degree of enthusiasm, if guarding them at all. The non-cattle emigrants were quietly accused of permitting the Caw Indians, to help themselves to an occasional beef animal.

I assigned Kenny, Nimrod, Pleasant, and John to extra night guard duty, "Until we clear the Caw country" The four young men would crawl into the wagons at dawn and try to sleep until the noon stop. With this added precaution, we did not lose any stock. The Caws did not view themselves as thieves. It was just their culture to steal if they could, and when they could.

"Heck," Gabe said, "they would steal from each other just as fast."

Two highly respected emigrants, Pierson Reading and Martin McCarver, confided in me that in their opinion, "This conflict over the loose cattle will eventually cause a split in the train." They both thought a "division" was imminent. I took the matter to Peter Burnett and proposed a compromise. "Peter, why don't you see if the cattle men would agree to provide meat for any family in dire need, or if they need an oxen replacement if their animal broke down. A fair price could be determined by the Committee."

Peter thought it was a solid proposal, and took it to the cattle owners who agreed. Peter mistakenly felt that this compromise solved the issue. But it only served to delay the inevitable "division". My proposal was a mite disingenuous since my loose stock was primarily horses, and I didn't think anyone would elect to eat a horse.

Gabe was not as certain. "Remember, I once said that there could come a time when we would be thankful to have a horse to eat. The wolfhounds go first, but then the horses one at a time."

"Never," Joe Hess said, "We will starve first."

"Spoken like a man whose children are not starving to death. It has always amazed me how big the eyes seem to become when a person is starving, particularly the eyes of children," Gabe reflected.

"I'll not listen to any more of this nonsense," Joe said, and stomped away.

"I pray you will not be proven right, Gabe," I said.

"And so do I." Gabe replied. "There is a big difference between being hungry and 'starving'. I know, I have been there. Hell, everybody has been hungry, Joe has been hungry, but he has never been starving."

Almost at once Peter, our new Captain, was experiencing some frustration with his new undisciplined army of emigrants. He insisted that the wagons all proceed in single file thus stretching us out nearly four miles. This is a very poor defensive arrangement to say the least. But it was the dust more than anything that caused irritation. Many of the drivers, including the Keizurs, wanted to spread out so we wouldn't all be eating dust all day, but Captain Burnett would not allow that. At one point several muleskinners started racing, passing ox team after ox team. It certainly was a waste of energy, but most of the emigrants enjoyed the fun. Poor Peter nearly had a stroke trying to rein in "this foolishness". Peter insisted that we circle and chain our wagons every night. This process took a good hour if everything went as it should, which it seldom did. There was no danger from Indians at this point in the journey, so people resented this extra effort.

"Perhaps he is just giving us practice against the time when we will need to circle the wagons," I said.

"That's a good point," John Ford said. "But if that's it, he should share that with us."

"Sharing ideas, is not going to be Peter Burnett's strength," Mary observed.

After the crossing of the Kansas River the route slanted northwestward to the Red Vermillion crossing and then on to the Black Vermillion. The banks of both of these streams were steep, but they did not present much trouble, nor any delay to the Company.

Captain Burnett reorganized the train into four "Divisions", with a Captain over each Division. Captain Burnett then promoted himself to the rank of Colonel. Each Division was comprised of approximately sixty wagons. Each Division was further divided into fifteen "Platoons" of four wagons each.

Each Division made their own wagon circle at night. This was a better plan than trying to keep us all together, but even so, tempers grew short and several small disputes erupted into shoving matches and even fisticuffs. When a dispute broke out and the circle of onlookers formed, Burnett would race up on his horse shouting, "Break it up! Break it up!" Then another shoving match would develop further down the line and off raced Burnett again to "successfully" break up the fracas.

On one of these brawl-subduing races, Gabe hailed Burnett down. "Say, Colonel, there may be a way to stop all these young toughs from wanting to fight each other."

"Well, I'm listening," an exasperated Burnett, demanded.

"The next time a pushing match starts, you ride the other way," Gabe suggested. "When the boys realize that they might actually have to proceed, at the risk of getting a broken nose, or a split eyebrow, they will stop on their own."

About that time another circle of on-lookers was forming around a renewed shoving match. "Colonel! Colonel! A fight! A fight!" several yelled out.

"Stay right here Colonel and watch," Gabe advised. The two would-be combatants exchanged words and shook hands. That was the last potential fight that took place along the entire trail, although often cross words were exchanged.

"Gabe, why aren't you the Colonel?" Burnett mused aloud.

"Because I'm smarter than you, and besides just for your information, I am already an actual Colonel, having received a battlefield promotion."

It was completely out of character for Gabe to brag that way, or to show any disrespect for the leader. It was a sharp rebuke from an old soldier to a man who, after all, had promoted himself.

Gabe failed to mention, however, that his field promotion occurred in the five weeks' Mormon War, and that it was his friend that promoted him.

CHAPTER 16

Prairie Storms

On June fourth, as we were approaching the Big Blue River, the sky to
the north turned an ugly black. We made the crossing in record time with
a stiff wind gusting to hurry us through. By four in the afternoon the
sky turned from black to orange and the wind picked up. We circled the
wagons early, because we knew the sky was going to open up. It should
be the guide's responsibility to pick the nooning place and the evening
campsite. But the Colonel had taken this assignment away from our pilot,
Gantt. Three things are necessary for a good evening campsite, i.e. water,
wood, and grass. Burnett had not selected a good site yet. On this occasion he located us in a steep swale. Perhaps he reasoned that the swale
would protect us some from the wind and the oncoming storm that was
fast approaching.

The Keizur family had drilled for just such a force of nature. No attempt was made to start an evening fire. It would be a waste of time. "It's
cold flour biscuits tonight," Mary shouted above the increasing wind.

The wagons were turned into the wind as opposed to broadside with
the wind. Slack was pulled out of the wagon covers and the side tents were
not set up, but rather dropped from the wagon to the ground and staked
down. "Stake the wagons down with tie ropes," Joe Hess shouted. John
Brooks had the boys already digging a trench around the wagons. "Dig

the trenches wider and deeper tonight," he ordered. The women started putting hobbles on all the horses. Pleasant, Kenny, and I made the oxen lie down with their tails to the oncoming storm. This was all accomplished in half an hour because we had practiced it. Everyone had assigned duties and we all went about doing our part. Mary Louise and Matilda were in charge of the small children and got them into the wagons and bedded down. It is amazing how often children get lost in times of confusion like this, causing precious time to be wasted looking for them. This was not going to happen with Mary Louise and Matilda in charge.

When the front hit and the clouds opened up, some emigrants were still trying to start an evening fire. Tents half raised, went flying, several wagons tipped over when the wind hit them broadside. Too many had ignored the obvious signs of the impending storm, or just didn't know what to do.

Plan as we had for most eventualities, there is one the Keizurs had not planned for. Reeda Ann went into labor. Marcus Whitman had not arrived yet, as Reeda had hoped, but she had the best midwives west of the Missouri River, in her mother and her three sisters.

At two AM June 5, 1843, amidst the crackle of lightning and the rolling of thunder with a faucet of water pouring down, a fine looking boy, Tilman Keizur Ford, was born.

When mother and son appeared in the front opening of the wagon, the entire Clan shouted and cheered. Fortunately the other emigrants did not hear our cheers over the shrilly wind or they would have surely thought that "trail madness" had overcome us all. It was a very joyous night for us.

Tilman Ford was the first baby born in the emigration of 1843, but he wasn't the last. Little Tilman was the first baby born on what would become known as the Oregon Trail.

Mary Louise's six year old son, Tillman said, "But Aunt Reeda, we already have a Tillman,—me."

"This is true, but perhaps by naming my son Tilman also, he will grow up just as strong as you. And we will spell his name with one 'L'. You have two L's in your name." This seemed to please Tillman Hess.

Besides Tillman Hess should have realized that we had two Marys, two Sarahs, two William Harrisons, and three Thomases already in the family, so there would be nothing unusual to have another Tilman. The names sometimes even confused me and I don't think that Gabe McGee and Kenneth O'Regan even tried very hard to get us all straightened out.

Two situations concerning our oxen, caused discussion among our emigrant neighbors. After the first heavy downpour, six of the Keizur children went to work currying the oxen with their wooden toothed currycombs. An oxen's hair is naturally matted but when it gets wet it can be combed to lie in straight furrows. The rainwater will then run off quickly in tiny rivulets, thus keeping the hide of the oxen nearly dry. The oxen love to be curried except on their flanks. The Keizur children know this and they skip the flank areas. The children ages four to thirteen take on this assignment. It is quite a sight to see eight children scurrying around the huge animals talking to them, and calling them by name with the children's rubber slickers dragging in the mud. It is a showstopper. This did attract attention from the other emigrants. One old emigrant called out, "If there is a fair in Oregon, you kids will sure have your oxen ready to show."

But the other task of interest surrounding the care of our animals, was what our neighbors referred to as the "evening toe picking". They were referring to the older boys digging the mud and pebbles out from between the cloved hoofs of the oxen. John Brooks, Nimrod Ford, Pleasant, and Kenny O'Regan, did this chore at the end of each day's travel. The procedure was quick. The young men tapped the hoof and the ox would raise it and bend it at the ankle spreading their hoofs wide apart as they did so. With a quick downward motion of the cleaning stick the hoof was usually left free of dried mud and sharp rocks. However, if the ox knew there were pebbles lodged deeper they would not set their hoof down until "the toe digger" did a more complete job. And this was the time the men inspected each oxen shoe for its tightness, etc.

As a result of these few minutes of animal care each night, our oxen were not experiencing split hoofs, and swollen infected hoofs as were so many other oxen teams in the Company. More than one ox had gone lame because of infected hoofs, but not ours.

Several other drovers tried to copy our routine. However, for the most part they had a hard time getting up the nerve to walk behind their oxen to lift their hoof and treat it. They didn't relish being kicked by a 1500-pound ox. However, they should have known what our men did, that a bovine cannot "kick back" without first bringing his hoof forward. This forward motion should give the person ample time to know that a kick is on its way and to quickly sidestep it. It would be a terrible mistake to apply this same rule to a horse or a mule, because they can and do kick straight back, with little warning. Most of the drovers watching our boys were amazed, but remember we had spent ten months training the oxen.

The storm on the fifth of June dumped ten inches of rain into the swale where Peter Burnett had established our camp. It did not stop raining the sixth or seventh of June and the travel was slow as wagons bogged down hub deep in mud. Many treasured belongings were jettisoned to lighten the wagons. The lady, who wanted to take her pump organ, lost her argument as the organ lay on its back in six inches of mud and rainwater.

Thousands of pounds of flour, oatmeal, and cornmeal, were dumped by the emigrants as it got wet. These were valuable life saving commodities that would be sorely needed later on. We had one barrel of cornmeal that somehow got water into it. But my resourceful wife baked the wet cornmeal with a little flour for binding, into hard little biscuits. The biscuits were hard as rocks, but tasted fine when soaked in a cup of warm milk.

Pleasant offered a suggestion, "If we ever get in a fight with the Indians and run short of lead, we can just grab some of Mom's cornmeal biscuits and continue loading." This brought a roar of laughter from everybody, including Mary. But the point is, we didn't lose this important source of food. Mary just modified it a bit.

And still it rained and tempers grew short as the teams wallowed belly deep in mud. On the night of the seventh, after making only eight miles that day, Colonel Burnett again selected a terrible site to camp. He circled us up in a smooth spot with lots of grass, however, it was a peat bog. By morning the wagons had sunk into the peat with only the wagon boxes holding them up from sinking completely out of sight.

Two wagons split from the group to cross to the other side of a small stream. Another storm was coming and the emigrants in the two wagons in question felt it would be better to cross before the creek expanded, as it surely would.

Colonel Burnett ordered them to stop, but they weren't inclined to do so. The Colonel deputized two men and ordered them to stop the errant wagons. "How do we stop them?" one man asked.

"If they don't follow my orders, shoot to kill."

The two deputies caught up with the wagons and explained to the drivers that they had orders to, "shoot to kill" if necessary, but they must return to the main camp.

Rifles began to poke out from under the canvass tops of the covered wagons. "You tell the good Colonel that if he wants to stop us with lead, let him come to do it."

"I think you have a good reasonable approach to this matter," a deputy replied while looking down the barrels of a number of rifles. The riders rode back and reported to Colonel Burnett.

Peter Burnett had gone too far and he knew it. On the morning of the eighth of June, after only one week in charge, Peter Burnett notified the Governing Council that he was resigning, citing "health reasons." The Council accepted his resignation with no hesitation.

As an interesting footnote, Peter Burnett continued to use the title of Colonel for the rest of his life.

CHAPTER 17

Changing Leaders

William Martin was immediately elected Captain and like his predecessor, promoted himself to the rank of Colonel, but that is where the similarities ended. Martin was a wise leader and a good listener. He informed the Council that he would take charge until the train reached the California cutoff.

"I am going to California, not Oregon, so be thinking who you will pick to lead from that point on."

William Martin immediately called a meeting of all the emigrants driving ten or more head of loose cattle and announced, "For the good of all, we must divide the train."

There was no disagreement, well almost none. Alex Zackery didn't like the idea.

"Jesse, will you head up the column with the cows?" Martin asked.

"Only if the rest elect me," Jesse Applegate replied. We gladly elected Jesse Applegate as our Captain.

"I guess I will stay with Martin," Alex Zackery declared.

"You are driving ten or more head of loose cattle, you will go with the cow column," Jesse said. "Or you can go it alone, but make up your mind now."

"I'll go with you and see how it goes," Zackery replied.

"We will act and travel totally independently of the main column," Jesse went on, "we will set up our own rules and have a way to change them if need be without threatening one another. From now on we will be known as 'the Cow Column.'"

"We will keep in touch with each other for defensive purposes," Martin said, "and be ready to assist in any emergency."

Since we Keizurs certainly had more than ten head of loose stock we became part of the "Cow Column" of sixty wagons and over 2,500 head of stock. We were officially the Applegate Party, but unofficially we called ourselves, "the Cow Column".

The Division was a wise decision and probably saved the lives of many emigrants. The second day after the Division, Jesse Applegate paid our camp a visit.

"Thomas, could I have a word with you?" Jesse began.

"You can indeed," I said. "Come sit by the fire for apiece. What's on your mind?"

"We are now about a half day behind the main column. That doesn't worry me too much, because now that we are organized we will keep pace."

"I agree. I never thought it was the loose cattle that were slowing us down. Oxen can only go so fast, about two miles an hour or about 16-18 miles a day. Whereas, we can drive cattle twice that fast without a problem. So I never thought the loose cattle was the problem. There were just too many of us and everything took longer, from circling the wagons at night, to getting rolling in the mornings. Sometimes we were strung out over miles of trail which makes defense a worry."

"It is our defenses that I want to talk to you and Gabe about," Jesse began. "You both obviously have had military training. I am just a farmer and a part time surveyor. I don't know sound military operations."

"Heck, Jesse, Martin was a storekeeper, and an indebted one at that," Gabe said.

"My military background is very limited. I served less than two months

119

in the Missouri Militia. But I did have an experienced officer that taught me much. His name is Colonel McGee and he is sitting right beside you."

"Gabe, you're an army officer?"

"I have served some time in the military," Gabe acknowledged.

"What should we be doing? I feel we are more vulnerable since the split. It is our horses and cattle that is the attraction to the Indians. I wasn't too concerned with the Caw Indian tribe, but we are entering Pawnee territory and they are a different matter," Jesse pointed out.

"I agree, Jesse," Gabe said. "Ever since we discovered the young Pawnee Brave that the Caws murdered and then mutilated, I knew we could expect a war Party of Pawnees to our area. If the Caws had just shot the young Indian, it would have been one thing, but they cut off his ears, scalped him, cut off his nose, and other manly appendages."

"Gabe! For goodness sake, there are children present," Mary scolded.

"The Pawnees will seek revenge for that act of savagery, and that will put them right in our path," Gabe continued.

"What suggestions do you have, Gabe?"

"Well, let's start with the night watch. Order the night guards to stop building little warming fires. I have never seen anything that stupid. The guards will get cold and they are supposed to get cold. They are not supposed to be comfortable. Have the guards dismounted and posted just below the ridges, not on the rim where they are silhouetted against the sky. You should have two line guards mounted going in opposite directions all watch long."

"Do they need a password?" Jesse asked.

"Good thinking, only I suggest they use their first name. They won't get confused and forget their name. Also, tell every night guard that if they are caught asleep on duty, they will be court-martialed and shot in the morning."

"Gabe," Mary interrupted again, "some of those night watchmen are just boys. You can't be serious about having them shot."

"Tell them they will be shot, and tell them in a way that they will believe you. If you are very convincing you will never have to shoot one. Tell them that the old excuse of 'I'm not sleeping, I'm just resting my eyes', won't work."

"I can do that," Jesse said.

"And another thing, we change our night guard always at the same time and all at one time. This is not a good idea. The Cheyenne always hit us at a change of guards. And another thing, no one should leave his post unless he is relieved. If a replacement fails to show up, the guard takes another shift."

"Tell Jesse about our weakness at the creek and river crossings," I suggested.

"You bet. We should never, I repeat never, cross a creek or river without first sending an advance party across. If I were Chief Big Feather I would love to catch you in a river crossing. The advance party should scout out the bank and take a stand at least an arrow's distance from the pull out area."

"How far is an arrow's distance?"

"About fifty yards."

"And while I'm waxing on, we follow the creek banks too close. That is where the grass is the best and it is tempting, but you should run the column away from the brush and trees or other cover, again by an arrow's distance. Most Indians I have fought are masters at ambush and diversion."

"Explain diversion to me."

"They will divert your attention in one direction then attack from another. For example, if I was Chief Big Feather I would set the rear wagon on fire with pitch arrows, and wait for all the pale faces to race to the fire and then hit you in the front. Or I would make a big war whooping charge just out of rifle range from the left, while my main force was coming on the right, without the war whoops. And for God's sake tell your eager young invincibles to never chase 'the cowardly red skins' over the hill and out of sight of the Column. First of all, they are certainly not cowards. That's why they are called 'Braves.'"

"I think I'm catching your drift," Jesse said. "But you keep saying I should instruct the men. Wouldn't it be better coming from you and Thomas?"

"Absolutely not!" Gabe and I both said in unison.

"You are our Captain. You must act like a Captain. You give the orders. We need your leadership. Don't defer to us or anyone," I said.

"However, Jesse, don't become arrogant and afraid to ask questions. That's what got Burnett in trouble," Gabe added.

Mary interrupted again, "Do you want to be our leader?"

"Yes, Mary, I do."

"Good," Mary said. "And remember if no one follows you, you are not a leader."

"I understand your point," Mrs. Keizur.

Jesse really put the guards on alert, perhaps too much so. That evening about ten o'clock eighteen year old Nate Sutton fired a shot that reverberated through the dark night. Nate came running in shouting, "I shot an Indian! I shot an Indian!" Jesse ordered a doubling of the guard and instructed Nate to return to his post until he was relieved. Needless to say we all slept lightly that night.

The next morning Jesse said, "Come on, Nate show me the Indian."

Nate led us to the spot in the tall grass, "Be careful, I may have just wounded him," Nate cautioned.

In the grass with its neck broken was one of the Martin Brothers large, three hundred dollar, yellow, Kentucky mules, as dead as dead could be.

The young men razzed Nate for the next three months, "Say, Nate, have you shot any four legged Indians today?" and on and on.

Being the "trailing" Column had certain advantages. We had a trail to follow, so we didn't need to scout the route, but more importantly, many of the small creeks that fed into the Blue River that we were following, had steep approaches. The Light Column, (which the main Column preferred to be called) had to dig down before they could get their wagons across. This backbreaking work was already done for us, which made our crossing easy. However, the area of travel was usually grazed down, forcing the

Cow Column to go further a field.

We often camped within sight of the campfires of the Light Column. This made it easier for several young Romeos to slip ahead after supper to meet the "more charming" ladies. In some cases the relationships were mere dallying, but in several instances lasting romances budded, proving that even the rugged life on the trail and the long exhausting hours left some energy for the more basic instincts of young men and women.

Some of the emerging relationships brought evaluations from their emigrant friends and neighbors.

"I hope Elizabeth McGary and Asa Lovejoy continue their friendship," Reeda commented. "They make such a handsome couple and Asa is such a gentleman." Asa had made the winter ride with Marcus Whitman and was returning to Oregon.

"And Lettice Millican with Ransom Clark," added Matilda.

"Ransom Clark is too old for Lettice, she is barely fifteen and he is over thirty-five," Reeda offered, "He is a Fremont man, and just watch, when Fremont moves on, so will Ransom Clark, leaving a broken heart behind.

But the major discussions involved the Millican twins, Mary and Melvina not yet twelve years old.

"All the boys are buzzing around the Millican twins like bees at a hive. Even Pleasant and Kenny hang around them." Reeda said with disdain in her voice.

"A couple of the boys got into a shoving match over the girls," Sarah reported.

"And I bet the girls just loved it," Reeda said.

"Mrs. Millican has made the girls promise they won't get married until they are thirteen, but unless she puts a high fence around Mary and Melvina, that promise won't be kept," Mary added.

"Let's work to keep our nice boys away from the honey pot because some one is going to get stung," Reeda suggested.

"I say Amen to that," Mary added.

CHAPTER 18

Forced March to the Platte River

For two weeks straight, the rain continued, as we moved northwest following the Little Blue River. This is terrain over which we should have made good distances, but the rain had turned the ground to a mud lolly and the travel was greatly reduced. There are many small tributaries to the Little Blue and each presented a different challenge.

On the Republican Fork of the Blue River, the members of the Light Column encountered their first buffalo. We were two miles behind in the Cow Column, but we heard the gunfire. At first we thought the Light Column was under attack because the firing was so rapid.

Jesse ordered an immediate circling of the wagons although it was only mid afternoon. John Brooks, Nimrod Ford, Lewis Cooper and John East led by Jesse Applegate, all heavily armed, raced forward to give assistance. Jesse left me in charge of our Column.

Two hours later the men returned with the story of the buffalo kill. It seems that Jim Nesmith and Captain Gantt, our guide, had spotted an old bull. They and some others, gave chase for about a mile. The story goes that the "hunters" fired seven shots into the hapless beast before he dropped to the ground. That was the gunfire we had heard. There didn't seem to be a person among them who knew anything about butchering an animal. In the Cow Column many of the men had experience in butchering, but the men in the Light Column literally hacked off portions of meat to distribute to their group.

Jesse was offered some of the meat, but he declined all but the tongue, which the Light Column was going to just discard, not knowing that the tongue is one of the prize pieces. Jesse said he would have liked to have had more, but they had made such a mess of the butchering that he wasn't interested in more of that "old critter." We learned later that the meat was so tough it was barely edible.

Jesse and Lindsay Applegate had a better idea. One of the yearling heifers had been stifled earlier in the day's march and could no longer keep up with the herd and so they decided to butcher the heifer. Lindsay and Jesse were experienced butchers, having butchered many an animal on their farms.

Every family received some fresh beef. The amount was dependent on the size of the family. Jesse gave the tongue to the Blevins family, but he kept the tail, which he skinned, for himself. So the Applegates had ox tail stew. They deserved the best I thought. The aroma of freshly cooked beef floated from our campfires and we knew it was far superior meat to the bullet-ridden buffalo. The wolfhounds had nice leg bones on which to gnaw.

We began seeing many antelope in the distance. It was tempting to send a hunting party out after them, but Gabe advised us that the amount of meat obtained would not equal the energy expended by horse and man.

"If you get within range, which I doubt you would, you will get little meat for your effort. They are only the size of a goat. You will fatigue your mounts for little gain,"

The Light Column under Colonel Martin sent out hunting parties each day but they were not successful.

On June 17 a Pawnee hunting party met us. They were curious and so were we. They had known Mountain Men and other white trappers, but our children and women took them back. By sign language we were made to understand that they were locating buffalo for their annual hunt. They explained to us, that we would not see many buffalo until we reached the Platte River country. We were impressed with how handsome and sturdy of body they appeared. On a signal, the Braves swirled on their mounts and disappeared over a knoll, and were gone as quickly as they had appeared.

"What do you think, Gabe?" Jesse asked.

"They weren't a war party but the next time we see them they may be painted. I would add night guards tonight and put the 'out riders' further out tomorrow."

"I'll see to it," Jesse said.

The Pawnees had communicated to us that we were about thirty miles from the Platte River. That evening Jesse rode ahead to talk to Colonel Martin and Captain Gantt regarding our visitors, and to see if they had any visitors. As Jesse rode past our wagon I remarked to Mary, "He won't get back until way after midnight. The day of a good Column Captain never ends."

"Jesse is always thinking ahead for the welfare of the Column," Mary replied.

Jesse returned sooner than I had predicted. When he arrived about nine o'clock, he immediately called for an impromptu meeting of all the heads of households.

"I've just returned from a conference with Martin and Gantt. What the Pawnees were conveying to them was for the next thirty to forty miles there is no water. There is nothing to drink between here and the Platte River. There are no springs, no creeks, and no water. Captain Gantt rode ahead two days ago, all the way to the Platte River. He says it is sandy ground all the way. He estimates it to be about thirty miles, which verifies what the Pawnees were trying to tell us. The Light Column is planning on two to three days to cross this stretch, but I think, if we take that long, the loose cattle will suffer too much."

"What do you suggest?" Charles Applegate asked his younger brother.

"I suggest we force march the loose cattle. They can go four to five miles an hour, but the oxen pulling the wagons can only go about two miles an hour, if we are fortunate. I will need all the men we can spare to drive the cattle. Incidentally, prepare your people for a cold camp there are no trees or any wood for fires.

"Those of you who are going with me, be ready to ride out and start pushing the cattle at 4 AM, that will be before daylight. I'm leaving Thomas Keizur in charge of the Column. Do you have anything to say Thomas?"

"Not much, except if you have spare oxen, yoke them on in the morning. Fill your water kegs yet tonight. We will spread the Column out five or six wide if we can. We don't want to eat anymore dust than we have to, and we won't be sinking deeper into the sand. It will be a very long day, but don't try to force march the oxen. They will go their own speed. But I can tell you when we get within ten miles or so of the river, the oxen will begin to quicken their pace. Be ready for them to break into a run when they see the river."

"Jesse, does Colonel Martin know you are driving the herd through his Column?" Charles Applegate asked.

"I hope to have the herd past their camp before they break out in the morning. We will skirt their camps if we can, otherwise we will drive through as quickly as we can. And yes, the Colonel knows we are going to drive the cattle ahead, and he is not too happy with the idea. Get some sleep now and be ready to ride before dawn. Tomorrow you will learn why they call this, 'The Great American Desert'."

After we retired to our fire, I said, "Gabe and I will lead our wagons and Mary Louise can drive Gabe's buggy. That means Joe, Samuel, John Brooks, John and Nimrod Ford, Pleasant, and Kenny will go with Jesse to help drive the herd."

Francis stood up, "I'm thirteen and I want to go with the drovers. I can ride and I can shoot, and I am as tall as Pleasant."

"One thing you're not, Francis, and that is shy. If you want to go, be ready at four. But I better never hear that you didn't carry your weight," I said.

"Francis will not disappoint you, Thomas," Mary, a proud mother said. "We will see you on the Platte River."

As the Keizurs scurried to their bedrolls I pulled John Brooks aside. "John, look after your brothers."

"Don't worry, Dad, I already had that in mind."

Gabe quietly said to Mary, "If I had had a Dad like Thomas, I would not have left home when I was Francis's age."

"They were all boys when they left Independence, but they will be men by the time we get to the Willamette Valley somewhere in Oregon," Mary sighed.

Jesse had the herd moving by 4:30 AM and I had the Column rolling by 5:30. By seven we were at the Light Column's campground. It didn't look like they would be underway for another hour or so. They were still filling water barrels and the like.

I was hoping to get in front as soon as possible, because once the crust of the sand is broken, the wagons will pull much harder. As we pulled through their camp there was cheering and some cat calls. Generally we heard "See you on the Platte!"

"I hope so, I dearly hope so," I said under my breath.

Mary Louise and Reeda came up alongside the wagon I was leading. They were mounted and each carried a rifle across her saddle. "We need some 'outriders', Dad and that's Reeda and me," Mary Louise announced. "I turned the buggy driving over to Matilda she needs more to do."

"What about your babies?" I knew Mary Louise was still nursing little William, and Reeda's baby, Tilman was not three weeks old.

"Grandmother Keizur is on baby duty," Reeda replied, "When it's time to feed them, Mom will wave her bonnet and we will come in for awhile."

"Thank you, girls," I said. Having outriders to warn of any intruders was certainly a blessing. An outrider stays off about a quarter of a mile and keeps a sharp eye on the horizon. My girls knew their responsibilities and to see them to my right and to my left gave me a great sense of security not just for the Keizurs but also for the entire Column.

The day wore on hot and boring. I stopped the train at 11:30. The sun was on high without a cloud in the sky, except for the cloud of dust raised by the wagons. I sent the word down the train to not unyoke, but to take the time to regrease their running gear. The temperature had already risen to above 90 degrees by my estimation, and the grease on the running gears was liquefying and dripping off. "When you have greased up, continue on", I shouted. Mary put all the children in the wagons. They had already been walking for over seven hours and about ten to twelve miles.

By five in the afternoon I figured we had covered about 22-25 miles. We had been on the move for eleven hours. The oxen were suffering greatly as were the women and children. But as I had expected, the oxen had slowly but surely picked up their pace. They could smell water. I waved Reeda into my wagon.

"Reeda ride back and tell each family that we are not stopping for an evening camp. The oxen smell water. So we must be less than ten miles from the river. Tell them to allow the oxen to accelerate at their will." In fact, we were only six miles out from the river.

At half past nine with the moon rising in the east, we crested a brow of a ridge and there was the Platte River. It looked more like a lake than a river. Up from the river came eight Keizur riders whooping at the top of their lungs, sweat stained and dirty but happy.

"We saw your dust at four o'clock. We knew you would come on in yet tonight," Francis shouted.

Reeda and Mary Louise came riding in from their stations. "Go back down the line and tell the drivers to drive right into the river. Tell them not to unyoke the oxen. We need to soak those wheels."

Joe Hess added, "Tell them Jesse said we will lay over tomorrow."

By ten at night the camps were quiet as a church. Everyone crawled slowly into their bedrolls under the stars. No one set up a tent that night. Jesse's men who had arrived much earlier and were somewhat rested ,stood guard for the rest of us. Jesse had not lost a single animal in the thirty mile drive. During the early morning moonlight I heard wolves howling for the first time on our trip. The wolfhounds came in closer to the fire tonight. They heard their distant cousins too, and didn't like what they heard.

We got our first good look at the river by morning light. We had arrived at the head of a substantial island called Grand Island, by the Mountain Men. The island stretched further than we could see. The river itself consisted of many small rivulets. The bottom was three to five miles wide. In a few places the water was running fairly swiftly, but generally the water ran lazily.

Sand bars hundreds of yards long and five to six feet wide gave the river a striped appearance. Another feature which is a concern, on our side of the river, or the south side, there were no trees or brush. The Island is covered with willows and cottonwood and on the north bank there are trees and brush. Why the south bank had no trees has never been explained to me.

No one knows for sure who first described the Platte River as "a mile wide and a foot deep" or "too thick to drink and too thin to plow" but they are apt descriptions.

The name "Platte" was given to the river by a French fur trapper. It means "flat". Joe Hess said, "It would be a good river if it was set on edge."

CHAPTER 19

Buffalo Stampede

As I have said several times before, three items are important in setting up a camp site on the trail. I'm sure you remember those three items are water, grass, and wood, or I should say fuel. We soon discovered, that along the south bank of the Platte River, there was no wood. So another fuel had to be obtained, or there would be no cook fires, let alone warming fires.

But we are in buffalo country. The droppings left for years by the buffalo would be our source of fuel. Fremont's French Canadians say "*bois de vache*", our farmer friends say, "buffalo dung" but the pioneers called it "buffalo chips". The "chips" are an excellent source of fuel. They burn hot, much like charcoal. In fact Mary called the chips "prairie coal". A few of the women, but not Keizur women, were squeamish at first in handling the chips, but they soon got over it or their men would be eating only cold suppers.

The children often do the gathering in the evenings. The preferred method is to take a bed canvass and throw the chips onto it from as wide an area as they could throw the chips. The best method is to sling the flat chips underhand and with a little practice to get the right ark a good chip thrower could hit his target from forty feet away. More than one chip fight entertained the gatherers. It takes three to five bushels to supply the evening fire. That is a lot of buffalo chips, but usually there was no shortage.

We observed the method used by the Pawnees in making the most efficient fire. The Pawnee's method was to dig a ditch eight to ten inches wide and three to four feet long and set the fire in the ditch. The ditch is oriented against the evening wind so that the breeze blowing across the ditch supplied the right amount of oxygen but with out scattering the embers. Buffalo chips burn hot, with very little smoke, and no odor.

We were now sighting small groups of buffalo several times a day. The oxen became distressed, if their wild cousins got too close, or if we crossed a fresh buffalo trail. One time we laid bye for an hour, waiting for a fresh trail to cool. The oxen snort and paw the ground, and in some cases they seem like they would like to follow the buffalo.

I remembered bringing our cows down the lane to the barn when I was a boy in North Carolina. The cows always walked in single file led by a boss cow, never led by the bull. By walking in the same trail night and morning, the cows soon wore a trail about six inches wide and three or four inches deep right down the middle of the lane. I recalled this when I watched the buffalo. They do exactly the same thing. They file down to the river morning and night in single file, not led by a big bull, but by a buffalo cow. Over time they have worn ruts down about eight inches deep and a foot wide. The edges of these trail ruts look like they were carved smooth by a huge knife. I mention all of this because along the Platte River these ten-inch deep ruts are found about every thirty yards. The wagons bounced and jolted across these ruts. The muleskinners that sat on wooden seats were jarred from tooth to toe. Everyone walked who could.

Colonel Martin with the Light Column commissioned twenty men to go on a hunting party after buffalo to obtain fresh meat for both Columns. Nimrod Ford was the only man selected from the Cow Column.

"Nimrod is not our best marksman," John Brooks lamented, "several of us can out shoot him."

"Remember," Gabe coached Nimrod, "you don't drop a buffalo by shooting at his head."

"Where should I hit them?" Nimrod asked.

"You try for a spine shot or a heart shot," Gabe said. Nimrod knew that Gabe had hunted more buffalo than Colonel Martin and all twenty of his hunters, had ever seen.

"Anything else I should know, Gabe?"

"Well, buffalo have very poor eyesight, but a keen sense of smell, so always approach with the wind in your face. When you think you have gotten a good shot in, back off, don't continue the chase. Don't expect the buffalo to drop in its tracks. They will keep going for even a mile or so. Just be patient. Don't get too close to them. Most mortally wounded bulls will charge you, and they can be very dangerous at that point.

"When they finally have to stop, they will start spreading their legs further and further apart. When they do that you know you will have buffalo steak for supper."

"Why do they spread their legs like that?" Pleasant asked.

"They are struggling to keep their balance and not go down and spreading their legs will keep them upright a little longer. The buffalo in-stinctively know that once they go down, they can't get back up. I will tell you, that the first time I watched a gallant old bull in his final death fight, trying to stay erect, I wished to God I had missed him, and we were very hungry too, as I recall. I have no problem with a hunter taking a buffalo when they need the meat, but I can tell you, I don't like this Sir Stewart bunch of so called sportsmen, shooting buffalo just for the hell of it."

Nimrod was anxious for more tips but Colonel Martin had summoned the hunters for their departure.

The Colonel seemed to select men without any direct family ties such as Nimrod Ford, James Nesmith, John Overton, and Pierson Reading as examples.

The hunters were gone for four days, but returned with a good supply of fresh meat. Nimrod reported that the hunting party had been caught in a series of sudden rainsqualls and they had spent several wet miserable nights without being able to start a fire.

"If the rain had been any colder it would have congealed," Nimrod remarked. "Next time you can go John Brooks, and I will stay."

June 24 was an extremely hot and humid day. An event occurred that affected the psyche of the Keizur Clan for years to come, and for some individual members the impact was for a lifetime. Such was the case with me.

We were the lead wagons that day and we were plodding our way along the Platte. Joe Hess was riding point. It all began with a low rumbling sound, like the approach of a major storm, but there was not a cloud in the sky. While we were pondering the meaning of this, Joe suddenly let out a yell, "Buffalo! Buffalo stampede!" And came racing back to the wagons. "There are thousands of them and they are headed directly into us."

"How much time do we have?" I shouted! "How much time?" I repeated!

"Twenty minutes, maybe less," Joe shouted!

Gabe immediately turned the teams of oxen into a row of willows and cottonwood. These were the only trees we had seen in some time. He motioned to the four wagons behind us to do the same. The oxen sensing the oncoming peril, responded faster than usual.

By this time the ground was literally bouncing, and the roar of thousands of hoofs was like continuous thunder.

"Hand the rifles down Mary! Everyone with a gun follow me. The rest of you go deeper into the cottonwoods!"

I ran to a swale that the Column would have been going through only twenty-five yards away. The swale was a depression about ten feet lower than the surrounding terrain and about fifty feet wide. Perhaps the swale had been a watercourse at some time.

"First row of rifles in a kneeling position," I shouted. "Second row stay standing."

We had gathered fourteen riflemen and riflewomen at the gap. All of my family, except for Sarah and the children, who she was herding deeper into the woods, was kneeling or standing in front of me across this narrow gap. The last I saw of Sarah she had William on one arm and baby Tilman in the other and she was running like a deer.

By this time, we could see the leading edge of the stampeding buffalo come over the rim of the hill. It looked like a brown bucket of molasses being poured down the hill directly toward us.

"We must turn them at the swale, or they will run right down the entire train, destroying us all," I shouted. I stayed in front with my revolver in the air. I had given my rifle to Thomas Cullwell, my ten year old son , who kneeled in the front line.

"Don't shoot until I do," I shouted! "Hit the leaders! We will try to roll them up across the swale." I stepped in front of my little army with my pistol held high in the air. Only fifteen minutes at most had gone by, but it seemed like an eternity.

At that moment Kenneth O'Regan, who had been our outrider on the left flank, came galloping up. His eyes were larger than dinner plates.

"Stay mounted!" I yelled. "Ride up the line and warn the rest of the train and bring us all the riflemen you can."

I will never know for sure, whether he heard and understood or not, I turned to give my attention to the oncoming stampeding buffalo, but I turned back to glance in Kenneth's direction and to my dismay, saw Kenny disappearing over the ridge in the opposite direction.

The stampeding buffalo were like fingers on a hand, moving this way then swaying back in another direction. The leaders swung back and forth twenty yards in one direction and then swung fifty yards back. The main body of the herd seemed to be veering slightly to our north. One finger of beasts swung toward us and came within twenty yards of our position.

I turned facing my grim family waiting their orders to fire.

"Steady! Steady! Steady!" I shouted over the din. But each time a finger of brown animals headed toward the swale they veered off in a slightly different direction at the last moment. We held our position for an hour and a half while thousands of 2,000-pound buffalos raced by. We could see their blood shot eyes, and smell their sweat, and hear the thunder of their pounding hoofs.

For some unexplained reason, the herd never broke for the swale. They came very close, but did not take that slight turn that would have put them on top of us. It is questionable whether we could have rolled them up by killing enough in the front if the stampede had turned through the swale. We would have probably been able to get off 20 to 25 rounds at the most, and even if every shot had been effective, their momentum would have carried them past our line. But if our shots were effective, and if some animals had started to drop, then others might have piled up behind them. That was our plan, and only hope.

Even the very youngest on the firing line knew, that in the event of a breakthrough, none of the Keizurs could survive a horrible death, and probably the entire Column would be lost. Little Thomas had wet the front of his overalls, but we all pretended not to notice.

When the stampeding buffalos had finally past, Colonel Martin and Captain Gantt came galloping up to us. The Colonel sat on his horse surveying our Party, which was sitting or laying, almost in a daze.

"Do you think you could have turned them?" Captain Gantt asked.

"I don't know. It wasn't likely," I replied.

Colonel Martin swung down from his horse, and without saying a word, shook the hand of every one of us. Others began gathering around. Jesse Applegate came up on his horse.

"Colonel lets lay bye for the rest of the day. We have many cattle to round up." He tipped his hat in salute to us.

Suddenly the Keizurs were alone. At that time Kenny O'Regan came riding in.

"Where have you been?" I demanded.

"I was scared," Kenny stammered.

"Didn't you understand my order?"

"I was scared," Kenny said, lowering his eyes.

"Do you think we weren't scared? Do you think I wasn't scared? But we did our duty. We didn't run like a rabbit." Kenneth sat with slumped shoulders.

"You are a coward, Kenneth O'Reagan."

"I was scared."

"Is that all you have to say? You're sitting on my horse. Get off my horse. There is no room in my family for a coward. You are banished. Get out of my sight. And that rifle you're packing belongs to me too. Give it to me."

Kenneth appeared stunned as he handed over the rifle.

"Thomas," Mary said with a plea in her voice.

I raised my hand to stop her. "Now go, Mr., you are not welcome here."

Kenny turned to go but then hesitated, reached into his pocket and took out the twenty dollar gold piece that Mary had given to each of us to carry to Oregon and handed it to Mary.

Mary hesitated but took the coin and was about to hug Kenny, "Mary, no," I commanded.

Kenny turned and started walking away toward the brow of the hill, and then he broke in to a jog and disappeared over the ridge. The family was stunned into silence, and Mary turned away without a word. One by one the family turned to follow Mary. Only Gabe remained with me.

"Thomas, you have done wrong. He is only a boy. You have set him out on foot unarmed. You have sentenced that boy to death."

"Gabe, I have never done anything so hard in my life, but he needed to be disciplined. His actions could have cost me my entire family and we could have lost the entire Column."

"It was too harsh, Thomas. Would you have banished him had it been John Brooks, or Pleasant, or Francis?"

"Yes, Gabe, Kenny was as much my son as any of the others."

It was a quiet supper that evening. Jesse came up shortly after supper. "I understand you banished the young Irish lad," Jesse opened.

"Yes, I did."

"You have no authority to have done that. That is a decision that only the Council can make. He should have had a trial. You exceeded your authority."

"Don't lecture me, Mr. Applegate. This is a family matter."

"His scalp will be on a Pawnee pole before the week is out."

I walked away from Jesse, and from the light of the campfire, into the darkness surrounding us.

I did not sleep well that night, but finally slipped into a light slumber, about one in the morning, only to be awakened by Pleasant shaking me. "Dad! Dad! A rider is leaving the camp trailing a horse!"

"Is the horse being trailed, the pony that Kenny usually rode?"

"I think it may be. The rider looks like Reeda."

"I am not surprised."

"Shall I stop her? She's carrying a rifle too. Do you want me to try to stop her?"

"No, I don't think so. Go back to bed, Son. And let's not discuss what we saw tonight."

Mary reached over and patted my hand. "Thank you, Thomas. He will have a chance now," she whispered.

"I pray he makes it to Oregon, but realistically, it is not likely. *It's a long way to Oregon,*" I said.

At four thirty in the morning I heard Reeda coming back into camp leading her horse in order to be as quiet as possible.

"She found him! Thank God," Mary whispered.

"Go back to sleep, Mary, we will have to be underway in an hour."

In the weeks ahead, no one mentioned Kenny, at least not to me, but when there was a storm, or when the wolves howled at the moon, I wondered about him.

CHAPTER 20

South Fork

We were now following the South Fork of the Platte River. The South Fork was not the quiet, shallow, slow moving stream that the main branch was. Captain Gantt, while with the hunting party, scouted the river for a suitable fording place, but found none. We traveled an estimated 85 miles along the South Fork, which was taking us further and further from the direction we needed to be going. We gave up looking for a safe fording place on the 29th of June, and set up camp in a willow grove.

"Does anybody know how to build a boat?" an old Kentuckian mumbled.

The river was about a mile wide at this point and carried five to eight feet of water from bank to bank.

The plan we came up with was to tack "green" buffalo hides, flesh side out, to the bottom and sides of the wagons. The sun, which was scorching hot, dried the green hides. Women and children rubbed buffalo tallow and ashes all over the hides to make them still more waterproof.

By Saturday July 1, we had used all the green hides available. Our boats were ready. We attached long towropes to the front of each "boat". Three men waded or swam beside each wagon using guy ropes to steady the wagon. When a wagon was pulled out on the other side the buffalo hide was torn off and returned across the river to be affixed to another wagon.

Jim Nesmith, at six foot eight inches, became a most valuable man in this operation. He could wade nearly the whole distance tugging on the guy ropes, whereas the shorter men could wade much less, before they had to swim. "Just call me high pockets," Jim quipped.

Elisha Applegate, the thirteen-year-old son of Lindsay and Elizabeth Applegate, was an excellent swimmer, and along with Pleasant and John Brooks, who were also strong swimmers, swam the river numerous times and was very helpful.

Many of the men gulped their stomachs full of river water and became really quite ill with a high fever. Pierson Reading was totally incapacitated due to the fever. Reeda was kept busy treating the ill.

The crossing was consuming too much time and the men were all fighting fatigue. A decision was made to load the wagon contents onto the makeshift ferry and take the empty wagons up stream to a spot much wider but shallow enough that the wheels would be on the bottom for all but the very center of the stream. The wagons were raised and blocked about eight inches higher than normal. Sam Penter advised us not to raise our wagons by blocking. "Blocking up the wagon beds could be very risky. They could float right off the blocks. Besides our wagon boxes are watertight. The water could come up several feet on the box without a worry to us".

From twenty to forty wagons were chained together, with a towrope in front and sway ropes in the back, held in place by oxen. It was a risky plan, but as we had been going, it would take many more days for this crossing.

Even with the tow rope and sway ropes the wagons finally pulled out of the river a full two miles downstream from where they had entered. But the system did work.

The only really serious accident was when John McHaly's wagon broke loose and rolled over and over. The men with the buffalo skin ferryboats downstream knew that something was amiss as McHaly's belongings started showing up down stream. By some near miracle the men at the skin boats grabbed onto almost all of McHaly's belongings, all which floated at least.

To add to our concerns a party of some one hundred to a hundred and twenty Braves lined the bluffs overlooking our crossing. They sat on their ponies watching.

Captain Gantt, with his spyglass, determined they were Pawnee and that they were not wearing war paint. Nevertheless, the Column leaders set up a skirmish line a hundred yards off the river. The men fell cottonwood trees to form a breastwork. This pulled forty men off the crossing detail where they were sorely needed. Men rotated off the crossing party to the skirmish line to get a little rest. When the last wagon was finally pulled from the river we heard a long whooping call, almost like a Swiss yodeler, coming from the watching Indians.

"I swear, I believe that was a salute to us," Jesse said.

Some of the women waved their sunbonnets back at the Indians as they disappeared out of sight. "Most Indians respect bravery, and they saw this little operation as being so foolhardy, as to be courageous in their eyes," Gabe suggested.

We were six days in crossing the South Fork of the Platte River. In fact, it took so long, that another small wagon train that started from Independence the first week of June, caught up with us. Captain J.B. Chiles led this party. The Chiles Company planned to turn off at Fort Hall to go south to California. Chiles had been with the Western Emigration Company that took fourteen wagons to Fort Hall in 1841. They left their wagons at that point and went south by pack train. Chiles came back east and organized this Company to return to California.

In addition, Overton Johnson and his small group of eight men, who had broken off at the Kansas River crossing and had wandered around a bit, rejoined us. And so our delay on the South Fork crossing allowed several straggling groups to catch up with us.

"If we wait much longer, half the state of Missouri will be here," Gabe lamented.

Perhaps the most exciting addition to the Oregon Emigration Company was baby Catherine Stewart, daughter of Peter and Rebecca Stewart. This was their first child for the newlyweds. P.G. Stewart was a watchmaker and a jeweler and he and Rebecca were part of the Cason group. Usually the mother of the expectant would assist. However Mrs. Cason, Rebecca's mother was just not up to assisting, although she had several children of her own.

Reeda Keizur Ford arrived and asked, "Can I be of assistance?" Peter was somewhat concerned and hesitated, "But you are so young and didn't you just have your first baby?"

"Yes, Tilman is not quite a month old. But I assisted my first birth when I was twelve years old. I have been a mid-wife seven times since then."

"For goodness sake, Peter, let Reeda in, and you get out," Rebecca ordered.

While little Catherine Stewart may have been the most exciting arrival, the most important one was Dr. Marcus Whitman.

Dr. Marcus Whitman came riding into camp on a big white stallion carrying very little visable gear. He didn't even have a rifle. Everyone felt they knew Marcus Whitman and some actually did know him. For example Peter Burnett had met Whitman twice. Colonel Martin also knew him. Dr. Whitman's thirteen year old nephew, Perim Beza Whitman accompanied him. Asa Lovejoy heard that Dr. Whitman was not far off and rode seven miles back over the trail to escort him in to camp. Asa had accompanied Whitman on his winter ride east in 1842, but had not seen him since he left St. Louis.

Marcus Whitman hailed each wagon and family, like he had known him, or her, forever. When he reached our wagon he stopped. Asa said, "This is the Keizur Clan. Their daughter Reeda Ann Ford is the young lady I told you about. She has been our doctor."

"Is Mrs. Ford available? I would dearly like to meet her."

Reeda, was standing in the rear, somewhat awed at seeing the famous doctor, stepped forward. "I am Reeda Ford. I am so honored to meet you,

Dr. Whitman."

"I understand you attended to the birth of a little girl last night," Marcus Whitman said.

"Yes, but we didn't know you were that close or we would have sent for you," Reeda explained.

"It is my understanding that everything went well for the mother and child and they are doing, fine," Whitman said.

"I believe they are," Reeda confirmed.

"Where did you get your medical training?" Marcus asked.

"I have had no formal training. It seems I just have a knack to get people feeling better."

"Your gift of healing is well recognized. It is a *gift* not a 'knack'. There are perhaps as many as a thousand souls in this train rolling into history. Some will get sick, some will be injured, babies will be born, some will meet their Maker, but there is one thing for certain, one doctor cannot tend this flock without help. Will you spend the time with me and assist me and let me teach you as much as I can? Can you bleed a patient?"

"I never have, but I would like to learn," Reeda said.

"The color of the blood is important, but I will show you. Have you ever set a bone?"

"Only on animals."

"We will have that challenge sooner or later you may be sure of that." He reached into his saddlebag and extracted a leather-covered manual. "Can you read, Mrs. Ford?"

"Please call me, Reeda, and yes, I can read."

"This is a book on anatomy. Study the illustrations and don't worry about the Latin terms. It is alright to say the big bone, or the small bone."

Reeda took the book in both hands.

"I will teach you how to properly cauterize a wound, a most useful skill, and heaven forbid, how to amputate."

A young worried rider came into the camp and spoke up, "Dr. Whitman, my wife is doing poorly. What is your fee?"

Dr. Marcus Whitman turned to the crowd and raised his voice so that more could hear his answer. "My fee is a small portion of your evening meal and the warmth of your camp fire when it is cold. Reeda, do you have a horse and can you ride?" The entire assemblage roared with laughter. "I guess my question has been answered. Let's go talk to this pilgrim's wife and see if we can make her feel better."

Thus began a unique relationship between Dr. Marcus Whitman and Reeda, that lasted for the duration of the emigration. To most in the Company they were referred to as the doctors.

The Keizurs were extremely proud of Dr. Reeda and her "gift of healing", which she so willingly shared. But none was more proud than John Ford, her husband.

Marcus Whitman's arrival was a morale lift for everyone. He was a man to be trusted. His contribution to the welfare of the train was far more than his medical knowledge. He and Asa Lovejoy were the only ones on the train who had actually been to Oregon. They knew the way.

Marcus Whitman wasted no time in giving advice to Jesse, Colonel Martin and Captain Gantt. "Gentlemen, get this wagon train moving. It has got to move faster. You are barely making ten miles a day. You will have to average fifteen miles a day, so some days you will have to make 18-20 miles. Send men ahead to prepare each creek crossing. Why do you wait until you get to the crossing to begin the preparations? And I see most of the Company lays bye on the Sabbath, and those that don't, wait for those that do, to catch up. That will cost you fifteen miles a week. You will pay for those delays in the lives of your neighbors. If you want to do the Lord's work, save as many of these good people as you can, by keeping them on the move seven days a week. The Lord will understand. We will celebrate His day, a little differently for a few months. You must be through the Blue Mountains before the snow falls."

Chiles was joined by the Waldo group and took Whitman's warning to heart. They joined with others making a train of about 18 wagons and moved on about three miles further, before they camped. Many thought this "break off" was tantamount to desertion. The Keizurs did not pass judgment.

Old Alex Zackery was one who moved his wagons ahead. Pierson Reading said, "I will shed no tears getting rid of the Old Prairie Chicken." We were glad to have this obnoxious man out of our sight and hearing. Reading's moniker for Zackery stuck. Everyone referred to him as the "Old Prairie Chicken".

Our next big hurdle came at a place we named Ash Hollow, because of the grove of ash trees growing there. In the grove was an excellent spring with the sweetest water in the world, but to get to this setting we had to go down the steepest grade that we had encountered. The only other option was to travel on the bluffs for an extra two days. The men all gathered on the crest of the hill to offer their own theories on how to best navigate this hill.

The hill was an awesome sight. It slanted at a 45-degree pitch for three hundred yards before it leveled off. Some planned to tie trees on behind their wagons to serve as a brake. Many inserted timbers between the spokes of the wheels. Many chained the wheels down. We didn't like any of the ideas that gave the wagon a sled effect, like tying the wheels down, and so forth. We reasoned that we wanted the front wheels to roll free for steering purposes, but just not roll too fast. A great deal of time was wasted trying to figure out some sort of a windlass device, such as digging a wagon in, and using the axle on which to wind the rope. The problem with that, as we saw it, was even if the buried wagon withstood the strain, 300 yards of hemp rope tied together was not a good idea. It would break sooner or later, and then it would really be a disaster. Our solution was to hitch three yoke of oxen to the rear of the wagon and one yoke to the front and hope that the power of the animal's legs could hold back a half loaded wagon. We also put drag ropes on each side and the entire family helped slow the wagons down. The oxen in the front were primarily to keep the wagon tongue from digging in and snapping.

This was the method that most of the other families used. Some had trouble hooking up their oxen to the rear of their wagons since that was not a normal role for them. But we had little trouble because of our animals being so well trained. Gabe had no problem with his buggy with all the Keizurs hanging on to guy ropes to slow him down.

I learned later that subsequent wagon trains did rig up a windlass and, in fact, this hill was named, "Windlass Hill".

The next fifty miles was a gradual climb with many gullies to cross but we had water, wood, and grass. Dr. Whitman rode from party to party urging everyone to, "Travel! Travel! Travel! Nothing else will take you to the end of your journey; nothing is wise that does not help you along; nothing is good for you that causes a moment's delay."

We listened to him and so did Jesse who said, "His advice is based upon knowledge of the road before us."

Someone had estimated that we had traveled 500 miles since leaving Independence. So far we had not lost a person but gained two babies. We knew that record would not hold.

CHAPTER 21

Rock Formations

Following along the south bank of the North Platte, we entered an enchanted land of unusual sandstone and clay formations. Only Marcus Whitman and Asa Lovejoy had ever seen these sights. For the most part the emigrants were all "flat landers". To us the Great Smokies were big mountains. Little did we know what "real" mountains and rock formations would be like.

The first strange sight was a rock formation of many tiers. Near it, but detached from it, was a lesser, but interesting formation. The children all had their special names for these rocks such as, "Castle Rock", "Cathedral Rock," "Ghost Rock", and so forth.

Our trail ran parallel to this rock for miles. When we approached what appeared to be the nearest point, everyone including the Keizurs, were clamoring to go to it. "It appears to be about two miles off," I said. Gabe and I will keep the oxen moving and the rest of you can ride or walk over to the rock and explore it a bit and then catch up with us further down the trail."

"The truth is, Thomas, I would like to see it up close too," Gabe said.

"You go ahead, Gabe. I will lead our second wagon," Mary volunteered. "And I will drive your buggy and team," Sarah said, "someone must stay with the little ones."

"We should be back in two hours, I would say," Gabe said.

It was quite a caravan that left for "Cathedral Rock".

Mary Louise had six year old Tillman and four year old Mary Jane up behind her on her horse. Joe Hess had little Sarah, just three years old, hanging on to his belt loops behind him. Matilda had Thomas, four years old, on behind her. John Brooks had his little sister Elizabeth, eight years old, behind him and John Ford had his nephew William Henry, only four, up behind him. Thomas Cullwell, ten, insisted on riding his own horse. Altogether we saddled seven horses for the sight-seeing trip. Since the rock formation was estimated to be only two miles away they didn't need to take canteens of water or heavier clothing and certainly food was not necessary because they would be back by suppertime. The caravan finally got under way about two in the afternoon.

We laid bye, at about six. Mary, Sarah and I ate our supper by seven, but with no sign of the return of the sightseers. By eight at night Mary said, "They are three hours over due. Something is amiss. I have a bad feeling about this. I think you should organize a search party at once."

"I'll go check with Jesse Applegate and see what he thinks," I said. I was back in a very few minutes. "I can't consult with Jesse, he and most of the Applegates went to the rock formation too, as did half the Company it seems. No one is back yet. This is not good. They had no water, they weren't armed except I know that Joe Hess and Gabe would have their Militia revolvers on them."

We built our campfire higher to serve as a beacon in case they were temporarily confused with their directions and we paced and paced.

At 11:00 PM one of the night watchmen shouted "Riders coming in, twenty minutes out". It was too late to circle the wagons. Campfires were quickly doused, up and down the line, and women started handing down rifles to their men. We were totally exposed in the open. "How many riders?" somebody shouted.

"At least forty to fifty, maybe more, they are not coming hard, yet."

Mary and Sarah each took down a rifle and kneeled beside me.

"Don't shoot for God's sake! It's me, Jesse Applegate. Don't fire! Don't fire!"

The Keizurs straggled in about a half hour later. Others kept straggling well after midnight.

John Brooks explained the situation to us. "The rock formation is not two miles away it was at least fifteen miles. The formation is not fifty feet high it is more like 200 feet high. The distances are very deceptive with the rock rising from a flat plain. But it is worth the effort to see this wonder up close. The rock is about 200 feet long by 150 feet wide. On the north side a person can climb nearly to the top with ease. Some of the fellers climbed all the way to the top, but Gabe and Joe wouldn't let us. We all cut our names and the date into the soft sandstone. There were other names already there. Gabe said he recognized the names of some of the Mountain Men. And that's not all. Joe said not to mention this, but I want to. We saw carved in the sandstone 'Kenneth D. O'Regan of Cork'".

"Dad, Kenny is still alive! He was there!"

"Did he put the date?" I asked.

"No, he did not put the date. But he was sure there."

"Kenny is a strong lad," I managed to say.

"Tomorrow morning early, I want to go to the rock," Mary said.

"And so do I," I said.

"You will not regret the side trip," Joe said. "We will keep the wagons rolling while you're gone. But just remember it is much further away than it looks, take water."

As I understand it, later emigrants in other wagon trains dubbed these rocks as "Courthouse Rock" and "Jailhouse Rock" because they reminded them of the new courthouse in Independence. There was no courthouse in Independence when we left. It had not been built yet. So to the members of the Oregon Emigration Company of 1843, it was always called either "Cathedral Rock" or "Castle Rock".

Cathedral Rock was not out of sight before the next strange rock formation appeared ahead like a giant's finger beckoning us to come forward.

Only fourteen miles west of Cathedral Rock a slim stone shaft thrust into the air some 500 feet high. The base is surrounded by great heaps of debris that was once part of the "shaft". Everyone described it in his, or her, own terms. Some said it looked like a chimney in a burned out building, or a pole in a haystack, or a church steeple, or an inverted funnel. However it is described, it is a wonder to be sure.

Once again we all rode over to get a closer look. The distance was not as great as the Cathedral Rock and this time we were not fooled, but still it was a good ten-mile ride. Up close we could see that the shaft was spindly only about fifteen feet in diameter at the top and about forty feet in diameter at the base of the shaft. There appears to be an enormous crack in the top. I am glad we got to see this before it crumbles to the ground from erosion.

Pleasant and John Brooks decided they wanted to determine the distance around the main base of rubble but neither wanted to walk the whole distance. Their solution was to start back to back and walk in opposite directions each counting their strides until they met. Adding their steps together they came up with 10,040 strides. Assuming each stride was a yard, they estimate it to be about two and a half miles in circumference. Jesse Applegate, being a surveyor by profession, encouraged the boys in their curiosity.

Carving our names was much easier in this formation because the rock was softer. We scouted the initials and names of previous carvers looking for Kenny's name but we did not see it.

Only twenty miles further the wagon train came to Scott's Bluff. This rock outcrop was one of the few that had been named before us. Scott's Bluff is the last of a string of large rock formations and by far the largest. We passed through these rock "wonders" as we continued along the Platte River.

Scott's Bluff is enormous. We estimated it to be 800 feet high. The Indians call it "Me-a-pa-te", meaning, "hill that is hard to go around".

"Who was Scott?" Francis wanted to know.

Marcus Whitman, who was well read, indicated that Washington Irving, the famous American writer wrote about the naming of Scott's Bluff in his book about the fur trade, which he titled *The Adventures of Captain Bonneville*. Since none of us had read the book, we asked Dr. Whitman to tell us the story.

"There are several stories about the naming of this enormous rock formation and who can say which is really the correct story. But all the stories do have a common thread to them. So I will tell the one as related by Washington Irving.

"It seems in about the year of 1828, fifteen years ago, a group of trappers were making their way to the Green River rendezvous when one of their group became very ill. His name was Hiram Scott. Two men were assigned to stay with him and to catch up with the other trappers on their return trip. The assigned trappers wandered for days with many hardships. All the time Scott grew weaker and weaker, to the point that he could no longer sit a horse. The group realized that they had missed the meeting place where they were to join their returning friends. Scott was in extremely bad shape and they reasoned he was soon to die. The men also knew that if they waited with him they would quite likely also perish. And so they made Hiram Scott as comfortable as they could and without saying "good bye" the two trappers slipped away at night. This was at these bluffs we see in the distance.

"When the trappers finally caught up with the other trappers going east they reported that Hiram Scott had died and they had buried him at the Bluffs. The story might have ended there, except the next summer, Bill Sublette, the same Bill Sublette, who is now the guide to the nearby Stewart Party, was traveling through the area and found the remains of Hiram Scott, with undeniable identity on him. But the spot he found Scott was miles from the place where the two trappers had said they buried him. Obviously the two men had lied. Hiram Scott had crawled many miles before he died.

"It is my understanding, that Bill Sublette has never revealed the names of the two trappers that left poor Hiram Scott to his fate. Well, that's the story as best I can relate, that Washington Irving wrote about."

CHAPTER 22

Fort Laramie

Our forward scouts advised us that we were within two hard days travel of Fort Laramie or three easy days. With Marcus Whitman urging us on, we decided on the "two hard days". The terrain was gradually gaining in elevation and we were now about 4,500 feet above sea level as reckoned by Fremont using scientific instruments. In the distance was Laramie Peak the forerunner of the "Great Stony Mountains" or more commonly known as the Rocky Mountains.

Somebody commented that when we reach Fort Laramie we will have traveled 640 miles, which would mean we have not gone one third of the way to Oregon and the Willamette Valley. We should, therefore, have two-thirds of our food supply left, but we did not. We had less than half of our commodities remaining. Our stock was holding up fine but many of the teams of horses and some oxen had broken down and it can only get worse.

The emigrants had different expectations of Fort Laramie. It was the first sign of civilization we had seen since we left Independence, Missouri.

Gabe had words of caution, "Remember, this is a fur trading fort. They are geared to supply trappers and Indians, not 1,000 hungry emigrants."

Gabe had never actually been to Fort Laramie but he knew the story of the Fort.

"The Fort was originally named Fort Sublette after Bill Sublette, who recognized the site for its strategic location. But Bill Sublette, being a modest man, felt it should be called Fort Anderson, after William Anderson who had actually built the first fort on this spot. They compromised by naming it Fort William after both men. Then the American Fur Company took it over and renamed it Fort John. But to all the Mountain Men from the very beginning it was 'Fort Laramie'.

"The Fort sets on the main north south Indian trail that has existed since the beginning of time. With the desert to the east and a worse desert to the west the location at the confluence of the Laramie River and the Platte River makes this a virtual oasis with good water and excellent grass."

"Is Laramie an Indian name?" Mary asked, "It sounds effeminate."

"The Laramie River was named after a French trapper by the name of Jacque La Ramee who camped on this river twenty-five years ago," Gabe explained. "Interestingly enough no Indian tribe has ever claimed the territory so they all come through in relative peace because it 'belongs' to no one. At rendezvous time you will see many different tribes here. All except the Blackfeet which no one welcomes."

We pulled past the fort about a mile to get better grass, although the grass was plentiful. In the early evening we all walked back to the fort to take in the excitement. Gabe was right; the area was filled with Indians and traders. We found out that the Indians had come from as far south as the Gila River and north from the Red River, and the Columbia River to the west. There were representatives for the Sioux, Mandan, Crow, Snake, Pend-Orielle, Nez Perce, Cheyenne, and even Delaware. Camped near by were French Canadian trappers and American Mountain Men with their squaws and half breed children. Many of these people had fought each other and would again, but not here at the oasis on the Laramie River.

The walls of the fort were made of adobe and they were about fifteen feet high. There was one large entry that wagons can drive through one at a time and a much smaller entry, which would admit only one person at a time. Above the main entrance there was a square tower with loopholes for riflemen. Opposite each other were two more square bastions situated so when manned by riflemen they would have a clear sweep of the entire area. The main bastion housed a cannon. The cannon was more useful for psychological warfare than anything else. The trappers told us that the Indians had a great fear of the "big gun" and the "loud talk."

Many of the emigrants felt the fort was a big disappointment. Matilda perhaps said it best, "For not having seen a house or a living abode, other than a teepee, for over 600 miles the fort looks quite civilized to me." The Keizurs all agreed. The fort was only two years old so the adobe walls did not show much weathering.

Interestingly, a rival fur company had built a fort only about two miles away, but closer to the mouth of the Laramie River. This was called Fort Platte. Their prices were just as high, but Fort Laramie had a blacksmith's shop, and this service enticed most of us to this facility.

However, Fort Platte sponsored a "ball" in our honor. They boasted two fiddles and a banjo plunker. Mary and Joe, Sarah, Matilda, and Sam, John Brooks, and the Fords all walked over to enjoy the evening. There was not enough women to go around so the trappers and single emigrant men danced with each other.

The prices were outrageously high, unless you understand the rule of supply and demand. For example, watered down whiskey was $64 a gallon; sugar $1.50 a pint; tobacco $2 a pound; making sugar and tobacco the same price per pound, and coffee $1.50 a pound. A common blanket brought $20, a cotton shirt $5, and calico $1 a yard, and it was quite inferior.

"We can't afford the prices at the Fort, and they don't have much we need anyway," Mary reported.

"But the Indians do have what we need, and that is food supplies," Gabe declared.

We found trading with the Indians easier than trading at the fort. The Indians wanted anything made of iron. We had a broken knife and several split horseshoes, and Gabe's supply of large needles was in great demand.

We traded for three well-cured buffalo robes, 600 pounds of dried buffalo meat, and 200 pounds of venison jerky. We were very pleased, although the process took a long time.

Little Elizabeth Jane, our eight year old, decided to get into the trading business. She observed the interest that a group of Indian children showed toward Elizabeth's stuffed rag doll. In an hour's time she had traded her rag doll for three beautifully beaded Indian dolls. She gave one doll to her nephew, Tillman and one to her niece, Mary Ann.

In the process of trading the dolls, 15-20 Indian children surrounded Elizabeth to enjoy the activity. She promptly organized them into a game of "ring around the rosy". The Indian mothers all gathered on one side to watch and the emigrant mothers on the other side. This was a major break-through in our relations with the natives.

The game led to some Indian boys enticing our young men into foot races. It became rather apparent that over the hundred-yard course our boys were no match for their Indian counterparts. Yet in a strange show of sportsmanship, the Indian boys lost every race in the last five yards of each contest, regardless of their lead midway in the race.

At this point a young Cheyenne Brave indicated he wanted to show his prowess as an archer. A gourd eight inches in diameter was hung from a tree limb about 30 yards away. The gourd was set to swinging. He took six arrows to place in his quiver. The six arrows were in the air before the first one had hit and five of the six arrows were left sticking in the gourd and the sixth one barely missed. The Brave was obviously pleased as were his circle of fellow Braves. The young Cheyenne then removed his quiver, which had been slung over his shoulder and placed six more arrows in the quiver. And handed the quiver and the bow to Joe Hess. Joe looked the bow over, tested the bow string, and then quickly pulled his Missouri Militia revolver out of its holster and pulled down on the arrow impregnated gourd and with one shot blew the gourd into a million pieces and scattering broken arrows. His second shot broke the limb the gourd had been hanging on, then he discharged his revolver three more times, in three seconds time into the air. The Indians had never seen a revolver before, let alone any gun that could fire that fast.

The circle of young Indian Braves melted away at once. The game of "ring around the Rosy" came to a halt and the children and their mothers scurried away.

"You are stupid and vain," Gabe admonished Joe. "That unnecessary display of showmanship may cost someone his life. And it could very well be someone in your own family."

"Don't call me stupid, Old Man," Joe said in anger. "I knew exactly what I was doing. Within a week every Redskin within a hundred miles will have heard of this. It will save lives, not cost lives. The word will go out not to mess with the Keizurs. This will save lives I tell you."

"Maybe, maybe, time will tell," Gabe said and stomped off.

CHAPTER 23

"Turn Backs" and Tragedy

For a variety of reasons, a number of the Oregon Emigration Company turned around to go back to Independence. In some cases I think the realization, that we had only come one third of our journey, and that it was closer to go back now, than to continue on to the journey's end. In several cases I think they had discovered how ill prepared they were, and thought the long trail ahead was just too much for them.

In one case love over ruled. Thomas Cochran returned to marry his fiancée, but with a vow to return in '44 with his bride.

The brother and sister team of Luther and Nancy Dickerson and her husband James Welch along with their three boys gave no reason for turning around. They left after dark, perhaps to avoid their neighbors trying to dissuade them.

John Bacon returned to get his family that he had left in Missouri. Young Archibald Wilkes had essentially all the adventure he needed for awhile. He also left at night. He didn't have a wagon so we didn't miss him at first.

There were others such as F. Luger, Jackson Moore, Alex Francis, and Stephen Fairly. There may have been others, but these were the emigrants that we knew the best.

Two other young men left at this point, but not to go back east. They turned south to go to Taos, which is part of Spanish America. They had a plan, but they never shared it with us. Nicholas Biddle and J. Loughborough rode off together for Taos.

We heard much later that several gave "Indian Troubles" as their reason for turning around, which is interesting, since to this point we had virtually no confrontation with the natives other than some minor thievery at the hands of the Caws. But even that inconvenience occurred very early on our journey. Perhaps they needed a reason to tell their families and friends back home to explain their return.

At the supper campfire, on the eve of our departure from Fort Laramie, Pleasant asked his older sister, "Well, are you ready to turn around?"

"You can turn around if you want to," Reeda said. "We wouldn't miss you, until plowing time next spring. And it would certainly save a lot of food for the rest of us." This jocular conversation was the only mention of ever turning around by any of the Keizurs.

On July 17, three days out of Fort Laramie, in an area called Red Buttes, so called for the blood red color of the rocks, tragedy struck the Hembree family. The Hembrees were attached to the Cow Column, so we knew them well. There were fourteen members of their Clan. Joel and his younger brother Absalon brought their wives and children from McMinnville, Tennessee, to the jump off point, in time to join our Company in 1843. Sadness and despair were not strangers to this family. Sarah and Joel Hembree had already had their share of sorrow. Just before leaving Missouri they had lost their two year old daughter, Sarah. They never talked about it and we didn't know the particulars, but they were depressed most of the time. But there was much more for this family to endure.

While traveling along a rough section of the trail young Joel Hembree, only six years old, was riding the tongue of his father's wagon. He shouldn't have been doing that, but he was probably just bored walking beside the oxen. Older boys had been known to ride the tongue without incident. Suddenly the wagon went into a chuckhole, spilling young Joel from his perch. Before the men could stop the wagon, both iron-rimmed wheels had rolled over his small body.

Immediately a rider was sent for Dr. Whitman and Reeda. Reeda got there first, followed by Marcus Whitman within minutes. A tent was raised to shield the boy from the scorching midday sun. The Hembree wagons pulled out of line, but the rest of the train had to roll on. What else could they really do?"

Little Joel was conscious and in terrible pain and could not suppress his screams, although the little boy tried.

"Reeda," Dr. Whitman confided, "there is nothing I can do. There is too much internal bleeding, his spine and pelvis area are crushed. We will do whatever we can to reduce his pain and that's all I know to do."

Sarah Hembree, little Joel's mother, who was enormously large with their eighth child, laid down on the ground canvas and held her little boy close to her, until he died.

James Hembree the seventeen year old brother of little Joel left the tent and circle of family members and began carving his brother's name on a slab of Red Bluff rock.

Joel Hembree bravely fought for life through the long night, but slipped away before noon on July 18, 1843. His was the first death of the emigration of 1843. Rev. Enoch performed a short but very moving service for Joel Hembree. It had to be short because all the Hembree wagons had a major "catch up" effort ahead of them.

Nine days after the death of Joel, his mother Sarah, gave birth to a daughter named Nancy Jane. This was July 26, 1843, with Dr. Marcus Whitman and Dr. Reeda assisting.

To every member of the Keizur Clan, the object lesson given by Gabe McGee, when he had our loaded wagon run over a stout oak limb on the day of our departure from Sugar Creek in Missouri, came back to each of our minds, but we never spoke of it.

CHAPTER 24

Sweetwater River

We crossed the North Fork of the Platte River like we knew what we were doing. The wheels got a good soaking. Our only incident was William Newby losing control of his wagon, but it was recovered downstream with minimum loss of belongings.

Water has become a serious issue. The potholes containing water that the cattle usually drank from, had evaporated to a fraction of their normal size. As the water evaporated in the hot July sun the remaining water is heavily laden with alkali to the saturation point. If there is other water available, cattle will not drink alkali water, but when the cattle are crazed for water, you have to beat them away from the alkali water.

Adding to the misery of man and beast was the alkali dust. The dust rose in a cloud over the wagon train, which unfortunately had to go in single file through this stretch of the trail. We did rotate the lead wagons often, which helped some. Dr. Whitman was very concerned with dehydration. White crystals of alkali encrusted the nostrils of every breathing animal, man or beast. Keeping the animals out of the deadly alkali water was a never ending challenge. The alkali water looks just about the same as pure water.

Jesse sent scouts out ahead of the Columns to search for a source of good water. The scouts returned with good news of a substantial spring only two days ahead. They reported that the spring flowed about a mile before disappearing into the burning sand.

Jesse made two quick, but very important, decisions. "We will drive all night. It will be hard on the animals but we will be at the spring in the early morning. Secondly, I want about a dozen men to ride with me to prepare the spring. We will dam the spring with rocks, or logs, or what ever we have, every fifty yards over the entire length of the flow. My purpose is to make a series of pools. Otherwise the cattle will dry up the supply too soon. I want Lindsay to go with me and I need about a dozen more men. Thomas Keizur is in charge until you get to the spring. Keep the train moving, Thomas."

Jesse had no problem in getting willing volunteers to prepare the spring. Pleasant and Sam Penter was our contribution to Jesse. We needed every one else to keep the cattle moving and out of the alkali potholes.

We were about four miles out at three in the morning when the oxen started picking up their pace. They could smell good water. We entered a green valley about 4:30 AM to see in the half-light, a series of little lakes stretching a mile or more. I sent John Brooks down the line to tell the wagon drivers to spread out at the "lakes" so as to not overtax any one particular lake giving it a chance to recharge itself.

Jesse ordered a lay bye for the next day, over Marcus Whitman's protestations. We had grass, good water, and wood. What more could you ask for?

Normally, we would expect to find game in such a fertile valley, but if there had been buffalo or deer, Sir William Stewart's band of "sportsmen" had driven them out several days before our arrival.

We left Willow Springs, as we dubbed the place, on July 26 for an easy day's march to a tributary of the North Platte River called the Sweetwater River. The water in this stream was so pure and clear that you could count the pebbles on the bottom.

We had another "division" tonight. Some of Martin's Light Column members and some "deserters" from the Applegate Cow Column elected

Lewis Cooper as their new Captain. The split consisted of nineteen wagons all told.

"Lewis is a good man. They elected an older leader, more mature, I think," Mary offered. Lewis Cooper married late at 44, only two years ago. He and his wife, Elizabeth put everything they owned in their wagon to go west.

"I think they should have been forced to stay with either Martin or Applegate. It spreads our evening guard and our drovers too thin," Joe Hess complained.

"How are you going to 'force' anyone in the train to do anything they don't want to do?" Mary Louise said to her husband. "These people are free spirited, no one ordered them to go to Oregon, no one can stop them from going, and no one can 'force' them to align one way or the other."

John Ford added, "We are still Americans, although we are beyond the protection of our government, we should not be beyond the influence of our forefathers who died to give us the right to go where we want to and with whom we want."

"I hope you remember your fine speech as you draw extra guard duty at night," Joe mumbled.

"But why did they split off?" Pleasant wanted to know.

"They weren't pleased in not having a say with the decision for a forced night march," John answered.

We had another birth on the trail. One of Molly Moo Cow's granddaughters "freshened" with a very small bull calf. Because it was so small we decided to have it nurse only until the fever was out of the milk, which usually is by the sixth milking. Then we will butcher the bull calf as a vealer.

"We will have veal strips just like a fancy French eatery," Gabe said.

We had planned to have two cows freshen on the trail, which is good since one cow was about dry. That cow is down to only two cups of milk at a milking. She is bred back and should freshen about the time we reach the Willamette Valley.

Of the five cows we started with from Missouri, one is nearly dry, one has just freshened, one we butchered after she injured her stifle joint, and the other two are still producing, but not nearly as much as when we started, which is no surprise since they have been on the trail all that time.

From the three producing cows we were still getting enough milk for a large cup of warm milk morning and night, for everyone. We were also supplying the Hembree baby with two cups of milk a day. Mrs. Hembree was nursing the little girl but she could not get enough from her mother alone.

One day Elizabeth Jane was delivering the cup of milk to the Hembrees four wagons behind us. She tripped and fell, spilling the contents of the cup into the dust. Elizabeth broke into tears, which was the first time she had cried since we left Sugar Creek, which is saying something for an eight year old girl.

Mary splashed a little water into the cup to wash the dirt out and silently handed the empty cup to Tillman who splashed a little of his milk into the empty cup and passed the cup to his cousin Thomas, who splashed a little more milk into the cup and moved it on to his cousin Francis, who moved it on to his brother Thomas Cullwell, who gave the now full cup back to Elizabeth.

Elizabeth carried the full cup in both hands like she would a baby robin and delivered it to the Hembrees.

The entire adult Keizurs, who had not even been solicited for a single "splash of milk", drank their cup of milk in silence and with pride.

Old Gabe, who was getting soft, either by old age or by living with the Keizurs, walked away from the campfire so no one could see the tear escaping down his grizzled face, but Mary and I saw it and smiled at each other.

Independence Rock was the next wonder we encountered. From the distance it looked to us like a large black turtle shell. Legend has it that the famous Mountain Man, Tom Fitzpatrick named it. Apparently he had cached some furs there on Independence Day July fourth, 1824. It is hard to believe that there were people out here nearly two decades before us.

The Rock is a long narrow mass of red and white feldspar and mica. It appears to be about 190 feet high at the northern end sloping to about 165 feet at the southern end. It stretches about a half mile in length. Once again the boys stepped off the circumference and claimed it to be 1550 yards around or just under a mile.

Many names had already been inscribed on the rock, but the rock was too hard to carve so in most cases names were painted on the rock using a variety of substances for the paint. We used axle grease and gunpowder.

Some of the names and dates we could make out, was Father De Smet, July 5, 1841; Bill and Milton Sublette; Bonneville; A. J. Miller 1837; Lansford Hastings 1842; and A. L. Lovejoy 1842. "The Fremont Cross," which was made with melted India rubber, was quite visible.

"That Cross is such a brazen Papist symbol that it could cost him the Presidency which he so ardently seeks," Dr. Marcus Whitman stated. "I can't imagine that this great nation would ever elect a Roman Catholic as president. It just won't happen." Most heads nodded in full agreement.

We saw the names of Mountain Men, explorers, and missionaries painted on Independence Rock, but I believe we were the first emigrants to do so. We did not see Kenneth's name, although we looked carefully.

"Just because his name is not painted on the rock does not mean he didn't get this far," John Brooks pointed out. "What would he have used for paint. He wouldn't have axle grease on anything."

Lewis Cooper's new train of nineteen wagons stayed on an extra day to dry meat "and to get organized" but we moved on again, with Whitman's encouragement.

One fallout of this most recent split was that "Orderly Sergeant Nesmith" was not needed in that role. Jim Nesmith at 23 was elected at Fitzhugh's Mill at the very beginning of our journey. As the Orderly Sergeant, he had many responsibilities including posting the night guard duty list. He performed this task with such an even hand that there were few complaints or conflicts. Another task was to keep a running record of all the people with the Company. Martin kept a record of all males over the age of sixteen, or in other words all of fighting age, for a registry of who could vote, but he had no reason to keep data on women, or children, or slaves (Of which there were several). James Nesmith, on the other hand, kept a record of everyone including births and deaths and "turn backs" and the record of each "division".

Jim was gone away with a hunting party when this latest division occurred. When he returned, he was informed, that his position had been eliminated and that now he would have to take night duty like everyone else.

"If that is the decision of the majority, I shall abide by it," Jim said.

No vote had been taken, as far as we knew, and the Keizurs would not have supported the change had we the opportunity to vote. The Keizurs were quite fond of this young man.

"I do hope he maintains the registry because someday it may be important," Mary commented.

Several of the men had contacted a strange fever while at Fort Laramie. Dr. Whitman was at a loss to identify it. Pierson Reading tried to bleed himself, but more or less botched it. However, Dr. Whitman with Reeda's help performed the bleeding correctly. Dr. Whitman offered the same procedure to Clayborne Payne, but he wanted no part of it.

Mr. Reading slowly recovered, but Mr. Payne grew progressively worse. Dr. Whitman diagnosed the problem as "inflammation of the bowels". Reeda, with Dr. Whitman's approval, mixed up a tea of powdered Cascara bark, but even that had little effect. Reeda reported that evening to the Keizurs, "Mr. Payne will not survive long."

On August fourth, Clayborn Payne became our second fatality. He left a wife and five little children. Their twin boys were barely three years old, and thus would be spared most of the sorrow. Miriam Payne, Claiborne's wife, was only twenty-five.

Daniel Matheny had packed long planks in the bottom of his wagon. "I knew I would be building a coffin for someone. I didn't know when or for whom. But I knew the planks would be needed. I guess they are needed now."

John Brooks and Pleasant offered to help Daniel. "We could hold boards or something like that," John Brooks said.

"If you want to help get the twins away. They're playing in the shavings. It bothers me greatly to have them play in the shavings of their father's coffin. Elizabeth Jane and her aunt Matilda lead the little boys away to play elsewhere.

"Miriam Payne is absolutely no help," Matilda reported, "She sits by their wagon in a stupor smoking her pipe."

Reeda sat beside her with her arm around the young woman's shoulder. Miriam rested her pipe on the wagon wheel during the service.

Mary said, "Under the circumstances it was a nice service."

After her few friends had left, Miriam again sat and stared into space. Finally she turned to Reeda and asked, "What is to become of me and my children?"

"If you want to go back to Missouri, Miriam, my Dad will send one of our men with you to drive your team."

"Why to Missouri? I don't know anyone there. We were from Tennessee."

Reeda was grave, as she considered what she thought her Dad might do. What if he sent John or Nimrod? In either case it would be two years before they would be reunited.

"I think I should go on to Oregon", Miriam said very slowly. "I have never driven a team, but I could learn. I must learn all the things that Clay did for us. Daniel and Mary Matheny said they would help us. They have twin boys too, you know."

"I am sure that between the Mathenys and the Keizurs we will get your family safely to Oregon."

"Will you teach me to shoot Clay's gun?"

"I'm not the best one to teach you that, but my sister Mary Louise is. She can outshoot most men."

That evening Marcus Whitman took supper with the Keizur family. We always looked forward to those opportunities to discuss things with him. The men could talk politics or ask questions about The Blue Mountains, or Fort Vancouver, or Dr. John McLaughlin and he could answer on a first hand basis because he had been there. And the children were always on their very best behavior.

"This is just like having the Queen of England for supper," Francis said.

"More like President Polk, I think," Pleasant replied.

In the course of the evening the discussion turned to the recent death of Clayborn Payne.

Dr Whitman said, "We need to put this death in its correct perspective. There are between 800 and a thousand souls in the Oregon Emigration Company, depending upon whom you are talking to. That's counting the 'turn arounds'. We have been on the trail for two and a half months and we have lost only two, the Hembree boy and Clay Payne. I know there will be more. But, if all of these folks had stayed home on their farms, or running their stores, and so forth, I would wager that more than two of them would have passed away. Now mind you I don't wager. The deaths have been tragic, but the mortality rate on our journey has been remarkably low."

"You make a good point, Marcus," Gabe interjected. "I know if I had stayed in Arkansas trying to farm I would have died of boredom."

"I would rather talk politics," I said.

CHAPTER 25

The Water Flows West

The travel along the Sweetwater was relatively easy. Again the three main elements of a good trip was present, that is water, wood, and grass. Time went by quickly with new wonders of nature at either hand. The scenery we were going through inspired us.

By mid-morning, after leaving Independence Rock and after covering only four miles, we came to the next point of interest called "The Devils Gate." The "Gate" was made by the Sweetwater River dashing through a narrow cleavage in towering cliffs four hundred feet high. The entire river was squeezed into a thirty foot wide space with a run of about 1300 feet. The chasm was about 300 feet wide at the top of the cliffs. Fortunately we did not have to go through the "Gate". An Indian trail of thousands of years went around the mountain. The Fremont and Sir William Stewart Parties had recently gone around the mountain several days earlier. Many of our Company scaled the cliffs to the brim, just to look over from the top.

There were many theories expressed on how the gash in the mountain was formed. Some thought an ancient earthquake left this fault in the earth. Others reasoned that a flash flood at some time had washed through the rock formation. Many thought it had been formed simply by erosion alone. Gabe had an interesting theory; "By just looking at the Gate one could think that the river wore this cut through the mountain. But I think the river is right where it has always been. I think the mountains raised, the river merely kept pace with the uplifting. In other words, the river broke the back of the mountains."

We did not tarry long at the "Gate" because it was not noon yet and besides the next wonder was already in sight. Looking straight ahead was a mountain with a split at the top. "Head right toward that split rock," Captain Gantt ordered.

On Friday August fifth, at just before noon we experienced a strange occurrence. A ball of fire passed directly overhead trailing blue smoke in a cloudless sky. Not everyone saw it, but we all heard a tremendous BOOM like a very large cannon going off. Some took it as an omen good or bad. It was most likely a meteor.

Due west of the split rock the emigrants had a choice to make. We could continue over, "the deep sand route" which meant days of hard pulling in deep sand under desert like conditions, or we could take the "three crossings" route. This route required three crossings of the Sweetwater River because of the meandering of the river. No one looked forward to a triple crossing of the Sweetwater, but that was the decision, and we thought it was a wise one.

We slanted to the northwest and crossed the Sweetwater. We continued along the north bank for a mile and a half then cut south to cross the river again. We barely got to the south bank before we drove into the river once more. The river was running only two to three feet deep and the bottom was solid. The moisture from the crossings tightened our wheels and spokes which was excellent for our running gear.

We followed the Sweetwater River for about 120 miles and we were becoming quite fond of it. But now we began a steady uphill climb, not too steep but steady. We were headed for what we were told was the South Pass through the Great Stony Mountains. The Indians had known of this pass for centuries. Members of the Astor Party, going from west to east some years ago discovered the pass.

We had heard for months about the pass, but we didn't know just what to expect. Perhaps, a narrow rocky ledge, hovering over dizzying canyons, and so forth. We were into the so-called Pass without even knowing it because the climb was so gradual. If there had been no South Pass it would have been impossible to take wagons through the mountains that we saw in the distance. Fremont had a special interest in the South Pass and actually sent his men back through it several times. He surveyed the pass and mapped it, and it is said, studied where artillery batteries would be placed some day.

The evenings were frigid with a heavy frost in the mornings. So it was not a big surprise to find a bog frozen solid. Many emigrants actually dug down about eighteen inches and removed blocks of ice. We continued our gradual ascent for the next four miles and camped by a spring that our forward scouts had alerted us about.

John Brooks came running back to our Party shouting, "The spring flows west! The water from the spring flows west!"

"We have crossed the great divide," Mary exclaimed.

We camped at "Pacific Spring" for a day because John Pennington's wife who was expecting, was having a very hard time. Dr. Whitman and Reeda managed to turn the baby successfully and Mary Jane Pennington was born. Baby Mary Jane joined her sister Martha who was barely one year old herself. "Just imagine Mary Jane can tell her grandchildren that she was born right on the great divide," Elizabeth declared.

Three days later Edward Stevenson died. He was one of the three men who had become ill at Fort Laramie. Of the three men that came down with the "Laramie fever" only Pierson Reading survived. Ed Stevenson had been traveling with Andy Masters and his wife Sarah and it was in their wagon, after suffering for many days, that he just passed away. He asked Mary Masters, as he lay dying, "Does the water flow west yet?"

"Yes, Ed it does."

"Then I am in the Oregon Territory. I knew I would make it to Oregon." He died a few hours later. He was a long way from his home in Kentucky.

Pierson Reading was the only one of the three that was bled by Dr. Whitman and he was the only one who lived. "Masters and Payne might have lived if they had only let us bleed them," Reeda lamented.

"Was Mr. Stevenson right? Are we in Oregon?" Francis asked.

"When we crossed through the South Pass, and the streams ran west to the Pacific Ocean, we were officially in the Oregon Territory," John Brooks explained.

"Is it down hill the rest of the way?" Francis wanted to know.

"Yes, except where the trail goes up hill," John Brooks laughed.

CHAPTER 26

Fort Bridger and Fort Hall

It was here that Father Devos and Father Hoecken, two Catholic priests along with three lay brothers, left the train to go north into Flathead country to Christianize the Natives. We caught up with them way back at the Kansas River crossing and they had traveled with us since that time. Their outfit consisted of three two wheeled carts pulled by single mules. They kept apart from the emigrants and were barely noticeable. Yet it was rather sad to see the little group depart from the protection of the main body, and to head into territory where they would be completely on their own.

After crossing several tributaries of Sandy Creek with little difficulty, we headed towards Hams Fork traversing a stretch of "true desert". Many wagons were experiencing loosening of wheel spokes and rims and the serenade of squeaks was a melody of trouble. Fortunately, we had traded the Indians at Fort Laramie out of a quantity of buffalo tallow, which we applied frequently to our running gear. Driving wedges between the rims and the wheels tightened the wheels, but you can do that just so long. Temporary repairs were the best we could manage while on the trail. We looked forward to arriving at Fort Bridger, where we understood they had a blacksmith shop with a forge and anvil.

Finally on August 14, our lead wagons rolled into Fort Bridger. Fort Bridger was brand new. It was built by the old fur trader Jim Bridger and his partner Louis Vasquez.

They started construction of the fort in the spring of 1843, only a week before we left Independence. The fort was finished just in time to greet us. Jim Bridger had not as yet received eastern backing, which he had counted upon. Thus, supply trains had not reached the fort and the shelves were bare. However, the blacksmith shop and anvil were busy day and night with light from lanterns and the fire at the forge.

Jim Bridger and Marcus Whitman had a great reunion. The year before Whitman had removed an old arrowhead from Jim's shoulder that he had carried for a number of years. The arrowhead was deep in his shoulder and required cutting to get it out. Dr. Whitman had an audience of Indians and Mountain Men and all were amazed at Whitman's skill and Bridger's courage. Jim Bridger delighted in showing people the long scar left on his shoulder.

The emigrants going to California had planned to stay for a number of days to hunt and stock up on meat. However, the Sioux and Cheyenne had run off all the game, so they aborted their plan to stay over. In general we were disappointed in Fort Bridger. We knew that in time the fort would be very successful and a welcomed sight to other emigrants, but we were the first to visit and we came a year too early.

The Cory family all came down with a sudden and retching illness. All members of the family except the infant, Miles, became sick. The father, Miles Cory Sr. and his wife Cyrene, and three year old William recovered but Catherine, Williams's twin sister did not. She died after a short intense illness August 15.

This death was particularly demoralizing. We were not surprised when Clay Payne died after being ill so long. We were prepared for it. But Catherine was playing and healthy one day and died the next. The Cory's young black slave girl that they brought along, took Catherine's death particularly hard. She had been the primary care person for the Cory children.

Dr. Whitman suspected that eating tainted meat caused the illness.

The infant was the only one that did not have the same meal. "Reeda, you go one way down the train and I will go the other to warn the other families. Tell the women that burned meat is good, partially cooked meat is bad. Go tell them."

We left Fort Bridger and crossed the Muddy River over a steep divide to the Bear River, which runs north and south for over forty miles, before it turns south to eventually reach The Great Salt Lake. The Bear River is a beautiful stream about twenty yards wide and three to five feet deep.

The Valley of the Bear River was like a green oasis to us. It ranges from two to eight miles wide. We took a full week to travel slowly through the valley to give the oxen and other cattle a chance to fill up on the wild grass that reached the cattle's bellies. And for a short period Dr. Whitman was not telling us to "Hurry! Hurry!"

We were beyond the buffalo range, but we found deer and elk in great abundance. We added two new foods to our diet, namely bear meat, and mountain trout. Few of us had ever eaten fish before and the fish proved to be a delicious respite from buffalo jerky.

Lieutenant John Charles Fremont with his party of 39 men and their two wheeled carts rejoined us in the Bear River Valley. The United States Army Corps of Topographical Engineers, as they were officially known, had taken a side trip down the Bear River to The Great Salt Lake, exploring for a second pass through the Rockies. They had followed our trail through the South Pass and caught up with us here in the Bear River Valley.

"The 'Great Pathfinder,' as Fremont likes to be called found only one path as far as I am concerned," Gabe commented, "and that was the path we made."

In spite of Gabe's dislike for Fremont, he and his troop of young French Canadians were welcomed by most of the emigrants and they gave us a feeling of safety as we traveled through Sioux country. It was as if we had our own military escort. Fremont had started from Missouri a full week behind us, but he caught and passed us several times. Fremont was a cartographer, an engineer and surveyor by training.

"Fremont is so ambitious that it concerns me at times," Marcus Whitman said. "He is certainly well qualified for his mission, which is undoubtedly military."

"His number one qualification for getting appointed to these 'exploring' missions is the fact that he is married to Jessie Benton, Senator Thomas Hart Benton's lovely daughter," Gabe added.

"Indians! Indians!" a warning cry went up and down the Columns one midday. The Indians were Shoshone or Snake, as they were more often known. They rode exceptionally fine horses and moved in slowly in a non-hostile manner. Obviously they came only to visit and trade. They were eager and willing to trade horses for knives, blankets, and shirts. Trinkets did not interest them. "It certainly breaks the monotony of the trail," Mary said.

Accompanying the Indian band was a trapper as old as the hills. He was known as Peg Leg Smith. Peg Leg had married into the tribe and had lived with them for years.

He was well respected by his adopted extended family of Indians. He acquired his name, or so the legend goes, after amputating his own leg with his Bowie knife following an encounter with a bear trap. As I explained his name to the children I said, "It takes a lot of courage and a strong will to do what Mr. Smith did."

Gabe added, "You must do what you have to do in this country."

Our forward scouts had alerted us to more geological wonders to come. We came to a series of springs that were truly amazing. The Mountain Men called them "beer" springs but we called them "soda" springs. The water boiled to overflowing the spring basin from which it sprung, and then disappeared back into the basin only to start the process again in twenty minutes.

"It tastes just like soda water without the syrup," Pleasant claimed.

Not far away was the next attraction called Steamboat Springs. The water in this spring boiled up at half-second intervals occasionally shooting ten feet into the air. The entire process emitted a sound similar to a high-pressure steam engine at full throttle.

We left the beautiful Bear River Valley traveling twenty miles to the Portneuf, a tributary of the Snake River and the first stream entering the Columbia River drainage system.

"If the Bear River Valley was not so far from the markets I believe we could do worse than settling right there," Joe Hess said. "But we are farmers and farmers must have a market for what we raise."

We have now come an estimated 1,200 miles in three and a half months. That is an average of fourteen miles a day even with the layovers. "I would like to know what we have averaged since Marcus Whitman joined up," I pondered. Marcus is still saying "Travel, travel my friends! Hurry up! Hurry up!" It was August 27,a Sunday, when the first of our wagons rolled into Fort Hall. Fort Hall is located on the Snake River. This was our third fort, but the first one that flew the Union Jack flag. Fort Hall was under the control of the powerful Hudson's Bay Company, a British monopoly, and they flew the flag of the British Empire. The Hudson's Bay Company was in charge of the entire Oregon Territory, even though technically the United States and Great Britain had a "Joint Occupancy" treaty. In spite of any treaty, the "Company" controlled all aspects of life including the laws and rules pertaining to humane activities and commerce, and they liked it that way.

As we approached and saw the Union Jack flying in the breeze we were somewhat apprehensive. "I don't like the Britishers. Never did, never will" one emigrant exclaimed. That was the sentiment shared by most. After all we had fought the British in two wars in the last sixty years and a third one was brewing , if President Polk has his way.

So you can imagine our genuine surprise when Factor Richard Grant welcomed the trail weary emigrants with kindness and hospitality. Factor Grant was a Scotsman, but loyal to the crown.

"He seems pleased to be able to serve us," Mary observed. However, the Fort was soon unable to supply the total demand of so many and provisions were quickly exhausted. This happened in spite of the steep prices they were charging.

Late arrivals found everything was off the shelves. Grant, knowing that he and his men were facing a long winter understandably was concerned. Grant began holding certain supplies back and would not sell them at any price.

The California bound Company was agitated by two hot heads who threatened Richard Grant with violence if he refused to sell to them. Factor Grant was not intimidated and ordered them away.

"We will go, but we will be back with the American Army. I wasn't born in the backwoods to get scared of hoot owls".

It wasn't certain if Grant understood the "hoot owl" characterization, but he understood it better when Lt. John Fremont who was camped nearby but unbeknownst to the British, came riding in by two's heavily armed with mules pulling a little canon waving the American flag.

Martin and Gantt immediately raced out in front of Fremont to intercept him. Martin voiced concern, "Sir, what is this all about?"

Gantt was less diplomatic," What in the hell do you think you are doing?"

"I thought a little show of American force might be helpful," Fremont replied.

"Oh, you did, did you? And did you happen to notice the four riders that left the rear of the fort hell bent for leather?"

"What do these riders mean?" Fremont asked.

"You can be sure one was dispatched to Fort Boise and the other three to the nearest Cheyenne and Sioux encampments. We could have 3,000 warriors here in a day's time, all loyal to the Company and the Crown. My advice to you is to get your company of English hating Frenchmen who are so eager to spill redcoat blood, the hell out of here."

"Sir, do you realize you are addressing an officer of the United States Army?"

"And you are talking to the man in charge of getting this train of civilians safely to Oregon and *it's a long way to Oregon*. If you have a need to start an international crisis, go to Texas or to California," Captain Gantt said. With a motion of his hand, Fremont's men whirled and left in a gallop.

"Out of curiosity only, Mr. Gantt, who are your friends in Washington?" Fremont inquired.

"The people's choice and soon to be President, James K. Polk. I assume you have heard of him."

"I have, Sir, and I hope this incident is concluded."

"I do also."

Factor Grant surveyed the situation and opened his stores until they were empty. However, we are convinced he had wisely cached some stuff for his own winter's use.

We lost another member of our Company on August 31, just before we were to leave Fort Hall. Daniel Richardson was buried at Fort Hall. His wife and two children decided to struggle on, not that they had a real choice in the matter.

"We can help Mrs. Richardson ," Mary volunteered. "You boys can help yoke her oxen each morning." Others offered other assistance.

CHAPTER 27

The California Cutoff

The Company that was turning off for California traveled with us for two days along the Snake River, past Fort Hall. The parting was not going to be easy because we knew in all likelihood we would never meet again.

Captain Gantt, our faithful guide, said when he was hired, that he would be leaving somewhere near Fort Hall. Colonel Martin, the leader of the Light Column, and our good friend Pierson Reading, also turned off for California. Others that took the California cutoff were: John Atkinson, John Boardman, Joseph Buzzell and his wife Francis, the Constable brothers Benedict and Edward and Edward's wife Priscilla. Priscilla was the daughter of William and Molly Arthur, all the rest of the Arthurs continued on to Oregon, I. Dawson, E.A. Farwell, Bartholomy Hally and his wife Ann, Thomas Hensley, Milton Little, Julius Martin, William Martin, not the leader of the Light Column, but another Bill Martin, McClellan, John McIntire, Humphrey O'Brian, Joseph Walker, Isaac Williams and most significant to the Keizurs, was our own, Gabriel McGee.

Joseph Chiles with Old Joe Walker as their guide led the Company. The Company was called the Chiles Company. In all, there were 28-30 emigrants that took the California cutoff. Interestingly, no children were involved in the Chiles Company.

"I suppose there is little use in trying to talk you out of going to

California," I said to Gabe.

"No, Oregon is for farmers and family people who will settle the country. That's not me. I never liked farming before, and I am too old to start liking it now. But, I would be lying if I told you I will not miss the Keizur family, because I will."

At the actual cutoff place to California someone had posted a sign with an arrow-pointing west, which said, "This way to Oregon". Lower down on the sign post was an arrow pointing south, but instead of wording, it had a painting of something like a gold coin. The joke that went around was, "those who could read went to Oregon, and those who couldn't, followed the painting to California."

We all knew that sooner or later Gabe would be leaving us for California but it was not until we saw the signs that the realization sunk in, especially for the children, that the time was now. The evening before Gabe was to leave he sternly scolded Francis for swinging on an oxen's tail. "The ox has worked for you all day, he is tired, and he doesn't need some ungrateful boy pestering him. I don't want to ever see you torment an animal again," Gabe admonished Francis. Gabe very seldom had anything to say in a disciplinary way to the children, unless there was an issue of safety involved, this was primarily true because, the children were very well mannered and well behaved. But, Francis was crushed and had his feelings severely damaged. Then the very next day the children realized that Gabe was about to leave them. Francis paired those two events, and concluded, that Gabe was so disappointed in him, that he was going to leave them because he had misbehaved.

Francis was "too big" to cry although he probably wanted to. He waited until Gabe was by himself tying up his two trailing horses, as he always did each morning.

"Gabe, please don't go. I will never bother an animal again, I promise." Francis managed to get out.

Gabe had frankly forgotten the incident of the night before. "I know you won't Francis, because real men don't do those things, and you are going to be a real man. I'm not leaving because of that mishap last night. I'm leaving because California is calling to me just as Oregon is calling to your folks, but you will always be in my thoughts and prayers wherever I may be."

"I will always remember you too, Gabe."

Gabe shook the hand of every Keizur male, including the four year olds, and hugged all the girls and women. He pulled Reeda aside. "If you ever see Kenny O'Regan again, which isn't likely, but if you do, tell him that your Dad suffered over his banishment and that it left a hole in your father's heart."

"I will tell him," Reeda promised. "And Gabe here is a little pouch with a supply of rose hips in it. Take a few each day and you won't get trail scurvy." Gabe wrinkled his nose at the thought of the bitter little morsels, but took the pouch.

As the California bound Chiles Company pulled out they traveled parallel to our trail for a short distance. Just before their trail turned abruptly south Gabe stood up in his buggy and gave us a military salute. Joe Hess happened to be standing beside me at the time and we both snapped to attention and gave our best military salute in return.

"Imagine," Joe said, "A full Colonel saluting a mere Captain and a lowly trooper."

Their trail turned south at that point and we could see only the rear of the wagons and a cloud of trailing dust. We never saw or heard of Gabe again. We wondered many times if he got to California, because some of the Chiles party did not.

In the registry of names of the emigration of 1843, all it says about Gabe is: "McGee, Mr.: cutoff at Fort Hall for California."

It doesn't even list his first name. He is one of only two persons on the registry with just "Mister" in front of his name. The other was Mr. Kenitook whose only claim to fame was an accident he had with his gun.

181

CHAPTER 28

Three Island Crossing

As the Oregon Emigration Company strung out along the Snake River after leaving Fort Hall we were aware that we were making history. We were the first wagon train to go beyond Fort Hall. We had been told that Captain Benjamin Bonneville on his trip to spy on The Hudson's Bay Company in 1832, did cross the South Pass with twenty light wagons but they stopped at the Green River to build a fort. Four years later in 1836 Marcus and Narcissa Whitman managed to get a wagon, which had been reduced to a two-wheel cart, as far as Fort Boise where they were forced to leave it. In 1841 a train of fourteen wagons made it to Fort Hall and a year later eighteen wagons made it to Fort Hall but in all these cases the wagons were discarded for pack animals at Fort Hall.

Marcus Whitman was convinced that wagons could go all the way to the Columbia River. Factor Richard Grant of the Hudson's Bay Company rebutted his arguments. Grant advised us, as he had the trains before us, "that it simply is not possible to take wagons beyond Fort Hall."

Peter Burnett who was committed to California said, "While I wouldn't say it is impossible for Americans to make the trip to Oregon in wagons, I cannot see how it can be done." Dr Marcus Whitman countered Factor Grant's arguments just short of impugning his motives by pointing out that no other train had the resources available that we do.

Marcus confronted Factor Grant, "Sir, you encourage us to go to California over a route that no one here has traveled. I have traveled the route to the Columbia twice. A wagon can get through. At this late date getting through the Blue Mountains will be a challenge but the Sierra's is deep in snow now. Yet, Sir, you encourage us to go south via the Sierra Nevada Mountains. What possible reason would you do so?"

We all listened intently to the arguments and were persuaded by the man we trusted most, namely Marcus Whitman. When Factor Grant realized he was losing the debate he quickly switched positions and offered us the service of a Hudson's Bay employee named Remeau to be our guide. Marcus Whitman respectfully declined this offer.

"We signed up to go to Oregon and Oregon it is," Sam Penter said, in one of his very rare statements. Samuel Penter, Matilda's husband was not one with words but when he talked we did listen.

A few of our Company did switch to pack animals but in these cases their particular wagons had all but fallen apart anyway. If their wagons had been decent wagons they would not have switched to pack animals.

"I don't know if we will make it or not," I said. "But every mile we travel, every experience we have, both good and bad, will make it that much easier for other Americans to follow as they surely will. And getting more Americans to Oregon is important to me."

Our next challenge, and perhaps the sternest, was to cross the Snake River Plateau. Our animals were gaunt having had very little grass since leaving Fort Hall. Getting water was a major problem also. We followed the basalt cliffs along the river but there are few places where we could access the river. As John Brooks observed, "We are only 300 feet from water. Fifty feet to the edge of the chasm and 250 feet more straight down."

If you were a quarter of a mile to the side of the canyon you would not guess there was a river there at all. There are a few places where a trail goes down to the water's edge, but the trails down to the river are steep and over a mile long so it is a waste of energy to try to reach the water in most cases.

Fredrick Prigg decided to ride his mule down just such a trail. The saddle slipped over the mule's head, and down the cliff sliding and rolling went the mule and the man. By some quirk of fate neither was seriously injured.

James White lost an ox trying to go down a steep trail to the river. The ox fell and broke its neck and it was impossible to recover it and butcher it for meat. Leonard White, James's sixteen year old son, tried to scale down to the freshly killed ox with the thought in mind to butcher it for the meat. The family of six needed the meat. But his stepmother's pleading persuaded him, that his life was worth more to the Whites than all the ox meat in the world.

We had no water, we had sparse grass, and sagebrush was the only wood. However on the night of September 12 a sudden cloudburst occurred. When we went to bed that night the stars were shining brightly without a cloud in the sky. At two o'clock in the morning the heavens opened up in a full bore cloud burst, which continued until 10 AM the next morning. A thousand little rivulets ran across the plateau to drop 200 feet into the river below. Every man woman and child started damming up these little streams four to six inches wide. The animals all broke their slumber for their first good drink of water even though it was muddy water.

We set out pans and canvases to catch all we could for drinking water.

Many years later we would recall that downpour as a defining experience for the Oregon Emigration Company. It was no small blessing. Marcus Whitman always a devout person organized a prayer circle of "Thanksgiving" that evening.

The rain stopped just as suddenly as it had begun and soon the dust was blowing again, but our spirits were lifted and our animals had their fill of water.

It had been weeks since the children had curry combed the oxen. There had been no reason to curry dry animals. However, the children retrieved their currycombs and curried their beloved oxen. However, the last time the oxen were curried there was flesh on their bones and they enjoyed being curried. Now with ribs protruding two inches, the oxen objected to having a wooden comb raked across their ribs and back.

"I swear that the sage brush has grown a foot overnight," Joe exclaimed.

The sagebrush was an issue. The bushy plant stood as tall as the back of a mule. "and thick as the hair on a hound dog," Samuel declared. Fortunately the sagebrush was limber enough to bend over as the wagons drove over it. However the drag of the sagebrush on the bottoms of the wagons was very fatiguing for the lead ox team. Jesse ordered a rotation of lead wagons every hour. The lead team would pull out of line and let the rest of train move past. We went single file through the sagebrush, which slowed our progress to only ten miles a day.

"Not good enough," Marcus yelled, "we have got to move faster."

Many of the emigrants once again jettisoned unneeded items to lighten their loads. Many of the emigrants were very low on provisions, particularly the wagons that rolled into Fort Hall late after the provisions from the Fort had all been sold.

John Shively had decided to come west at the last minute after the sudden death of his wife in 1842 and so he was not as prepared as he should have been in the way of provisions. After leaving Fort Hall he was down to one gallon of unbolted flour and a gallon of dried serviceberries to last him the next 800 miles. When we heard of his predicament we gave him about ten pounds of buffalo jerky from our store. He pulverized the jerky, and with a spoonful of flour added, made soup. This soup was his breakfast and supper. At noontime he had the berries.

"I wish we could spare more, John," I told him. Fortunately, for John and many others, we soon came in contact with Indians, who were eager to trade dried salmon for almost anything.

The viewing of a series of spectacular waterfalls broke up the monotony of this portion of our travels. The first was called American Falls named long before there were many Americans in the region. But a group of Americans, left over from the Astor Fur Company disaster, decided to take to the river in self made boats against the strong advice of their Indian friends. They were caught up in the whirlpools and fast currents at this place and their boats capsized. Incredibly, a few actually survived and named the falls after their drowned comrades.

The falls appears to be 800-900 feet wide with a drop of about sixty feet over a 200 foot run. The water was 15 to 20 feet deep. Most of us had never seen a cataract such as this. We could hear the falls for three miles as we approached it.

Ten days and 139 miles later we came to Salmon Falls. It is aptly named. The banks were lined with Indians fishing for the huge salmon. Indian women were working in preparing and drying the salmon. The Indians were pleased to barter with us for their fish. These Indians were not interested in little bells or other trinkets. They wanted articles of clothing. The children could barely suppress their amusement seeing Braves wearing women's long dresses, pantaloons, and any other manner of clothing.

Properly dried salmon will keep for a long time, and pound for pound is just as nourishing as beef, and we didn't have any beef. We traded until we felt we had all we needed.

As we traveled along the Snake River and past the many falls our apprehension increased. We knew we would have to cross this raging river at least once and perhaps a second time. "How can we possibly ford this river?" I asked Marcus.

"There is a place where it is possible, not easy, but possible."

Thirty miles past Salmon Falls we came to that place. The river widened out into a sort of bay some 900 yards wide or just over a half a mile. The wagon train pulled over a bluff overlooking the Snake River. Far below in a valley, was the river, split by two islands and a partially submerged sandbar forming three channels in the river. I believe that every wagon paused at that point just to view the river below and all were silent in awe.

"It is not as foreboding when you get closer," Dr. Whitman, the consummate optimist, cheerfully shouted.

We were vastly more experienced in crossings than when we bumbled our way across the Kansas River over four months ago, but this was going to be a challenge.

"We had better select the right strategy for this ford. There will be little opportunity for corrections," Jesse Applegate stated the obvious.

The crossing is called the Three Island Crossing but the third island would be visible only in time of very low water. At this time the third island was a ripple over a gravel bar.

Jesse assembled a delegation to reconnoiter the crossing. He asked Marcus Whitman, his older brothers Lindsay and Charles Applegate, William Athey, William Doak, Nineveh Ford, and myself to join him and to take part in the decisions.

We crossed to the southern most island and went to the head of that island and crossed on a line to just touch the tip of the second island and then straight across the swiftest water to the north shore.

The plan was to follow this route with the wagons. The crossing to the first island was about a hundred yards. The bottom was good gravel and the water about wagon bed high on most wagons. To keep the loads dry we blocked the wagon beds up about eight inches. Our loads were much lighter now than on previous river crossings so we decided not to unload the wagons. We decided that when we crossed to the long island we would not push the cattle but let them graze slowly in very good grass to the end of the island.

Our little bell mare earned her keep once again. Pleasant led her across and all our horses obediently followed. They had to swim only a short distance in the deeper and swifter water. With our horses setting the example, the rest of the cattle began moving across to the luxuriant grass on the north shore. Now the challenge was to get the wagons and the oxen teams over the swift channel.

We placed several of the heaviest wagons upstream to deflect the current somewhat, and chained these wagons together. With riders on either side of each wagon; and with guy ropes to keep the wagons straight; and a rider on each side of the ox teams; and with angling slightly with the current; we managed a complete crossing with much less difficulty than we had feared. Placing the heavy wagons to break the current was my idea and the general conclusion was that it was a good idea.

I say we made the crossing with little difficulty but that is only partially true. Miles Eyers, a bull headed Englishman, decided that the crossing was too risky for his mule team. Eyers was always questioning orders and procedures and was not very well liked. He didn't like to associate with the "Colonials" and usually camped apart from the rest of the Column. He was very protective of his daughter, Mary, who had the eye of a young man named C.W. Stringer, who was traveling with his father, Cornelius Stringer.

In any case, over the objections of everyone, Eyers decided to take his mule team down the south side of the Snake River, with the thought of going all the way to Fort Boise, thus avoiding the crossing of the Snake River twice. For some reason the Stringers, both father and son, went with Eyers. The son may have gone because of his growing interest in Mary Eyers. We anticipated seeing them again at Fort Boise, but we did not.

A near disaster occurred to the Stoughton family. Alex Stoughton and his wife, Mary were in the front wagon with their thirteen year old son , John, in charge of their second wagon. The water was so swift that young John's horse lunged into deeper water. Marcus Whitman realized that John was in serious difficulty, wheeled his big white horse around and reached out and grabbed John's horse by the bridle and shouted, "Let go of the reins! Let go of the reins!" Marcus pulled the horse and rider to safety. Marcus Whitman was credited with saving John Stoughton's life.

Marcus Whitman was strong and energetic. He made numerous crossings helping others. In one such case he helped Ephraim Ford, no relation to our Fords, by putting a rope around the horns of Ford's lead ox and pulling him back into shallow water. Ephraim felt that Whitman saved him from disaster. Whitman was everywhere. He seemed to know intuitively where he would be needed next. As the emigrants finally reached the far shore they usually dropped to the ground in a state of physical and mental fatigue, but not Marcus Whitman, astride his big white stallion, returned again and again to the swift water to assist others.

After the Snake River crossing we traveled another eight miles into an area of good grass. Jesse ordered a day's layover. It rained hard that night and the Snake River rose making crossing by a few stragglers impossible. They had to wait for the river to go down or attempt the treacherous south side. They all went down the south side taking a little different route than Eyers had.

CHAPTER 29

Fort Boise

On September 18, the vanguard of our Company reached Fort Boise. We looked forward to arriving at Fort Boise just as we had at Fort Laramie, Fort Bridger and Fort Hall. Except for vastly improved scenery, Fort Boise was just as disappointing as the other forts.

Fort Boise was started to meet the needs of the fur trading industry and not for the purpose of supplying the needs of a large emigrant train. And as at the other forts, the "early birds got the worm", supplies in this case. Everyone could have received a little flour, sugar, rice, and so forth, but in fact the first few wagons got much, and the later wagons got none. This was the worst case of selfishness that we saw as of yet.

Fort Boise stands at the confluence of the Boise River and the Snake River. To reach the fort we had to ford the Snake again. This ford is called the Lower Snake Crossing. Fort Boise was established nine years ago in 1834, by The Hudson's Bay Company as a counter to Ft. Hall, which was built by Americans. The actual construction of the fort we are told was done by Thomas McKay, the step son of Dr. John McLaughlin, the "White Eagle" and Chief Factor at Fort Vancouver. The challenge to Fort Hall was effective and the Americans were forced to sell out to Hudson's Bay.

The Factor in charge at Fort Boise at this time was an old Astorian, Francois Payette. When the Americans were forced to sell Fort Astoria to the British during the war of 1812 Payette stayed on in the north-west. Eventually he hired out to the Hudson's Bay Company and moved up through their ranks. We found the old Frenchman, Francois Payette, friendly to the Americans and supportive to the limit of his resources.

The Cow Column had dropped behind to take advantage of the good grass along the Snake River. We were three days behind the Light column and we knew there would be little if any provisions left at Fort Boise. Our animals were rested and full and we felt that was more important than a few pounds of flour. We made the Lower Crossing without incident.

We did not tarry long at Fort Boise because we were deep into September and snow had probably already fallen in the Blue Mountains. We traveled northwest about twelve miles to the Malheur River. The word malheur means "bad luck" in French. Twenty-two more miles and we were at the Snake River again, but this was our last visit to this majestic water way. This place was called Farewell Bend. It is where we would say good-bye to the Snake River forever. Eight miles further and we entered the Burnt River Canyon. Burnt River also went by the name of The Brule and it was hardly a river, but more like a creek. But the creek corkscrewed through the mountainous country. We found ourselves crossing and re-crossing the deep gullies of The Brule.

"This is the worse road so far," commented Joe Hess.

This is the first stretch of trail that we had to double teams to make it up the steep grades. Many times we had to station members of the family above the wagons to tug on ropes to prevent the wagons from tipping over on the steep sides of the creek.

"We are taking wagons where wagons were not meant to go," Nimrod Ford complained.

"Stop the grousing," his brother John said. "We have excellent camp sites and with all our difficulties we still made twelve miles today."

"Some of the stragglers will never make these grades because many of them do not have enough oxen to double or triple up," John Brooks observed.

191

"Our oxen are still in relatively good shape because we have rotated and rested the oxen and they still have healthy hoofs because we have taken good care of them each night, no matter how tired we might be. This all brings me to the question of whether we should offer our oxen to double up with these families, who are not going to make at least three of these grades," I pondered.

"Your question needs no answer," Mary stated.

"Right. Joe, take one yoke of oxen back two miles to the grade there. It is not a long grade, but the wagons will have to double up or they will never make it. John and Nimrod take two yokes of our oxen to the long grade. I will take a yoke to this last grade, which is only about fifty yards long. Pleasant, you continue on the trail with our wagons. The scouts tell us we are through the worst of the trail. Then we will lay bye. Help the other wagons until dark then catch up with us, if the oxen are not too worn out. Joe, you have another assignment, which is to look over each wagon before you yoke on, if it is not stripped of foolish weight, don't double them up, but go on and help another wagon until they jettison the extra weight. Can you do that, Joe?"

"Absolutely, I can. I know foolish weight when I see it."

Our loyal animals did their job that day and into the evening. A number of wagons got through that wouldn't have otherwise.

But Joe reported the most significant thing that happened. "When they saw the Keizur oxen coming back to help, others stopped to share their animals too, as a result many more were helped, not just the few we were able to help."

"We have had the spirit of full cooperation since we left Fort Hall, where the early wagons cleaned out all the provisions in the fort to the detriment of the rest. Perhaps the philosophy of 'the devil take the hind most' is past." Mary said.

"I hope you are right, Mary" I mused

That evening Marcus Whitman rode by on his big white horse.

"Is someone ill? Do you need assistance?" Reeda called.

"No, not this time. I just wanted to say that your father is a good man. Sharing his oxen today was a Christian act."

"I know."

"Will you tell him so for me?"

"He knows it, but he will be pleased to hear it from you, Dr. Whitman."

From the sand and deep canyons, we entered the Valley of the Powder River. We were ready for this respite. The Valley is as nice as we have seen. It is about ten miles wide and about thirty miles long. The valley is rimmed with beautiful pine trees. It is crisscrossed with fresh flowing springs and creeks and grass that came to the bellies of the animals. In the distance the mountains are black with pine forest up to their summits, that were covered by a blanket of fresh snow. The valley was beautiful but the snow capped mountains and the dark clouds that swirled about them were ominous. That evening the campfires burned high, not because there was plentiful wood, but because of the nip of late fall that was in the air.

We did not hurry through this valley, but gave our animals ample time to graze. And for once Dr. Whitman did not prod us to "hurry on". Peter Burnett came down the line and pointed to a small speck on the horizon. "We can spread out tomorrow to make better time but steer toward that speck you see on the horizon. Tomorrow night we will camp by the 'Lone Pine'".

The speck of brush was like a beacon. By noon the speck revealed itself as a pine tree twenty feet high, by evening the twenty-foot pine was a 180-foot pine; "The Lone Pine".

It was a magnificent tree growing as a solitary sentinel over a vast treeless landscape. The pinecones of hundreds of seasons offered us kindling for our evening fire. The pitch smoke of the cones wafted down the hillside to the valley below. It was now September 28, and the snowcapped mountains warned us not to tarry.

Several days later we learned from Lt. Fremont who had been trailing us, that a straggler of our Company had cut the majestic pine tree to use the wood for their fire. The wood was green of course, and was useless as firewood. The giant pine had been a travelers' guide mark, for trappers, Indians, and for us, but now it was no more. Many a lost trapper, whether English, Canadian, French, American, or Native, gathered their bearings from this lone tree to guide them to safety. But now someone in the so-called "great migration" had chopped it down.

CHAPTER 30

The Blue Mountains

The spirits of the emigrants had risen. Hunting parties were bringing back fresh meat of deer and elk. We had good grass, good water, and lots of wood. The snow capped Blue Mountains loomed in the distance but we would face that challenge in due time.

We were nooning half way through the Powder River Valley when to our surprise a lone Indian Brave rode directly into our camp. He sat on the most beautifully marked horse. I had never seen such a horse, but I knew by hearsay what it was. I was looking at my first Cayuse pony. The Indian seemed to have a purpose and walked slowly leading his pony from noon fire, to noon fire, searching out each face.

Some one said, "Get Marcus". When he finally spotted Marcus Whitman he kneeled on one knee and lifted his arms, spreading them wide. Marcus slipped off his horse and caught the man under his outstretched arms and embraced him. They immediately started conversing in a strange tongue. Marcus called for some water and food. We gathered in a circle and just listened as the Indian Brave and Marcus engaged in what was obviously serious conversation.

Finally, Marcus turned to the circle of curious emigrants. "My friends, this man is Sticcus of the Cayuse Nation. He comes from Waiilatpu, my mission on the Walla Walla River near where it empties into the mighty

Columbia. He has informed me in Chinook Jargon that there is serious trouble at the Mission. The half-breed Dorian has spread the rumor that I am returning with an army. The Cayuse have refused to harvest the corn and wheat. My wife, Narcissa, has sent this loyal friend to bring me home in all haste. I am needed at my life's work place. I must go at once. I will leave within the hour."

"But how will we find our way through the Blue's," a woman whispered a bit too loudly.

"I told you I would guide you from Fort Hall to the Columbia River. This I cannot now do, but I will instruct Sticcus to guide you in my place. He is trustworthy and he knows the country like the back of his hand. I would trust him with my own life. You must trust him with yours. Could I have a word with the Captains?" Marcus asked.

Jesse and Peter joined Marcus Whitman a short distance away. Within a few minutes Peter called for James Nesmith and me to join them. "Sticcus tells me that there has been early snows and the passes have had deep snow drifts already this fall. He says the snow has melted somewhat this last week but there is much more on the way. It is doubtful that you can get the Columns through. If you had been caught a week ago in the Blue Mountains you would have been snowed in.

"You have two choices as I see it. You may stop in the next valley, which is called the Grande Ronde, prepare log shelters and winter over. There is game and grass at least until it is covered with snow. And most of you could survive. If your choice is to winter over, I will send provisions to you. Or you could try to accelerate your travel and push on through the Blues in the next two weeks or so. After that time you simple won't make it, the snow will be too deep. If you make it to the Mission our storehouses are full and there will be provisions enough for all. The problem with pushing on through, is the pine forest. Most of the trees are not large in diameter, but they grow as thick as hair on a hound dog. You will have to literally cut your way through. In either case I can't advise you any further. I must go now to give Sticcus his instructions. May God assist you in your decision and may God watch over you. Good bye until we meet at the Mission either in a few weeks or next spring." And with that he walked quickly back to the noon fire to talk briefly with the Cayuse and to instruct his nephew, Perim, to stay with the column. He then mounted and galloped toward the west. He never looked back.

Peter Burnett was the first to speak, "We have become too dependent on the good doctor, now we have been orphaned."

Jesse spoke next. "Of the two options suggested, I for one will take my Column on through, come hell or high water."

Jim Nesmith, the youngest of the leaders had this to say, "If we winter over, half of us will be dead before spring. If we get snowed in going through the Blue Mountains, half of us will probably freeze or starve. I am a single man I have no responsibilities for women and children. Having said that, I would push on hard for the next two weeks and if it becomes certain that we will be snowbound, I would leave the wagons until spring and put every man, woman, and child on the back of a horse, or mule, or even oxen, and ride for our lives. We have come a long way to stop now and I have talked too much for one who has only his own life to lose."

It seemed to be my turn to speak, "First, may I say to you Jim, that while it is true you do not have a family to care for, I believe your counsel has always been given for the good of all. If that were not so, you would have ridden out with Dr. Whitman.

"I have given a lot of thought to the Blue Mountains. But I did not realize until now that the timber is so thick that we will have to "cut" our way through. I have never seen a forest that you couldn't drive a team around the trees and between the trees with cutting only a few here and there. This forest is obviously different.

"But I have a plan to propose to you. I suggest that a party ride ahead in the morning to go as fast as their horses will allow, and have this party begin slashing out a trail for the Columns to follow. Perhaps they will be able to cut only a mile or perhaps ten miles, but however much trail is prepared , it could save the Columns precious days in the mountains."

197

"How many men would that take?" Jesse asked.

"I don't know 15 or 20 perhaps," I replied.

Jesse did not ponder the matter, but like the leader he was, he proceeded to launch the plan.

"Thomas, pick 40 of our best. They all have to be volunteers. Thomas, I'm asking you to lead such an effort. Will you?"

"Absolutely. Jim, will you go with me and serve as the second in command?" I asked.

"I am flattered that you have thought of me as being your second in command. Of course you can count on me to do what I can."

"Peter and I will stay with the Columns and keep them rolling," Jesse said.

"I wish Colonel Gabe McGee was still with us," I mused aloud.

"Return to your Columns now and tell them the plans. We will layover two hours while you get your work force organized," Jesse said.

I gathered the Keizurs around our noon fire and explained the change in plans.

"I want John Brooks, Pleasant, Joe and Nimrod to come with me to the forest. Samuel and John Ford will stay with the wagons. Mary Louise, you are in command. If there is a decision to be made Mary Louise will make it. She will speak for me."

"Mary Louise, you will have our full support," Sam Penter said. John Ford nodded in full agreement.

Over 100 men volunteered in the next hour. I chose four of the best mule- skinners along with their teams of mules. I chose to use mules rather than the stronger oxen because mules are more nimble and faster and I was interested in speed.

I chose 40 of the strongest men and ones a bit on the younger side, plus one man renowned for his hunting skills. His name was William Vaughan. The same William Vaughan who nearly drowned at the Kansas River crossing. That incident was long forgotten and we now refer to him as, "King of the hunters".

"Get your axes and crosscut saws and your all weather bundles. There is no reason to wait until morning," I shouted to my new recruits.

We left in a cloud of dust within the hour, with Sticcus leading the way, even though he had ridden all night and half the day to find Marcus Whitman ,and we knew he was nearly exhausted.

Philip Ruby begged to go with us. On September 30 he had lost his wife after a brief but severe illness and she had just been buried October 1, another victim of the trail to Oregon. I had great compassion for Phillip and his loss, yet I did not want a grieving man to accompany us. I explained to him that he had to stay with his wagon since he had no one else to drive it. He seemed to accept my rationale.

My battalion of tree cutters camped that night at the edge of the forest on the flanks of the Blue Mountains.

At daybreak I set the timber fallers to work at the most logical entry point. I paired the men into teams of two and spaced them 150 yards apart. They were instructed to cut a swath eight feet wide, which would give about a foot and a half side clearance for our widest wagons and two feet of clearance for most wagons. They were instructed to fall the edge trees away from the trail swath and trees in the middle to fall lengthwise to the trail, and to leave them where they fall for the muleskinners to drag to the edges. The hardest part was "flush cutting" the stumps to six inches or below.

I immediately dispatched our "offical"hunter, William Vaughan, to bring the crew fresh meat by nightfall if at all possible. Jim Nesmith, Sticcus, and I rode to the crest of the first grade to see where we should go from there. The timber was not large but very thick making the route difficult to determine. Beyond the grade we started on, there was a slight dip and ahead of that was a gap that would appear to be our next leg of the trail. Sticcus shook his head and pointed to the left and made a slanting motion with his hand.

"He wants us to by-pass the gap," Jim said.

"I'm not totally confident in his engineering skills," I quietly said to

Jim. "I will go with him in the direction he suggests but you go scout out the gap. This is not the time to make a major error in the selection of a route."

Jim caught up with us about two hours later. "A quarter of a mile past the gap is a bluff sixty feet high we would need to go three miles to circumvent the bluff," he reported. "What did Sticcus's direction turn up?"

"By going Sticcus's way we can use two meadows each about a half mile in length where there are few trees and no brush." Sticcus understood our discussions and smiled broadly that we realized his route was superior.

"In short, Sticcus knows the area and he understands the demands of the wagons. I am ready to fully trust his decisions," I said. And Sticcus smiled again.

At one place Sticcus indicated that if we could cut the bank of a stream we could then enter it and travel up the creek bed for over a mile. The creek bed was about twelve feet wide and had a good gravel bottom. In most cases the water was less than six inches deep.

I immediately dispatched two riders to return to the Columns to gather up some shovels to dig a slit in the bank.

We were still climbing upward. In one section five streams each separated by about a quarter of a mile cut the preferred route. Each stream had cut a deep narrow channel about twelve to fifteen feet deep and ten feet across. The little canyons presented a major problem. Sticcus tried in vain to communicate his solution, but I could not grasp his meaning. Finally Sticcus shook his head and took Jim by the hand and led him down the stream and out of sight. Presently Jim and Sticcus were back with Jim all smiles. "He took me downstream to a beaver dam," Jim explained. "He was trying to tell us to fall trees lengthwise into the gullies to fill them up. If we place the logs lengthwise, the water will continue to flow through and not dam up behind our log bridge. Just like the beavers do. Then if we pile the boughs from the fallen trees on top of the logs we will have level bed to travel over. It may be a bit bouncy, but I think it will work and look at the distance we will save."

I pulled workers ahead to begin the "fills". And so it went with our making good progress. The slashed trail was not a thing of beauty as it snaked back and forth using the principle of the inclined plane to go up and down the steeper grades, but it was passable and it saved the Oregon Emigration Company at least two weeks of precious time.

We worked from dawn to dark using every bit of daylight available, while a steady cold rain poured down. The rain was falling as snow on the mountaintops. One morning we shook six inches of fresh snow off our blankets.

Our hunter was either good, or lucky, because he supplied us with fresh elk steak morning and night. We did not stop for a noontime meal.

James Nesmith and I, along with our 40 workers received full credit for getting the Columns through the Blue Mountains, but Jim and I knew that it was Sticcus, the Cayuse who made it possible. The Columns rolled and bounced across the Blue Mountains in only four days of travel time. We did not lose a wagon or an animal.

As we broke out of the forest on the western flank of the Blue Mountains, the timber thinned at once and the traveling was easy. We camped Oct 7 near the Umatilla River. Friends of Sticcus were encamped about three miles away. The Cayuse were eager to trade particularly for items of clothing or any thing made of iron. The Indians brought corn, peas, potatoes, and wapato cakes to us. It was the first fresh vegetables we had tasted since we left Independence, Missouri five months earlier.

Coming down the grade to Whitman's Waiilatpu Mission, the Oregon Emigration Company separated into many independent groups. The concept of a Column or train disappeared. We were still 300 miles from our final goal, that is the Willamette Valley, and I thought the "train" should stay intact until we reached the Willamette Valley, but this was not to be. And still, *it's a long way to Oregon.*

CHAPTER 31

Whitman Mission

We were disappointed that Marcus Whitman was not at the Mission to greet us. He was off delivering a baby some place. And Narcissa, Whitman's famously beautiful wife, was at the Methodist Mission at The Dalles, down the Columbia River. But William Geiger the agent in charge greeted us in Whitman's absence. Geiger was a man about 27 years old.

"Welcome Americans! Welcome! I knew you were coming. Our harvest of corn, wheat, and oats was bountiful. Our storehouses are full. There are commodities for all. We can supply you with all you wish. We can talk about the rates later."

"What did he say? Talk about the 'rates' later?" Joe Hess sputtered. "We will have to buy our provisions?"

"I am sure the 'rates' will be most reasonable," I said. "You can't expect the Mission to not realize some compensation. We should be glad to pay for what we need."

"There will be ample grass for your animals at no charge," William Geiger announced.

"Such a blessing," Joe muttered.

"We can talk about the 'rates' and trading your spent oxen a little later," Mr. Geiger said.

The Mission was located on the Walla Walla River about twenty-five miles east of the confluence of the Walla Walla River with the Columbia River. The buildings at the Mission were built out of adobe bricks. The lumber used was all hand sawed and the joints were pegged together. Whitman was building a sawmill at this time. The mill was located twenty miles away on Mill Creek. Fields where corn and wheat were harvested this season surround the buildings. The potato and melon crops were in various stages of being harvested. There seem to be few fences, but then there are no trees from which to split fence rails. A poor perimeter fence was in need of serious repair. The fence encircled about 250 acres of which it looked like about 200 was being cultivated. There were two main houses and a scattering of other buildings, the most important one to us was the blacksmith's shop.

The most striking thing to us was the total absence of any native trees. To us farmers it appeared to be a strange place to locate a farm. The hills are rocky and barren. There did seem to be adequate grass along the Walla Walla River, but stray away very far and it was nothing but bunch grass. Now we know that bunch grass is very nutritious but it is very scanty here at Waiilatpu. The word Waiilatpu means "the place of the wild rye grass". Why would the missionaries put in the work that they obviously have, at a place like this, when not many miles away there is territory we went through with far superior soil, available wood, and setting on more likely crossroads for commerce. Waiilatpu was definitely off the road to anywhere, which raises the question why did we come this way when we could have cut off nearly 90 miles by following the Umatilla River to the Columbia. The answer is quite clear. We came this way because of the supplies we hoped to get at the Mission, but I never had it explained to me why the Mission is located where it is.

We were disappointed, even disheartened, when we learned of the "rates" that was to be charged, or should I say extracted, for provisions. William Geiger established the prices and they were not negotiable. One emigrant said to Mr. Geiger, "I think I'll wait and deal with Marcus Whitman."

Geiger replied, "You may have quite a wait, but that's your choice, except just remember Dr. Whitman and I work for the same authority, and that is the Mission Board."

"It sounds like Whitman has a whole bevy of babies to deliver somewhere," another emigrant grumbled.

So what are the "rates"? Beef was at ten cents a pound; pork fifteen cents a pound; potatoes a dollar a pound; and unbolted flour seven cents a pound. He offered wheat at a dollar a bushel. But it was livestock that Geiger wanted as much as our cash. He offered one fat beef for two of our trail worn cattle.

When it is all considered, perhaps the prices weren't exorbitant, but to many of the destitute emigrants, it was profiteering. The Keizurs had the funds, unlike most of the other emigrants, but we decided to buy only the minimal amount, just enough to get us to Fort Vancouver, and we were definitely not interested in swapping any of our livestock.

We decided to drive on past the Mission and camp half way to Fort Walla Walla, which was only twenty-five miles away. Jesse Applegate took his contingency right on to the Hudson's Bay Fort at the mouth of the Walla Walla River.

That night while we were camped, two of our horses came up missing. This was strange since they had been hobbled and couldn't stray. The next morning several Cayuse braves came in to our camp with our horses, which they had "found". In appreciation, we gave each Brave a shirt. That night we doubled our guard, but we still lost three hobbled horses. The next morning the Cayuse Braves came in to say how sorry they were to hear that some of our horses were missing again, and for another shirt apiece, perhaps, they could find the horses. Joe Hess was incensed, and told the Braves that hobbled horses don't stray away. They appeared hurt that Joe might be suggesting that they were thieves.

Against our better judgment we gave them the shirts. And lo and behold they found our horses and returned them within the hour. That night under triple guard we lost another three horses.

Mary observed, "We are almost out of shirts."

"And I am out of patience," I said.

Since we arrived at the Mission, all semblance of a Column was gone. We no longer had the advantage of strength in numbers in dealing with the Indians or any other problem. We were, in fact, scattered into little family groups over twenty-five miles between the Mission and Fort Walla Walla.

"Enough is enough" I said, "This is going to stop".

I sent John Brooks back to the Mission to locate our old faithful friend, Sticcus.

I signed to him, "Sticcus, can you arrange a powwow between me and your Chiefs?" He indicated that he could. The next morning John Brooks and I along with Sticcus rode about ten miles up Mill Creek to a large Indian encampment. As we approached the encampment John Brooks and I laid our rifles on a large flat rock in plain view. My first thought was to retain my revolver, but Sticcus motioned for me to lay it down too. Apparently the Cayuse were acquainted with revolvers, unlike their Cheyenne cousins that we had impressed with the revolver's firepower. Sticcus was becoming quite nervous and fidgety. He thought we would have many armed men with us. He explained that every Brave at our meeting would have knives under their blankets and although, they may appear to be unarmed, they certainly were not. He continued to explain his unique situation. He pantomimed that he was a Christian and the Chiefs resented his favored position with Marcus Whitman. Sticcus told us, "I will die first, then you and your son will die. You will die fast, I will die slowly."

I suggested that Sticcus stay by our guns and be ready to ride for help if there was trouble. Sticcus liked that plan. I advised Sticcus to ride to Fort Walla Walla rather than to the Mission. Jesse Applegate was at Fort Walla Walla.

"John, show no fear." We rode directly into a circle of Chiefs and dismounted. They were obviously impressed with our horses. John and I held up our empty hands in a sign of peace. "Do any of the worthy Chiefs speak English?" I began. One Indian stood up,

"I speak Boston. Do you speak Jargon?"

"No, I do not," I said.

"I have been schooled by the Queen's men. I am Chief Peu Peu Mox Mox of the Cayuse Nation and this is our head Chief Tiloukaikt. Chief Tiloukaikt wants to know why the squaw Indian, Sticcus did not come in to our camp?"

"He did not think he would be among friends," I replied. This brought a laugh from the Chiefs.

Peu Peu Mox Mox said, "We have gathered to hear you, but we are very busy. We have much to do before winter so do not take much of our time."

"That is good. We have much to do also and many more miles to go before the snow falls."

"You are not planning on staying at the Mission?"

"No, we are going to the Valley of the Willamette River, 300 miles from here."

"We know where the River that flows north is. This is good. Then speak."

"Thank you, I will. Worthy Chiefs of the Cayuse, we have given the last shirt for the return of our horses that your Braves have stolen. You and your people are welcome to come to our camp to trade or talk. But come while the sun is high. If you or your Braves come after the sun has set and before it rises, we will shoot you."

Peu Peu Mox Mox had to interpret very little of my message. The Chiefs understood my meaning.

One of the sub Chiefs named Tomahas asked in very good English "Are you a big Chief?"

"Yes I am. I am the chief of all the Keizurs."

"Is this your son?"

"Yes, this is one of many sons."

"He is brave."

"Yes, all my sons are brave."

"Return now to Sticcus, the white man's Indian. We will parley on

206

what you have said."

With that, we remounted and walked our horses back to where Sticcus was nervously waiting. Within a short while three Indian Braves rode out to us. They completely ignored Sticcus. Their spokesman said, "Perhaps your horses will not stray again. If they do it will not be Cayuse that finds them, there are Umatilla Braves that have been known to be thieves. If you want to shoot them, it will be fine with us."

"If they come at night they will be shot, and we will look in the morning to see what tribe they are from."

"The Cayuse do not need to steal such broken down horses. We have good horses already," the Brave said.

"Your horses are the finest I have seen," I said. "May we go in peace now?"

"Yes."

Sticcus could not vacate the place fast enough to suit him. When we were well away Sticcus signed that he couldn't wait to tell others how the Chief of the Keizurs stared down the Cayuse Chiefs.

In any case the horse stealing stopped, not just for us, but also, for all the scattered groups of emigrants.

CHAPTER 32

Return of a Lost Friend

Elizabeth Jane our eight year old came running and shouting like a bear was after her. "Amelia is here! Amelia is here and the other girls!"

Down the track left in the Walla Walla dust, a forlorn group of stragglers were limping into camp. It was Eliza Eyers, wife of Miles Eyers and her daughters, Mary, sixteen, Eliza twelve, and Amelia nine, also her son Thomas, fourteen. Also with them was Cornelius Stringer. Conspicuously absent was Miles Eyers and C.W. Stringer the son of Corny Stringer.

"Somebody go find Reeda, these folks need attention." Mary Keizur ordered.

"Give them each a few sips of beef broth, but nothing more," Reeda instructed. All six stragglers were emaciated with eyes deeply recessed and staring into space. They were all barefooted and caked with dust and dirt. They all collapsed at the edge of our camp. Their tongues were so swollen that speaking was a task.

Under Reeda's direction, the children were washed and carefully examined for any open wounds. All of them had horrible gashes on their feet that needed attention. Beds were made for them and they dropped off into a fitful slumber. Every two hours Reeda woke them up to give them more beef broth. It was late afternoon before she allowed them to take a little solid food.

The next morning they were feeling much better and felt like telling their story.

The last we had seen of the Eyers and the Stringers was at the Three Island crossing of the Snake River. Miles Eyers, against the advice of everyone, decided to not cross the Snake with the rest of the Company, but to strike out on their own down the south side of the river. Miles reasoned that using this approach, he could arrive at Fort Boise without ever having to cross the dangerous Snake River.

C. W. Stringer went along perhaps because of his growing interest in Mary Eyers. His father, Cornelius Stringer, went along because his son did.

Corny Stringer filled us in on the sad details of their ordeal. This is his story:

"As you recall, everyone advised against the south side route. I didn't think it was wise but my son wanted to stay near the Eyers in case there was some way he could assist them. Our first mistake was to take the riverbank trail when we should have stayed on the bluffs. Before long the trail we were following pinched out against the high basalt cliffs. At this point there was not enough room for Eyers to turn his mule team around, the trail was too narrow to maneuver the team. So Miles was forced to attempt a river fording at a much more dangerous place than at the Three Islands crossing. His family in total panic insisted that they be ferried over, which my son and I did, for Mrs. Eyers and the girls. And so we watched from the safety of the north shore as Miles Eyers attempted to swim his mules, with the wagon across. Promptly the wagon turned in the fast current and the mules became unmanageable, and turned up stream which would be the nature of most animals.

"My son, C.W. saw that Miles was in serious trouble and left the safety of the shore plunging in to help Miles. They were both swept away to their deaths within sight of their family. Their bodies were never found although we scouted the north side for two days. Miles Eyers was not a young man, he was in his sixties, I believe. He had married late and his wife was much younger. My son was strong and only thirty, but no one could have survived that river at that point. What made this tragedy doubly bad was the fact that old Eyers had all the family money strapped around his waist.

"But the drama of our story really begins here, after the drownings. I gathered Eliza Eyers, Miles's wife, the three girls, and the son, Thomas, and struck out at the right angle to the river hoping to intercept the main Column. We found the trail eventually but the Columns had already passed. We followed your trail, but could not catch up to you.

"We were left with only the clothes on our backs, no weapon, and no way to make a fire and with only my canvas canteen, which I had fortunately taken with me. We came across the wagon trail on the fourth day, but by that time the Columns were long gone. We knew we wouldn't get lost now that we had the trail to follow and frankly that was a great relief to me. Three different times we hid in the rocks or the brush, when we saw parties of Indians also following your trail.

"We found campfires that still had a bed of coals that we could fan into a fire to keep warm at night. And we sometimes found scraps of food around the campsites. We found a major butchering site in the Blue Mountains but the scraps of meat were putrid and I would not let anyone eat it. But the leg bones of the elk and deer that had been butchered were easily crushed with rocks and the marrow inside was still good and very nutritious, I think. In the Blue Mountains we also found berries to eat.

"We walked from first morning light until we could not see at night. At first we made good time, perhaps as much as twenty miles for the first several days. But the little girls simply could not keep up a forced march of that magnitude, and before long, if we made seven to eight miles a day, we were doing well. We were hoping we would catch up before now but we just couldn't go any faster."

Finally, Corny slowed down a bit in his story, and I interrupted, "Why didn't you get help at the Mission as you came past?"

"Mr. Geiger, the man in charge, was giving supplies to other destitute emigrants, but they had to sign a bill to pay for it later," Corny said. "Geiger said the Mission Board needed an accounting. But I could not sign, not knowing when or how it would be repaid. So we kept walking."

"Can Amelia stay with us until she gets rested?" Elizabeth Jane pleaded.

"They will all stay with us until Reeda says they have fully recovered," Mary said without any hesitation.

"And even after that if they wish," I added.

"I cannot speak for Mrs. Eyers and her family, but I do not know how I will be able to compensate you," Cornelius Stringer said. "My future is rather bleak."

"We have never asked for compensation from guests. You are our guests," Mary said.

"May God bless the Keizurs," Eliza Eyers whispered.

CHAPTER 33

Float the Columbia or Overland?

On October 16 we planned a visit to Fort Walla Walla for the entire family. The purpose was to get our first glance at the Columbia River. Everyone went except Sam and Matilda Penter who got the assignment of staying with the youngest of the clan. "You see one river you have seen them all," Sam declared. "How could it be any more impressive than the Snake River?"

We were impressed with the majestic Columbia. Never had we seen a river like this one. Not the Mississippi, nor the Missouri and certainly not the Snake could compare with the Columbia. Such a magnificent stream flowing such clear deep water without a ripple on the surface. It looked like a moving lake to us. The blue water was such a contrast to the barren hills that came right to the water line.

Jesse Applegate and his entire crowd were already building rafts and boats. To float "leisurely" down the river to The Dalles.

"Thomas, you would be wise to start building your boats," Jesse coached, "it will save you 120 miles of wagon haul over territory that everyone says is nearly impassable. We have already contracted all the available guides and still some rafts won't have a guide. But then how can you get lost on a river?"

"How are you going to get all your cattle on board rafts?" I asked.

"Mr. McKinsey, the man in charge at the Hudson's Bay Outpost has offered to take over our herd for a voucher that we can turn in at Fort Vancouver to Dr. John McLaughlin. He will trade straight across steer for steer, cow for cow oxen for oxen straight across. When you consider the shape of our cattle, I think he is being more than fair."

"It seems that he is, Jesse. Much more fair than any deal the Mission has proposed."

"How long do you figure it will take you to get to The Dalles on the river?" Joe asked.

"It will only take three to four days to float the river. We estimate that it will take us three weeks to build the boats, however," Jesse explained.

John Brooks started doing a little mental arithmetic and surmised, "If a wagon train averaged only five miles a day they would be on the dock to greet the Applegates."

We took in the whole scene and were reluctant to return that evening to our camp but we wanted to get back before dark. We had traveled only a mile or so when our old friend Sticcus caught up with us. He asked by signing, if he could ride with us. He said there are bands of marauding Cayuse out and about, and that he would feel safer riding with the Keizurs.

"No Cayuse would dare harass the Chief of the Keizur Nation." He didn't fully understand the hearty laughter of Joe, Pleasant, and the rest. As we rode we began to quiz Sticcus about the river and the overland terrain. For some reason none of us liked the idea of rafting down the river, but we needed much more information on the overland route.

"Have you ever been to The Dalles?"

"To Wascopan? I have gone every fall since I was a small boy. I went with my grandfather to trade for salmon and I have been several times to buy slaves. Wascopan is a very good place to buy slaves. Many slaves are sold there every year. My grandmother on my mother's side was of the Wishram Nation. The Wishrams control the mountain passes on the north side of the river. The Wishram seldom hunt or fish, but every Indian that goes to the great falls to fish must pay the Wishrams for going through their land. The powerful Yakima and their wicked cousins the Klicktitats could defeat them, but the Wishrams don't charge too much and there are plenty of fish, so it is just wiser to give the Wishrams a few fish. But then the Wishrams don't have to do anything." Sticcus was in a talkative mood for an Indian.

"Tell me then, how did you go to The Dalles? By boat or by horse?"

"Sticcus has gone both ways."

"If you were us, with our wagons, which way would you go?"

Without any hesitation Sticcus indicated emphatically, "By land, not by water."

Nimrod probed a little more. "The river looks peaceful enough, wouldn't it be easier just floating along down the river?"

"The river is not peaceful. It is dangerous. It is calm in front of the Fort but it is just resting for the mad race down stream." He took his hands to show how the river squeezes in at some places and demonstrated what we all perceived to be white caps that would be on the river.

"But going overland with our animals we need grass, and all I see is treeless barren hills. We are told that the cliffs along the river are barren of all grass for the entire distance to The Dalles." Nimrod kept pressing for more information.

"Sticcus is not a foolish Indian. He would not travel along the cliffs. Why would Sticcus do that?"

"Where would you travel then?" Nimrod continued.

"Sticcus would go east, inland about three to four miles, and there you will find much grass and wood for your fires at night. Sticcus would go to where the Umatilla River flows into the Columbia, then up the west bank for three or four miles, and then go west to Wascopan or as the whites say, The Dalles."

"Are there any rivers to cross going this way?"

"Yes, there are three rivers and several creeks. You will need to cross the Umatilla, the John Day, and the Deschutes. But you have crossed the Snake River twice. You will laugh all the way across these rivers and the waters of the rivers are always low in the harvest month."

"What would you charge to guide us?" I asked.

After a long silence, when I thought he was going to refuse any pay, he said, "I will lead you safely to within sight of The Dalles. But I will not go into The Dalles. My price is to pick one of your horses. One horse, and I choose the horse."

"You have a deal Sticcus, any horse except the little bell mare. You can't have her."

Sticcus offered his hand to close the deal as he had seen white men do before.

"We will leave by mid-morning. I want to spend the early morning seeing if others will form up with us," I said.

Eventually sixteen wagons joined us headed for the Umatilla River. The trail was not the best but with what we had been over we did not complain. We crossed the Umatilla, the John Day, and the Deschutes Rivers and several smaller creeks all with little difficulty. The rivers were low, as Sticcus had predicted since it was late October. It was on this stretch that we got our first view of Mt. Hood. Each wagon stopped at a particular viewpoint and all the emigrants just stared in silent awe. We could see at once that there would be no possibility of taking the wagons over the snow laden Cascade Mountains.

We made excellent time averaging nearly fourteen miles a day. We arrived at The Dalles on October 25. We traveled the last three days completely out of all commodities. Two of our cows still gave milk, but very little. Things would be better once we got to The Dalles because we had adequate funds to resupply.

It was time for Sticcus to collect his pay in the horse of his choice excepting our bell mare.

I had overlooked one other exception that I should have made.

"Dad, he is going straight for the stallion," Pleasant alerted us. We had brought only one stallion for breeding purposes. He was a fine Arkansas chestnut stallion. Five years old. Sticcus knew his horses. We all watched as he approached the big Stallion, which was hobbled at the time. He placed a bridle with no difficulty and threw his blanket over the horse's back and stooped to take the hobble off. When he stood up the blanket was on the ground. He threw the blanket on the stallion again, but the horse quickly dispatched it to the ground again with a quick bite to the corner of the blanket.

"He doesn't like the smell of Sticcus's blanket," Pleasant observed. "Should I help him?"

"No, helping was not part of the deal," I laughed. On the fifth circling try the horse had had quite enough, and quickly bit Sticcus on the butt. All the Keizurs tried to suppress their delight. Sticcus stared at the obstinate horse and the horse stared right back. Without a word but still rubbing his backsides, Sticcus with a quick motion, retrieved his bridle from the stallion. He then mounted his own Cayuse pony and took out a horsehair lariat that he had coiled to his side. With a quick and deft swing of his lariat Sticcus lassoed his second choice, a fine mare that had been bred back to the stallion. And a very good choice. With a wave of his hand Sticcus rode out of sight trailing his new horse.

Reeda immediately pulled a bunch of succulent grass and walked over to the stallion and gave him his reward. We were still laughing about the whole incident that night around the campfire. But we all knew we owed Sticcus our sincere thanks. He not only guided us unerringly through the Blue Mountains but also all the way to The Dalles.

We had our first view of the mighty Columbia since we had left Walla Walla, and we could hear the roar from the spectacular Celilo Falls. No raft would be going over that in one piece. The emigrants floating the river would have to land several miles above this site if they had any hopes of surviving. We stopped the train on the bluffs overlooking the falls. We had thought the various falls on the Snake were spectacular, and they are, but they do not compare in any way with Celilo Falls.

We learned much later that our decision to go overland, rather than floating the Columbia River, was perhaps the smartest decision we made on the entire 2,000-mile trip to Oregon.

Sticcus had advised us, that the easiest route down from the bluffs surrounding The Dalles, was to come straight down a creek called Chenoweth Creek. We found the creek and followed it. The two Keizur wagons had been the lead wagons the entire way from the Walla Walla River. If there was sagebrush to be broken, our wagons did it.

We came to a point where the trail widened out to where several wagons could move abreast. I stopped our lead wagon and waved to Nineveh Ford, no relationship to our Fords, John and Nimrod, but a very loyal single man, who had always done his share of the hard work. I motioned to Nineveh to pull his wagon up even with me. I yelled over to him, "Nineveh, do you have a sense for history?"

"I have always had an appreciation for history. Why do you ask?"

"Why don't we pull into The Dalles together, step by step? Ours will be the first wagons ever to be pulled from Independence, Missouri to The Dalles, Oregon. We are making history. Let's make it together. No one in the world will ever be able to say they were the first wagons into The Dalles but us. It could be noted in a book someday."

"It is a magnanimous offer, Thomas. I would be proud to share a page of history with you."

"It will be something your grandchildren will tell their children."

"But Thomas, I'm not married."

"Come on, the historians won't know."

So we preceded slowly together, wheel beside wheel. Soon other wagons behind us caught on and cheers went up. "Mary, do you hear that? By the Grace of God we have made it."

But the story of history in the making does not end there.

The third wagon behind us was pulled by a mule team of eight mules, driven by John Burch McClane, a young man 23 years old. When I stopped, and he saw Nineveh and me talking, he guessed what we were about to do. McClane whipped his mules up and passed both Nineveh and us. Our oxen could never have kept up the pace of the mules in the short run and we didn't even try. It would have been abusive to our animals. So, John Burch McClane was the first wagon from Missouri to arrive into The Dalles in October, 1843, not the Keizur, nor the Ford wagons.

But, if you asked anyone else in that wagon train, "Who was the first wagon into The Dalles?" quite likely they would say, it was the Thomas Dove Keizur wagon, or they would say it was The Ford wagon, but one thing you can be sure of, none will say it was the McClane wagon, even though it was the McClane wagon. In later years, as I understand it, even McClane stopped claiming the honor.

That evening we bought two fifty pound salmons from an old Indian. He was apologetic for having to sell "such small fish". We were in the process of frying huge salmon steaks in our giant frying pan when a rider approached the string of happy campfires. The rider stopped at each for a brief conversation and then moved on toward us.

"I believe you must be the Keizur Clan, I'm thinking," the man said in a thick Scottish brogue. "My name is Donald McDonald, first of Inverness, Scotland. Now of Fort Vancouver. I am a clerk to the Factor McLoughlin."

"A clerk?" Joe asked.

"Aye, but to you a clerk is a poor Laddy, who scribbles notes and keeps books and the sort. I am an officer in the employment of the Hudson's Bay Company under Royal Charter. Dr. McLoughlin is expecting several hundred Yankee emigrants to be coming our way over the next few months."

"More like a thousand, I believe," I said.

"A thousand? May the Saints be blessed? I have instructions to lend any assistance necessary to your needs, to you and any of the other emigrants from the Colonies."

"But may I ask, why did you single out my family?"

"On our flat boat tied up about ten miles west of here, there is a sack of spuds, a sack of good wheat flour, about forty pounds of beef jerky and two sacks of wilted vegetables, with instructions to give it to the Keizurs, should they be found, which I believe I have. Can you make use of these commodities?"

"Sir, this salmon is the first food my family has had for four days, except for half a cup of milk each morning and night. Our stores are gone but I must ask again, who knew we were coming? I mean, who specifically knew the Keizurs would be here? We don't know anyone at Fort Vancouver."

"It was a tall red headed Lad, Irish I would guess. He is a very popular laborer on the farm. A lad with a future with the Company, I would say. He didn't give his name. But we had room on the flatboat and I said I would find you if you were here by the time we leave. And when I heard that a sad looking lot of Yankees were coming down Chenoweth Creek, I reasoned that you could be among them."

"A tall Irish fellow with red hair?"

"Kenny!" Reeda and Sarah said in unison. "It was Kenny O'Regan. It has to be Kenny!"

"The boy made it then. Kenny O'Regan is alive, he survived!" I exclaimed.

"Praise the Lord! Praise the Good Lord," Mary declared. "You have been redeemed Thomas, for your harsh sentence, and he bears you no ill feelings. Praise the Lord!"

"Amen." I said quietly.

"It is sorry I am, to break into this family jubilation, or whatever it is, but I have more instructions and my day is not over by a far sight," Donald McDonald interrupted our enthusiasm.

"I have a fully manned flatboat at your disposal, which will leave the landing day after tomorrow at sunrise. We can take both of your wagons and your people, but we cannot take your livestock. Can you break your wagons down by day after tomorrow?"

"What do you mean 'break the wagons down'?" Joe asked.

"By removing the wheels and the running gear, so the box will sit flat on the boat. You will have to remove your canvas covers too. Can you do it?"

"I will need to know the proposed charge for such a service," I said.

"Dr. John McLoughlin said that there should be no charge since we will be returning empty anyway. If you reprovision at the Fort, there will be charges, but you will not have to pay until your first crops are harvested in a year or so, and then you can pay in wheat, oats, or cattle, because currency is hard to come by. I would make this trip, if at all possible, if I were you, because I understand there is a large party coming by the river and they will have to wait for more flat boats to arrive. Can you be ready the day after tomorrow?"

"We will be at the landing and ready, of that you may be sure," I stated with conviction.

Pleasant, stepped forward, "Mr. McDonald, Sir, may I shake your hand? I have never met a real Englishman before. And I believe you are a man of honor."

"I thank you, my Lad. I hope to be honorable, but I am a Scot, I'm not English, all Scots are honorable. I only work for the English."

Joe pulled Pleasant back, "Don't make shaking an Englishman's hand a habit. It will just make it harder when we fight them."

"Oh, another bit of advice. Double your guard tonight. The Columbia River Indians will steal the buttons off your shirt while you're still in your shirt. I'll be going now. I will see you at the landing, and welcome to the Domain of the Hudson's Bay Company." And he rode out of the camplight into the dark.

"Hudson's Bay Domain?" Joe Hess snarled, "We'll see about that. This land belongs to America and we are here to claim our God given land." Fortunately McDonald was out of hearing and did not know of Joe's political ranting.

"Pleasant and John Brooks, go tell our friends that we are going to circle the wagons for the last time tonight. We have not had to do that for some time. Place all the loose cattle inside the circle but they can leave the oxen on the outside. I want a guard posted at each wagon and I want several mounted outriders. We can't afford losing what little we have at this point in our journey."

I sent John Brooks with the women and children and the wagons on the flat boat, with instructions to get passage in some manner up the Willamette River to the Falls at a place they are calling Oregon City. "We will meet up with you there, as soon as we can drive the cattle and horses overland."

With me on the cattle drive would be Joe Hess, Sam Penter, John and Nimrod Ford, and Pleasant.

Mary was very much opposed to splitting the family. She did not like the idea of the women going by boat while we drove the loose cattle overland.

"Thomas, I implore you, leave the stock in The Dalles and come with us by boat. You can retrieve the stock next spring and by that time we will be located on our land and have a place to take the cattle."

"Your arguments are persuasive, particularly, in not wanting to split the family. But if we leave the horses, which we hope will be our future livelihood, there will be no purpose in returning for them, because they will have long vanished into thin air," I reasoned.

"Then let the women go overland with you, but don't split the family. We have come nearly 2,000 miles suffering all the hardships together and now within 200 miles of our goal, you propose a split?"

No one else in the family entered the discussion, but they all listened intently while their parents argued for the first time in their memory.

"The river, from this point on, will be the safest for the women and children," I argued, "And besides our only hope of getting the cattle to the Valley is to pull an almost continuous forced march. The women and children would frankly slow us down too much."

Mary tried one more argument but in vain. "And what will we find at this Fort Vancouver, another Fort Laramie, or Fort Boise, or worse? How do you expect emigrant American women to be received?"

"We have heard only glowing reports about Fort Vancouver and Dr. John McLoughlin, the man in charge," I rebutted.

"Just as we did before we arrived at Fort Boise, we heard glowing reports and then we saw the Union Jack flying, and we will see the British flag at Vancouver too."

"Enough, we will see you off by boat and start at once overland for Oregon City. We will look forward to seeing you at the falls on the Willamette. Incidentally, the gold still hidden in the false bottoms of the wagons should be split, with half of it going with us."

"No, Mr. Keizur, the gold stays with me. No one will be expecting women to be guarding gold. The gold stays with us."

"Alright, Mrs. Keizur, the gold stays with you."

The argument was over, and our children appeared relieved.

"Dad, would it be too much to ask for the use of your Militia Revolver while I escort the women and children?" John Brooks asked.

"Good idea, Son," and I immediately unbuckled the holster and gave it to John Brooks.

Joe Hess unbuckled his revolver and strapped his holster around Mary Louise's waist. "You can now match fire power with the entire Hudson's Bay Company and I feel sorry for anyone who crosses you."

We all laughed breaking any remaining tension, as the holster and belt kept slipping down Mary Louise's waist to her ankles. "This needs to be tightened up a little," she laughed.

CHAPTER 34

Fort Vancouver and Oregon City

The trip by boat down the Columbia River, as told by Mary Louise, was a pleasant four day adventure. John Brooks tried his hand at the oars to the complete entertainment of the skilled French Canadian boatmen. His experiment on the oars did not last long.

Donald McDonald provided English tea each afternoon at two o'clock for all the adults in our party and the boatmen. The tea was heated over an open brazier in the middle of the boat. Only the man at the sweep oar remained on duty at this time.

I noticed that our forward progress had slowed noticeably and the oarsmen were working harder.

"It's the tide we're bucking," McDonald explained. "The tide from the Pacific Ocean impacts the river as far as forty miles upstream from Fort Vancouver, but my men are used to it. Twelve hours from now the tide will help us."

We landed about five miles from the Fort, at the Hudson's Bay sawmill. "If the women and children would like to wash up, the mill stream is a good place to accomplish this," Clerk McDonald advised.

It was clear they wanted the Americans to be looking our best before we reached the Fort.

To our amazement there were three ships in the harbor at Fort Vancouver.

It looked as though one was fully loaded and was waiting only for the change in tide. To meet us at the landing was Mr. James Douglas, second in command to Dr. John McLoughlin.

Donald McDonald, in saying good-bye to us said, "Should any of you be in need of provisions or clothing you can obtain it here. Dr. John McLoughlin and James Douglas, who you are about to meet, are beloved and respected and deserve the gratitude of all people, regardless of their nation of origin. It makes no difference to them, or any of their employees, whether you are Russian, French, Sandwich Islander, or American."

"Mr. McDonald, you have been a gentleman, a kind and caring gentleman," Mary Keizur said, "and I am reluctant to ask anything more of you, but..."

"My dear lady, do not hesitate to voice a need. If I can obtain something for you, I will."

"The young man that gave you the commodities that you brought to us when we were so much in need, is named Kenneth O'Regan. How might we find him?"

"I guessed that this lad was special to you." Mr. McDonald said.

"He is like a son."

"I will see what I can find out. If he goes by his given name, and sometimes they don't, I should be able to locate him in the registry. In any case, I will try to locate him. I will be back to you tomorrow."

"Thank you again for all you have done," Mary Keizur said.

In less than two hours Mr. McDonald was back.

"I have good news. If it is a K. D. O'Regan you are looking for I can tell you exactly where he is."

"It is K. D.!" John Brooks exclaimed. "His name is Kenneth Darius O'Regan. How is he? Where can we find him?"

"According to the registry, he arrived the first of September. He worked a week splitting rails for his food. He caught Mr. Douglas's eye and he contracted him for a year as a laborer."

"The first of September? He made good time," John Brooks said, "Can we see him?"

"Of course. He is digging potatoes on Fourth Plain. We must get the potatoes dug before we have a frost. I can tell you this lad is well liked and seems rather bright for an Irishman. If you like, I will order you a wagon and team for the morning. Can one of you handle a team?"

"Every Keizur, man or woman, can handle horses. We handled horses before we learned to walk," Reeda said.

"I will have a team and wagon ready in the morning," McDonald said. "It is only about two miles northeast. This is First Plain where we are now and you need to go to Fourth Plain," Mr. McDonald explained.

That night around our warming fire all conversation was about Kenny. We all took turns recalling incidents involving Kenny, but not a word was mentioned about the incident that caused his banishment.

"I still don't see how he was able to walk all that way and get here a month and a half a head of us," Mary Louise pondered aloud.

"He didn't walk," John Brooks blurted out. "Reeda snuck his horse and rifle out to him."

All eyes turned toward Reeda. "John Brooks I would break your arm except I would have to set it. How did you know that?"

"Pleasant spied you and woke Dad to see if he should stop you. That's how. Pleasant told me."

"Dad knew?"

"Your Dad was well aware and was so relieved," Mary Keizur declared.

"Well I'll be blessed," Matilda said. "Are there any more secrets that this family would like to share?"

"I think Joe Hess has a jug full of secrets," Mary Louise laughed.

The morning ride to Fourth Plain was very pleasant under Indian summer skies. Mr. McDonald had even placed a basket with three loaves of bread and a small smoked ham in the wagon.

We drove through a young apple orchard and a newly cleared area where pigs were rooting and tearing up the remnants from the clearing activity. On the rolling hills we could see herds of milk cows and beef cattle grazing. The beef were a Spanish breed much smaller than our animals. Dr. McLoughlin recognized this difference and changed the voucher agreement reached at Fort Walla Walla to exchange the trail worn cattle for Hudson Bay cattle. The original trade voucher was "animal for animal" straight across. McLoughlin changed the deal to two Spanish breed animals for one American animal. He was quoted as saying, "Not only is this more fair but it will infuse our herds with superior stock. I only wish the Americans had brought sheep with them."

We found the ten-acre potato field and saw Kenny among the workers digging, sacking, and loading potatoes. It was easy to spot Kenny by his mop of red hair. Kenny was digging on a row going away from us. Reeda slipped off the wagon and quickly covered the distance to come in behind Kenny who was too busy to be aware of her.

Reeda covered Kenny's eyes with her hands and whispered, "Guess who?"

"Maria, what are you doing here?" Kenny demanded.

"Maria? Who in tarnation is Maria?" Reeda pretended to pout.

Kenny's eyes went from Reeda to the wagon full of Keizurs. "May the saints be praised? My prayers have been answered. The Keizurs are here! Hey, Frenchy, my family is here."

The man called Frenchy said, "Take your noon time early, Son, go visit your family."

It was a joyous reunion with hugs and tears. "We saw your name carved on Cathedral Rock," Little Elizabeth shouted.

"Bless you for sending us food at The Dalles. It was much welcomed," Mary said.

Suddenly a puzzled look came over Kenny's face. "But where are the other boys and Mr. Keizur and Old Gabe?"

"They are driving the livestock overland to the city at the Falls on the Willamette River. The women and children with John Brooks as our escort, came by Hudson's Bay flatboat to Fort Vancouver. They will be pleased we found you. Gabe McGee stayed by his plan to go to California. He left us near Fort Hall," Reeda explained.

"And will Mr. Keizur be pleased?" Kenny asked.

"He will be pleased most of all. Believe me Kenny, he will be pleased," John Brooks declared.

"We have so much to talk about, but I should get back to my work soon. The Company has been good to me. I love this farm work particularly the harvesting. Digging these praithies is work made for an Irishman. And look at this soil. I can bury the tines of my praithy fork with only a shove of me hand. I never have to put me foot on the fork. The whole country is like this. If the praithy is smaller than my fist we leave it for the pigs."

"Do you think we could buy fifty pounds of potatoes for seed? We ate our seed potatoes on the Snake River Plateau," John Brooks inquired.

"Fifty pounds you are wanting? I don't think Dr. McLoughlin would have us cut a praithy for anyone." Kenny laughed.

"The potatoes are huge, but not as big as your blarney," John Brooks retorted.

"Tomorrow is Sunday. We don't work on Sunday. I'll be going to early Mass at the Fort. They have a tidy little Catholic church that I attend. Why don't you join me?" Kenny suggested.

"I think the Keizurs will pass on that, but thank you for inviting us. But please spend the rest of the day with us. We have journeys to compare," Mary Keizur said.

"I would like to go to church with you,"Reeda announced, "only, don't tell Dad. Will Maria be there?"

"It is hoping I am, that she will." Kenny said, with a slightly redding face. "And don't worry if you can't understand the old priest. No one else does either. Then I'll be seeing you in the morning. I must get back to digging. I promised the Company a full year and I intend to see that they get a full and honest measure. But when the year is up I intend to go up the Willamette River and find a piece of land to clear and farm because farming is what I'm wanting."

"That is where we Keizurs are going too. Maybe we will be neighbors. Oh, I do hope so," Elizabeth said.

It was a good day for the Keizurs and one we will often recall in the years to come.

Narcissa Whitman described Fort Vancouver in her letters home, as the "New York City of the West" and we would soon see why. The scenery was beautiful and so different from the brown barren hills and cliffs of basalt that we had seen east of the Cascade Mountains. Behind the Fort the rolling hills are either under cultivation or covered with luscious spruce trees called locally, Douglas fir. This is more like what we had dreamed Oregon would look like. We have been told that the big timber goes all the way to the Pacific coast.

The Fort is located on the north shore of the Columbia River, a short distance from the mouth of the Willamette River, which pours into the Columbia from the south. Many of the Hudson's Bay men refer to the Willamette River, as the Multnomah River, named it seems, after a well-known Indian Chief. Lewis and Clark discovered the Willamette on their return trip up the Columbia River. It is hard to imagine how they could have missed it on their trip down the Columbia, but they did.

Dr. McLoughlin was put in charge of the Hudson's Bay enterprises, called the Columbia District, in 1824. At that time the headquarters for the Company was located at the mouth of the Columbia River at a place called Fort George. Fort George was the old Fort Astoria built and operated by Americans until they lost it to the British. Dr. McLoughlin moved his headquarters to Fort Vancouver in 1825, only eighteen years ago.

Looking from the riverside inland, are a series of wide benches called "Plains". The Fort itself is located on First Plain, just beyond the high-water mark at flood stage. The Fort covers an area 732 feet by 325 feet enclosed by a wooden palisade twenty feet high. Inside this enclosure are thirty or more buildings including the Factor's house, a Catholic church, a rectory for the priest, workshops, a powder magazine, a school house, a dining hall with a kitchen, a bachelor's hall with a sitting room, and even a small jail.

Outside the palisade are over forty small cabins, which house workers and the fur trappers, a hospital, barns, the piggery, root houses and several other buildings. They are building a bastion in the northwest corner that will house several three pounders.

John Brooks had an interesting observation, "I don't think the cannons are meant to defend the Fort against the Indians. It is intended to defend the Fort against Americans."

We heard that the barque Columbia was ready to sail to London with a load of furs. In talking to a worker he estimated the wheat crop to be 4,000 bushels, oats 1500 bushels, and barley 1700 bushels. He estimated the cattle to be at one thousand head. We learned that they were not pleased with their sheep and considered them inferior. "But the 3,000 head of milk cows are superb, producing enough butter and cheese to supply the Russian American outposts in Alaska," he said. "Hudson's Bay Company claims 300 head of brood mares."

But the thing that impressed us above all else was the apple, pear, and peach orchards and the vineyards heavy with grapes that they had not had the time to pick. We had our first taste of apples, ripe and red, since we left Missouri.

We met our host, Dr. John McLoughlin, on two different occasions. The first was the second day after our arrival, as he and his Indian wife toured us through their bountiful gardens. The second time was when we embarked to go to the falls on the Willamette River. He came to see us off.

Dr. McLoughlin is a most interesting man. He is imposing at six feet four inches tall and he weighs over 320 pounds. His snow-white hair drops to his broad shoulders, and it is his white hair that won him his Indian moniker of "White Eagle". He is only 46 years old but his white hair fools you into thinking he is much older. Dr. McLoughlin was trained as a physician, but somehow turned fur trader.

We rested and ate for a full week with no mention, not even a hint, at repayment. We heard that Mr. Day from our emigrant train had arrived at the fort very ill and was in the Fort hospital. We visited him but I do not believe he knew we were there. Reeda did not give him much hope, and indeed, he died the following day. We knew Mr. Day had a family in Kentucky or Missouri. He was going to establish a land claim and return for his family. We had no one to contact regarding his death. His family will wait for word that will never come. It is not likely that his family will ever know what happened to him.

The Hudson's Bay Company furnished us with a bateaux and men at the oars for our trip up the Willamette River to the falls. Again, there was no mention of a fee. We arrived at the falls and the new town of Oregon City on November 9, 1843.

Our final thoughts on Dr. John McLoughlin were, that although he had a reputation of being ruthless and dictatorial in business, and maybe he is, but to us he was kind and generous.

Mary philosophized, "To survive in the cutthroat fur trade and to have built the 'New York City' of the west, he would have to be part Saint and part dictator. We have seen the Saint side of Dr. McLoughlin."

CHAPTER 35

Overland to Oregon City by the Falls

The boys and I left The Dalles on October 27,1843, traveling almost due west. We camped the first night on Mosier Creek, having made only about ten miles. The grass was sparse until we reached Hood River. Within a very short distance, we left the pine and oak country and entered a towering forest of fir and hemlock. This change in vegetation occurred in the distance of a half a mile. It was just like some giant had drawn a line in the soil, and said to the world, the pine on that side, the fir on this side, but we knew we were crossing the divide of the Cascade Mountains. We knew that the clouds from the Pacific Ocean had to climb to get over the mountains and as the clouds rose they cooled down and became heavy with moisture and dumped the moisture on the west slopes of the Cascades. The fir trees thrive on the west side and the pine on the east.

As if on cue, a drizzle of cold rain greeted us, and followed us for most of our journey to Oregon City. We now had plenty of good grass in meadows and many small springs and creeks with water for the animals. Traveling through the forest was difficult due to the fallen logs, some as thick as six feet. The old dead and down trees had a layer of moss four inches thick over it, which made for very slippery footing. We didn't push the cattle, but allowed them to pick their route through the downed trees, but this allowed the loose cattle to spread out, and made herding them more difficult.

We crossed the Sandy River and eventually came to the Clackamas River and we knew we were not far from the Willamette. A day more and the Willamette River was seen for the first time. We came out on a high basalt bluff above the river. We could not see the falls because of a slight turn in the river, but we could hear it. A traveler shared with us that there was an easy route down off the bluff about five miles up stream and the trail led directly into Oregon City. We arrived at Oregon City November 5, ten days after we had left The Dalles and we had not lost an animal.

Below us on the flats above the falls nestled Oregon City. It seems that Dr. McLoughlin had filed a claim for the land around the falls in 1828. He was hedging his bets that England would eventually claim the land north of the Columbia where Fort Vancouver is located, but he thought there was a good chance that America would get the land south of the mighty river, and he thought it would be wise to have a foot in both camps. With the "Great Migration of 1843," McLoughlin privately conceded, that, "These Americans will probably win this wilderness struggle." In any case McLoughlin platted the east side of the river, at the falls, into blocks and lots and the town began to grow. He built a millrace for a gristmill, and a sawmill, and built a big house for him and his wife. Soon others came and by the time we arrived in 1843, there were approximately 500 white people and a sizeable Indian population living in, or near, Oregon City. There were two other gristmills and sawmills, four stores, two taverns, a hatter, a tanner, a physician, three lawyers, a printing office which printed a newspaper, a lathing machine and a brickyard. The center of social life was the new Methodist church and the two taverns.

John Brooks with the women and children, preceded us into Oregon City by only a day. Their last ten days was far more enjoyable than ours.

We had a joyous reunion of the family. We heard all about "the red apples and British gentlemen". The "Overlanders" had little to tell.

"Mary, the last ten days is the longest we have been apart since the Mormon War," I reminded her.

"Don't you think I know that?" she said.

CHAPTER 36

The Willamette Valley—Home at Last

Oregon City was too expensive to stay long and besides, the middle Willamette Valley was beckoning us on. We reassembled the wagons and repacked our belongings and were off down the east side of the Willamette River. We camped the first night where a little river enters the Willamette. Our next camp was at the tiny settlement called Champoeg. (Pronounced sham-poo-e). Wharfs were being built to receive the expected wheat harvest from the valley next summer. Most of the residents were French Canadian ex-employees of the Hudson's Bay Company. When a man had served his contracted time with the Hudson's Bay Company, they would return the worker to his home, or to wherever he had signed on. Most of their homes had been in Quebec but many of them had married Native women and had families here in the Oregon Territory. They all could see the end to the fur trade coming, but they also saw the potential in the land and wanted to be a part of it. Many of them lived on little farms nearby, at a place that became known as French Prairie.

Politics, at Champoeg, was the center of most conversations and had to be discussed before other matters were talked about. We were most interested in getting opinions about the best areas to locate, but most of the local people wanted to talk about the recent organizational meetings they had attended. Apparently much had happened since we left Missouri six months ago. In respect to the questions about where to locate we got the distinct impression that "any place is good, and some places are *really* good" and, "If you aren't satisfied at first, try another place."

But this is not to say, that area politics wasn't of interest to the Keizurs, because it was. Piecing the stories together we learned that two years previously in 1841 a settler by the name of Ewing Young had died, leaving a sizeable estate of land and livestock, but with no known heirs. Jason Lee, of the Methodist Mission in Salem, called a New England style Town Hall meeting, to determine how to handle the property. The meeting quickly turned toward the need to form some type of government, with laws and rules, other than those dictated by the British through the Hudson's Bay Company.

A resolution was passed calling for "drafting a constitution and code of laws for the government of settlements south of the Columbia River". Jason Lee was elected President and Gustavis Hines, another Methodist minister, was elected Secretary.

In the spring of 1843, about the time we were leaving Independence, Missouri, a second meeting was called here at Champoeg. The meeting was billed to develop a mutual plan to control the wolves, bears, and mountain lions that were menacing the settler's livestock.

"I do not like wolves," Mary stated emphatically. "If I had known that wolves were so plentiful I may have looked Texas over more carefully. I do not like wolves."

They called these meetings "The Wolf Meetings" but the discussions soon turned to the topic of establishing a government. The meeting was carried over for the next day, which gave the French Canadians living nearby at French Prairie, at the urging of several Catholic priests, time to come into the meeting. The ex-Hudson's Bay men, many of them still loyal to The Company, wanted to see what the Americans were up to.

The Americans argued in favor of forming a government and the French Canadians held out for the status quo. The pros and cons were argued with passion.

Finally, a big black haired ex-mountain man by the name of Joe Meek stood up and said, "We have heard the arguments, pro and con, go around the barn and back, several times. It is time to vote." Whereupon he picked up a stick and drew a line in the Champoeg dust. "All in favor of organizing, follow me."

Now this is where the story really gets interesting. There were 102 men in attendance and almost evenly split between the Americans and the ex-Company men. Forty-nine men plus Joe Meek stepped over the line. Slowly, but with conviction, two French Canadians stepped over the line making the vote 52 in favor and 50 against starting a government.

"If only one of the Frenchmen had come over, it would have been a tie and the resolution would have lost," John Brooks observed.

"According to the story, the priests did not vote and their vote would have made the difference," Mary Louise pointed out.

"Did the Methodist ministers, the counter part to the Catholic priests, vote?" Mary asked.

"Indeed they did," our informant replied.

"The first thing was to draw up a 'Bill of Rights'. The key items are 'Freedom of religion; the right to a jury trial; a ban on slavery; a provision for taxes which could be paid in wheat or cattle; and we enacted our own 'land law'".

"We have at least eight female slaves with the 'Great Migration'. What about them?" Reeda asked.

"Slavery is banned, that's all I know," our informant said.

"Explain the Land Law that was enacted, if you would," Joe suggested.

"Well, we pattern our new land law after the Linn Bill that Senator Linn of Missouri was pushing through Congress. However, we have learned only this last month that his Bill died in the House of Representatives. Senator Linn has vowed to try again however."

"What is the 'new law'?" Joe persisted.

"Each man will be allotted one square mile, in other words 640 acres, provided he stake the corners and build a cabin on the land within six months from the time he files his claim. Another meeting has been called for after the New Year, in Oregon City. I would plan to attend if I were you."

"You can be sure that the Keizurs will be there," I said.

We left Champoeg early the next morning with all the "new" information to think about. We were anxious to find and claim our square mile. We had not gone many miles south following the river when William Athey, a fellow emigrant, who had heard us coming, hailed us. He was excited and pleased to see us. William was a furniture maker and a farmer only about twenty-five years old. He insisted that we stay at his camp overnight.

"I have found my land to claim," he said. "I will claim that island right in the middle of the Willamette River. There are more than 640 acres. Why don't you claim the rest of the island and we would be neighbors. I have never seen such rich soil and the soil is over four feet deep. It will grow orchard stock without limit. We have named the island Grand Island."

"It does look rich, but I think we will go a little further upstream," I said, "but we will still be neighbors."

We continued on our way after a nice visit. Sam Penter was the first to speak, "It is certainly rich soil, but did you notice the debris up in the cottonwood trees about twelve feet off the ground?"

I had seen the brush and debris caught in the lower limbs of the cottonwood trees. "The entire island has been submerged and within the last few years, by the flooding river. Perhaps William could crop the island for many years before the next flood, but sooner or later everything but the huge ring of cottonwood trees on Grand Island, will be swept away in floods."

Another few miles and we saw Hiram Simkins waving to us from across the west side of the river. We could see the smoke from his campsite rising through the tall fir trees. Here the river had cut a channel and Hiram was standing on a little bluff overlooking the stream.

"This is fun," Reeda said, "to see all our old friends finding their places to carve out their farms."

"Hiram has a prime location it would appear. He will have some timber to clear before he can plant, but at the same time he will have plenty of timber for his cabin and his fences. He is young and he will do fine," I predicted.

A few miles further and we met the Daniel Matheny group. I say group because there are fifteen members in the family. He pointed out how both sides of the river had a low approach to the water. "We plan to claim both sides of the river. I haven't heard any rule against that. We will build a ferry and have it in operation by the time the crops on the west side are harvested. All the produce will have to cross to the east side to get to the landing at Champoeg and our ferry will have the strategic location for that. This is a natural crossing spot".

"You have a good plan. Just keep your rates reasonable and you will prosper," I commented.

Daniel informed us that the Applegates had gone through and he thought they weren't too far away. "We have seen freshly cut brush, floating past in the river so someone up stream is already clearing brush and I think it is the Applegates."

"How could the Applegates and these other emigrants get so far ahead of us?" Joe Hess wanted to know.

"I imagine they sent riders ahead to scout out the area," I said.

"Should we do that too? All the good land will be taken if we don't hurry," Joe worried.

Mary Louise said to her worried husband, "A shortage of good farmland in this valley is not going to be a problem. You could shut your eyes and drive stakes and not go wrong. It makes me immensely happy to see our friends that we labored with for six months, find their dreams, and we will find ours. There is no reason to be apprehensive. There appears to be enough land to go around in Oregon."

It wasn't until our meeting with the Mathenys that we learned of the terrible tragedy of the Applegate family. One of their rafts got caught in a cross current in some rapids and flipped over, coming down the Columbia

River. The drowning of Edward Applegate, Jesse's ten year old son, and Warren Applegate, Lindsay's nine year old son, was almost more than the Applegate brothers could bear. The accident happened in full view of the rest of the family. But they were totally helpless to assist. All three brothers were about to dive into the water in an attempt to save the boys when their women demanded, "Men stay by your oars".

The story of sheer heroism on the part of Alexander McClellan in trying to save the boys and surrendering his own life in the attempt, will never be forgotten. Uncle Mac, as McClellan was known to all the Applegate children, was 70 years old, and one of the oldest emigrants in the Oregon Emigration Company. Their bodies were never found.

The Applegate brothers vowed they would find another route to Oregon so future emigrants would not have to come down the "terrible Columbia".

"They almost made it to the Willamette Valley. It is so sad." Mary lamented.

Another sad story reached us having to do with Corny Stringer. After they recuperated with us in Walla Walla for a few days, Mrs. Eyers and the three girls returned to the Whitman Mission where they made arrangements to stay until the next spring when they planned to come to the Willamette Valley, but Corny made arrangements to come down the river on an emigrant's improvised boat. As he was boarding the boat he fell into the Columbia River, panicked, and drowned. Just think what that man had been through, only to lose it all in the final days of his journey.

The Applegates stayed the winter of 1843-44 at Mission Bottom on the Willamette River in the three old abandoned mission buildings left by Jason and Daniel Lee when the Lees moved their operation up stream to Mill Creek, at Chemaketa, or Salem.

We stopped at the old Mission site on our journey from Oregon City up the Willamette River.

We were not received as graciously as we had thought we might. The Applegates were concerned that we might ask to share their mission buildings, and they were already very crowded, and generally not in a good physical or mental state. But when we reassured them, that we were going further up the river and would not be staying, they did seem to be restored to their old demeanor of friendliness. It frankly hurt us a little, because we knew that if the tables had been turned, they would have been invited to share whatever we had. But our family was all intact. We didn't lose two sons as they had. We agreed among ourselves that considerable allowance should be made for that.

We found the Willamette Valley all that we had hoped and dreamed of. We pushed past the Applegates at Mission Bottom and continued up stream for about five more miles. Up stream is going south. This took a little getting used to. Most rivers in America flow east, west or south but the Willamette River flows north where it meets the Columbia, which of course flows west. The Willamette River is one of the few rivers in America that flows north. The river would be our major transportation link to the markets and we knew we wanted land that had access to this wonderful natural feature.

We found an excellent fording place just a few miles south of Mission Bottom. The river widened out slightly and ran over a gravel bar making a pleasant little ripple in the river. We called it "The Rapids", but that is a bit of a misnomer, it was more like a ripple in an otherwise smooth running stretch of clear water. We crossed the Willamette easily at these "Rapids" and set up our winter camp on the west side of the river. We knew almost intuitively that our permanent home would be back on the east side. But we needed to have time to scout the area to come up with the best land possible.

On our second night on the west side of the Willamette River Mary cooked a huge apple cobbler that she called her apple "crunch" because it scorched a bit over the open fire. She used delicious Hudson's Bay apples. We all sat around a big warming fire waiting with our tin plates for our serving of the apple dish.

Mary Keizur said, "Could I have everyone's attention please. I have a reminder for you."

"Mary, we said Grace. Could you serve the apple crunch now?" I asked.

"The apple crunch can wait. This won't take long. When we left Sugar Creek, Missouri six months ago, we divided our resources and put half in a recessed box in the floor of each wagon."

"Yes, yes, we all know that," I said tapping my tin plate.

Mary continued, "We did that so if we lost a wagon in a river crossing we would not lose everything."

"Yes, yes. That was your plan Mary, and it was a good one. Fortunately we didn't lose either wagon. Now, before those apples completely burn up...," I implored, tapping my tin plate a little louder and joined by a chorus of light tapping around the fire.

"But there was more to the plan," Mary ignored the drumming of fingers on tin. "You remember that I gave each of you, excluding only the very youngest, a twenty dollar gold piece to put in your pocket to carry to Oregon. Remember how I cautioned the children not to lose their gold piece? And remember that I said I would collect the coins again once we got to Oregon? Well, we are here! By the Grace of God we all made it to Oregon. So.."

"Does anyone remember that?" I asked.

"I certainly don't."

"I think I lost mine in the Snake River."

"I don't think I was there when you passed out the gold pieces."

"I thought you said something about a Christmas gift."

"Are you positive it was twenty dollars? I thought it was a ten dollar coin."

"This is a vile conspiracy," Mary Keizur whined.

"Grandma, I still have mine that you can have back," Little Mary Jane Hess said, putting a bright gold coin into her Grandmother's hand.

"And you, my dear, shall have an ample helping of my apple crunch. And if any one else wants any, it will cost you one gold twenty dollar piece right here in my hand."

"This is nothing short of extortion," I complained. "But I have just found a gold coin in the bottom of my pocket."

Very soon Mary Keizur had a stack of shiny gold coins and we all had a serving of delicious apple crunch.

We built a three-sided log shelter using our worn wagon canvas as the roof, and we added a lean-to shed off the backside. It was not the best of arrangements, but we knew we could survive. Fortunately, the winter of 1843-44 was not very severe. We had two small snowstorms, which deposited perhaps three inches of snow, but it did rain, and rain, and rain.

We spent our time scouting the terrain for our new farm; hunting for game which was plentiful; moving the cattle from one small meadow to another; and fending off the wolves. We were amazed that the grass was green all winter long. We had never known that before. And we were also amazed at the number of wolves and how aggressive they were.

As the river dropped slightly after the spring runoff, we moved back across the Rapids to the east side of the river. This was to be our home, our claim. Soon a small area was cleared for our log house, at a spot where we could view the beautiful Willamette River. Shortly after the cornerstones were in place and the first of the logs were notched, ten pink rose cuttings were planted. All ten Keizur children survived the ordeals on the trail to Oregon and so did ten tiny rose cuttings. And very important to Mary and the entire Keizur family, the family Bible was all intact, although water stained.

Joe Hess and Mary Louise, with their five children, found a place in an area called Newberg and left to go there. We were sorry to have them leave but they wanted to branch out on their own. The place they picked was on a cold running spring, just right for a still set-up, I suspect, but I didn't share that thought with Mary.

Our journey of over 2000 miles is over and we are tired. We lost Gabe to California and Kenny to the Hudson's Bay Company, but we gained baby Tilman, Reeda and John's first child.

"Thomas, you said in the beginning that you would get us all to Oregon and you did. You brought your five sons and five daughters along with their husbands and our grandchildren to Oregon safely," Mary commented.

"We have come a long way from North Carolina. If I had known all the hardships you and the children would have to endure, I am not sure I would have been up to putting everyone through it." I said.

"Did you ever think we were too old for this? Did you ever think about turning around and going back?"

"Only once, Mary."

"When was that?"

"When we rolled out of Sugar Creek, Missouri, that first morning and I thought, *it's a long way to Oregon.*"

THE END

WINNING THE WEST—PETTICOAT PERSPECTIVE

By Norma Benson

How often do we give our thanks
For those who've trod before
To make this land a better place
Some came from shore to shore.

The common call was "Westward Ho"
In eighteen forty-one
For men it was excitement pure
For ladies, 'twas not fun.

I sometimes think of those dear souls
Through sickness, death and weather
Who staked their claims in this great land
Of which, there is none better.

They left their homes first sign of spring
To start their westward move
At times they drove ten miles per day
Their mettle, they did prove.

No pampering the westward gals
Her diaries do relate
For many, it was not their choice
For MAN decided fate.

She gathered wood and buff'lo chips
Then baked and cooked the meal
She washed the clothes and drove the team
Gave birth along the trail.

She had to be a hardy soul
No weakling could survive
At times there was no food at all
No stamps to subsidize.

She traded with the Indians
Some friendly, some were not
She struggled mile on weary mile
With only what she brought

They traveled on for months and months
They thought 'twould be but four
They found it took from six to eight
And winter came before.

They rode in wagons without springs
Through weather of all kinds
The canvas top did not protect
From heat and snow and rain.

The diaries show the graves they left
In lonely emigration
The loss of life of westward move
Beyond our comprehension.

They suffered from the cholera
From hunger and from fear
From dysentery and the flu
And death was always near.

The modern gal would wear her slacks
To cross this mighty nation
She'd stop wherever she did choose
At modern service stations.

Courageous were our western gals
Long skirts were what she wore
She trudged along through mud and dust
No privacy for her.

She bore the hardships of those times
Each day by weary day
She longed for friends and family
Remembering to pray.

They mostly came for homesteading
To claim it for the states
Our song could be : "God Save the Queen"
Let us appreciate.

They later came in search of gold
Their fortunes, they did seek
This land could now belong to Spain
And we'd be saying "Si"

If this is in your heritage
Or even if it's not
Thank God for faith of pioneers
Who gave us what we've got.

A CAPSULAR HISTORY OF OREGON (1579-1850)

1579   Sir Francis Drake visits Oregon (allegedly)

1765   First use of the word "Ouragon" in Maj. Robert Rogers' *Petition to Explore the American West.*

1775   Capt. Bruno Heceta sees mouth of the Columbia and names it Rio San Roque

1778   Capt. James Cook makes landfall at Cape Foulweather

1779   Jonathan Carver's book refers to the "River Oregon"

1792   Capt. Robert Gray enters and names the Columbia River (After his ship the Columbia)

1803   Louisiana Purchase extends the United States to the Rocky Mountains

1804   President Jefferson dispatches Lewis & Clark Expedition

1805   Lewis & Clark explores Snake and Columbia Rivers and establishes Fort Clatsop

1806   Lewis & Clark Expedition returns to the United States

1811   Pacific Fur Company establishes Fort Astoria

1812   Astorians discover the South Pass (going west to east) later route of the Oregon Trail

1813   Astorian William Wallace establishes Fort Wallace (in present City of Keizer)

1814   Treaty of Ghent resolves the war of 1812 between Britain and United States

1817   William Cullen Bryant refers to "Oregon" in poem *Thanatopsis* U S. and Great Britain agree to "joint occupancy" of Oregon (ten year treaty)

1819   Adams/Onis Treaty cedes Spain's discovery rights north of 43 degrees to the United States (California/Oregon border)

1824   U.S. and Russia agree to 54-40 degrees as southern boundary of Russian America (southern tip of Queen Charlotte's Islands)

1824   Dr. John McLoughlin begins tenure as Chief Factor for Hudson's Bay Company

1825   Hudson's Bay Company builds Fort Vancouver

1827   U.S. and Great Britain agree to indefinite "joint occupancy"

1829   Dr. John McLoughlin establishes claim at Willamette Falls (Oregon City)

1830   Fever pandemic begins calamitous death toll of Indians (estimated 90% Mortality)

1832   Newspapers report four Indians from the Pacific Northwest in St. Louis in search of the Bible

1833   First school opens at Fort Vancouver

1834   Jason Lee establishes Methodist Mission near Wheatland on the Willamette

1836 Whitman-Spalding mission parties arrive overland via what was to become The Oregon Trail (Including Narcissa Whitman and Eliza Spalding). Washington Irving publishes *Astoria*

1837 Priests Blanchet and Demers arrive overland from Canada

1839 Catholics establish mission at St Paul

1840 Ewing Young's death leads to public meeting to establish laws

1842 Methodist establishes Indian school north of Salem (forerunner of Willamette University)

1843 First large migration of over 900 emigrants arrive overland (via what would become the Oregon Trail)
Lt. John C. Fremont makes reconnaissance of the Oregon Trail
"Wolf Meetings" lead to Provisional Government

1846 Applegate Trail opens as alternative route to the Oregon Trail

1846 Oregon Treaty affirms U.S. sovereignty to Pacific Northwest

1847 Cayuse Indians attack Whitman Mission

1848 Organic Act creates Oregon Territory
James Marshall in California discovers gold

1850 Congress passes Oregon Donation Land Act

WHAT BECAME OF.......

The following is a capsule of the lives of some of the emigrants of 1843, after they reached the end of the trail to Oregon. This is by no means a comprehensive listing of their accomplishments.

The emigrants of '43 immediately became involved in all civic affairs of their new home. For example, of the eleven members of the Oregon Provisional Government, seven had emigrated in '43. Of the original 21 members of the Oregon Rangers (the first military organization in the Oregon Territory), twelve were emigrants of '43 and three of that number were Keizurs.

In this body of pioneers we find a future candidate for the Presidency of the United states, governors, legislators, founders of cities, military veterans, doctors, lawyers, educators, heroes all.

Applegate, Charles—The oldest of the Applegate brothers. He farmed most of his life near Yoncalla, Oregon. He and his wife Melinda emigrated with eight children and had eight more in Oregon for a total of sixteen offspring. He was not involved with his brothers, Jesse and Lindsay in establishing "the southern route". He died at Yoncalla in 1879 at the age of 73.

Applegate, Jesse Grant—The youngest of the Applegate brothers. He ranched near Yoncalla, Oregon and became known as "The sage of Yoncalla". Jesse and his brother Lindsay worked with Levi Scott to establish a southern route through the Cascade Mountains. This route is now called "the Applegate Trail". Jesse and his wife Cynthia emigrated with six children and had six more after reaching Oregon, for a total of twelve off-spring. Jesse died at Yoncalla, Oregon in 1888 at the age of 77.

Applegate, Lindsay—The middle brother by age. He moved to Yoncalla, Oregon with his brothers, but later moved to Jackson County, Oregon where he established a toll road over the Siskiyou Mountains. He joined his brother Jesse and Levi Scott in opening up "the southern route". He served with General Lane; served as a special Indian Agent; raised a company of volunteers in the Rogue River Indian War; he was elected to the Oregon State Legislature, and served as the Indian Agent at Klamath Falls. He emigrated with his wife Elizabeth and six children. They had seven more children in Oregon for a total of thirteen offspring. Lindsay died in Jackson County, Oregon in 1892 at the age of 84. He was the last of the Applegate brothers to die.

Athey, William—Established a claim on Grand Island in the middle of the Willamette River near Dayton, Oregon. He was flooded out in the great flood of 1861. He died in 1897 at the age of 79.

Beagle, William—First settled at Linnton where West Linn, Oregon is today. He moved to Pendleton, Oregon where he was on the first Town Council. He died at Pendleton in 1887 at the age of 79.

Beale, George Polk—He was the first person hung in Salem, Oregon, Marion County, for the murder for money, of Daniel Delaney another emigrant of '43. Over forty fellow emigrants of '43 gathered to watch the hanging "and to picnic". No one would claim the body, so Daniel Waldo, another emigrant of '43 buried him on his claim at what is now known as Waldo Hills. Beale was 41 years old at the time of his hanging in 1865.

Burnett, Peter Hardman—He laid out the town of Linnton in 1843-44. When gold was discovered in California in 1848, he organized a group of Oregonians called "The Californian Party" of over 200 people, many of them emigrants of '43, to go to the gold fields. He became the first American Governor of California. He died in 1895 at the age of 88.

Cason, Tendall Carr—Settled at Oregon City. Operated a toll bridge over the Clackamas River. He served in the Territorial Legislature representing Clackamas County. He died in 1860 at the age of 61.

Chiles, Joseph Ballinger—Originally emigrated in 1841 with the Birdwell/Bartleson Party to California. He returned east to lead the "Chiles Party" to California. They traveled with the '43 wagon train to Fort Hall, where they took the California cutoff. He was a veteran of the Florida Indian War. He made a total of seven trail blazing trips from the east to the west. He settled in Chiles Valley, California (near Napa Valley). On one of his trips over the Sierra Nevada Mountains he brought a millstone, which he used for years in a gristmill he constructed. The millstone is now on display at the capitol in Sacramento, California. Because he established the gristmill, the Mexican Governor granted him 42 square miles of land (seven leagues). He led one of the first wagon trains over the Carson Pass in 1848; he pioneered the Humbolt Sink cut-off (known as the "forty mile desert") a popular route for the gold seekers of '49. He was one of the founders of Yolo, County, California where he established a ferry business.

Delany, Daniel Sr.—Became a prominent farmer in the Turner, Oregon area. He brought his slave Rachel with him to Oregon. His murder resulted in the first hanging in Marion County, Oregon. He died near Turner in 1865 at the age of 70.

Dement, William C.—He settled in Clackamas County, Oregon. He was the founder of the Oregon City Woolen Mill and the Oregon City Railroad. He was elected Sheriff in 1852. He died at Oregon City in 1865 at the age of 42.

Ford, Nineveh—(no relation to John or Nimrod Ford) Served in two Indian Wars, served three terms in the U.S. Congress representing Oregon. He fathered eleven children. He and T.D. Keizur brought the first wagons into The Dalles, Oregon. He died at Walla Walla, Washington in 1897 at the age of 82.

Garrison, Joseph McCullumn—Claimed part of the old Jason Lee Mission land in Mission Bottom. Across the Willamette River was the land claimed by Daniel Matheny. Joseph was elected to the Provisional Government representing Champoeg County. He served in the Cayuse Indian War at the rank of Captain. He became the Superintendent of Schools for The Dalles. He suffered a paralytic stroke and died in The Dalles in 1884 at the age of 71. His wife, Mary survived him by 24 years. They had six children.

Gilmore, Samuel Mathison—Served in the first elected Legislature of the State of Oregon. He was a delegate to the first Washington Territorial Constitution Convention. He was an active advocate for "Indian Rights". He died in Sherman County, Oregon in 1893 at the age of 78. Sam and Martha celebrated over fifty years of marriage.

Fremont, John Charles—After reaching Fort Vancouver in 1843, he led a party to Mt. St. Helens to map it. The mountain had been seen from Fort Vancouver, erupting on December 12, 1842. Fremont continued his exploration route from Oregon into California where he was heavily involved in the Bear Flag Revolt, which established California as a Republic.

Fremont became military Governor of California in 1847. He was the first U.S. Senator from California. He was the first Republican candidate for the U.S. presidency but President Buchanan defeated him. He was commissioned Major General in the Union Army by President Lincoln but later sacked by Lincoln for incompetence.

Fremont was Governor of the Arizona Territory from 1878 to 1881. Fremont died penniless in a New York hotel in 1890 at the age of 77.

Hembree, Absalom and his brother Joel—Settled in Yamhill County where they started the town of McMinnville, Oregon, which they named after their hometown of McMinnville, Tennessee. Absalom served as Captain in the Yakima Indian War. He was killed and scalped in 1856 at the age of 42.

Hembree, James—The oldest son of Joel Hembree married Melinda Millican (also of '43). Melinda promised her mother she would not get married before she was thirteen. Melinda kept the promise, but married one week after her thirteenth birthday.

They were married over seventy years. Melinda died in 1916 at the age of 84 and James died in 1919 at the age of 92.

Long, John Edwin—Was elected Territorial Clerk of the Provisional Government.

Looney, Jesse—Emigrated with his wife and nine children. Jesse was a first cousin to President Andrew Johnson.

Lovejoy, Asa—Made the winter ride east with Dr. Marcus Whitman and returned west in the emigration of '43. He met Elizabeth McGary on the trail and later married her.

Martin, William—During the Cayuse Indian War he mustered a company of volunteers from Yamhill and Tualatin counties. He served as Captain of the Company. Later he was Sheriff of Umatilla County. He was a very successful gold miner in the Canyon City area.

Matheny, Daniel Sr, and Henry—Married the Cooper sisters Mary and

Rachel. The Mathenys built and operated a ferry across the Willamette River at Wheatland. This ferry site has been in continuous use for over 150 years. Daniel Sr. died in 1872 at the age of 79. Henry died in 1849 in the gold fields of California of "camp fever". He was 49 years old.

McCarver, Morton Mathew—Founded the town of Linnton with Peter Burnett. He was a member of the Legislative Committee Government of Oregon. Managed the platting of Sacramento, California. He was a member of the Constitutional Convention for the State of California. He served as Commissary General during the Rogue River and Yakima Indian Wars. He founded the city of Tacoma, Washington and the town of Lincoln (part of Portland). He died in 1871 at the age of 64.

McLane, John Burch—Settled in Marion County, Oregon. He engaged in flour milling. He volunteered in the Cayuse Indian War and he was the first postmaster for Salem, Oregon.

Nesmith, James Willis—Volunteered in the Cayuse, Rogue River, and Yakima Indian Wars. He was elected to the U.S. Senate. He settled at Derry in Polk County. He died in 1885 at the age of 65.

Newby, William Thompson—He and his wife Sarah nearly drowned when their boat capsized in the Columbia. He founded the town of Mc-Minnville in Yamhill County. He built a gristmill and a store there. He served as a State Senator. He died in 1884 at the age of 63.

Owens, Thomas A.—Arrived in Oregon with fifty cents but became wealthy in ten years. He and his neighbors built a schooner and shipped Oregon produce to the California gold fields. He died in 1873 at the age of 65.

Owens, Bethenia Angeline—Daughter of Thomas. She was three years old in '43. She attended medical school in Philadelphia and became a pioneer woman physician in early Oregon. She established her own railroad station near Astoria. She was active for temperance laws and women's suffrage. She died in 1926 at the age of 86.

Reading, Pierson Barton—Took the California cut-off with the Chiles Party. He was in charge of Sutter's Fort when Sutter was gone. Redding California was named after him.

Shively, John M—Was a surveyor. He was commissioned by Dr. John McLaughlin to lay out the town of Oregon City. He founded the city of Astoria where he took his land claim. He died at Astoria in 1894 at the age of 90.

Smith, Isaac W.—Served in the Oregon State Legislature.

Stewart, Peter—Was a member of the Executive Committee of the Oregon Provisional Government. He died in 1900 at the age of 91.

Straight, Hiram A.—Was foreman of the jury during the Whitman massacre trial. The verdict was to hang the four Cayuse Indians that were on trial. He served in the Territorial Legislature.

Sticcus—The loyal Indian guide, who led the emigrants through the Blue Mountains in 1843, played various roles in the Indian conflicts. Sticcus was a friend of the Whitmans and warned Rev. Spalding of the pending danger to the Whitmans, but either the message never got through, or Whitman discounted the warning.

Sticcus served as an emissary to the "Volunteer" army on behalf of the Cayuse Indians, asking what it would take to end the Cayuse conflict? He was told that only the surrender of the Whitman murderers could end the war. Sticcus could not recommend that action to his fellow Cayuse and advised them to disperse into the mountains, which they did. Although it was thought that Sticcus was not directly involved in the massacre of the Whitmans, it was felt, that he had pre-knowledge that it was going to occur.

Whitman, Marcus—In November, 1847 Marcus Whitman and Narcissa, along with fifteen others, were massacred by the Cayuse Indians and forty seven women and children were taken hostage. The Mission, which served as a haven for many emigrants, was burned to the ground. These events precipitated the Cayuse Indian War. Many of the emigrants of 1843 served in the Volunteer Army including three Keizur men.

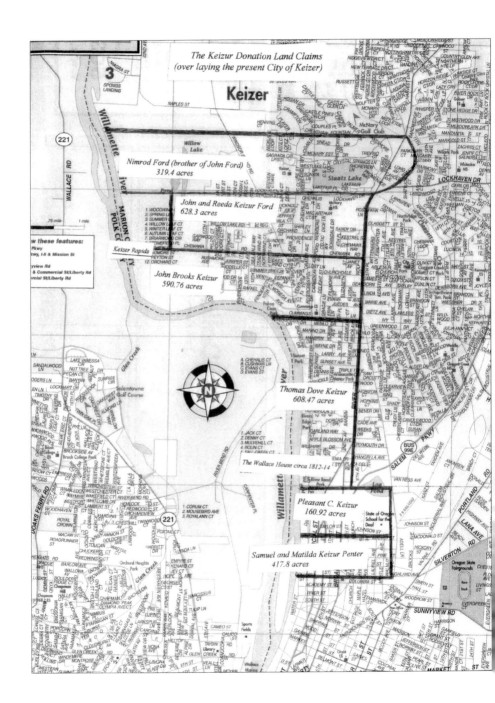

The Keizur Donation Land Claims
(over laying the present City of Keizer)

Keizer

Nimrod Ford (brother of John Ford)
319.4 acres

John and Reeda Keizur Ford
628.3 acres

Keizur Rapids

John Brooks Keizur
590.76 acres

Thomas Dove Keizur
608.47 acres

The Wallace House circa 1812-14

Pleasant C. Keizur
160.92 acres

Samuel and Matilda Keizur Penter
417.8 acres

AND WHAT ABOUT THE KEIZURS ?

After a difficult winter on the west side of the Willamette River, the Keizurs re-crossed the river at the rapids that would bear their name. On the East side the Keizurs took up land claims under the Land Act of the Provisional Government. These claims were later filed under the Donation Land Act of 1850, although the claims may have been slightly modified. (see map)

To the north, Nimrod Ford, brother of John Ford, claimed 319.4 acres, which went from the river on the west to Trail Avenue on the east.

John Ford and Reeda Keizur Ford claimed the next area going south, consisting of 628.3 acres. Their claim did not extend all the way to the river on the west but did go to River Road on the east.

The next claim going south was that of John Brooks Keizur. He claimed 590.76 acres. John Brooks's claim was the first claim surveyed with "metes and bounds" in the Oregon Territory under the "new" Donation Land Act. River Road bound his claim on the east and the Willamette River to the west.

The next claim going south was that of Thomas Dove Keizur. He claimed 608.47 acres. His claim was bounded to the west by the Willamette River, at the location of The Keizur Rapids (Current site of the Keizer Rapids Regional Park) to River Road on the east. The north boundary, (adjacent to J.B. Keizur's claim) is now Cummings Lane. Cummings Lane was the first road cut from the river to River Road by the Keizurs.

Pleasant C. Keizur claimed the next piece of land going south. His claim was 160.92 acres. His claim was also bounded on the west by the river and extended eastward beyond Cherry Ave.

The final claim of the Keizur Clan was that of Samuel Penter and his wife Matilda Caroline Keizur Penter. Their claim consisted of 417.8 acres extending from the Willamette River on the west to beyond Cherry Avenue, in what is now North Salem.

All together the Keizurs and their affiliates claimed 2,725.65 acres, which included over two miles of frontage on the Willamette River. This entire area was known for years as "Keizur Bottoms", which is interesting, since very little of their land was actually "bottom land". The intersection of Chemawa and River Roads was known for years as Keizer Corners. The community incorporated in 1982 (138 years after the Keizurs settled there). The claims of the Keizurs covered most of the west side of the present City of Keizer.

Thomas Dove Keizur served two terms as a Legislator in the Provisional Government. He represented Champoeg District. He was elected Captain of the first military organization in The Oregon Territory. They were known as the Oregon Rangers. The Rangers was the forerunner of the Oregon National Guard. The Oregon National Guard claims T.D. Keizur as their founding father, because he was their first commander.

Thomas Dove Keizer planted the first apple orchard in the Willamette Valley.

Thomas Dove Keizur died in 1871 at the age of 78. His wife Mary Girley Keizur died in 1853 only ten years after reaching Oregon. The Keizurs had been married 40 years. Mary was 60 years old at the time of her death. Thomas survived Mary by eighteen years.

A foot note in Bancroft's *History of Oregon-Vol I, Chapter XV page 398* had this to say describing Thomas Dove Keizur, *"Mr. Kaiser seems to have been a representative western man: vigorous, courageous, frank, and independent."*

Mary Louise Keizur Hess and her husband Joseph brought five children with them to Oregon and had eight more after arriving in Oregon, for a total of 13 offspring.

The Hesses settled near Newberg, Oregon, where they became wealthy through land deals. They lost almost all of their holdings via a series of run-ins with the law caused, at least in part, by a still he was allegedly operating.

Joe Hess was killed in northern California in 1870. He was hit over the head with an axe "in a strange accident". He was 58 years old at the time of his death.

Mary Louise died in Newberg in 1903 at the age of 86. She survived Joe by 33 years.

Sarah Lucinda Keizur Corzine was widowed the year before they left for Oregon. Her daughter Mary Ann was only two years old when the Keizurs emigrated. Sarah married Joseph Patterson in 1845. Sarah met Joe Patterson on the trail to Oregon in 1843. They had one daughter they named Sarah. Sarah Lucinda died in Salem, Oregon in 1850 at the age of 32.

Matilda Caroline Keizur Penter had two sons at the time of the emigration. One son was born shortly before they left for Oregon. Matilda had a total of five children. The Penters were divorced in 1870. She died in Salem, Oregon.

John Brooks Keizur claimed the first claim under the Donation Land Act in the Oregon Territory. He served in the Oregon Rangers and in the Cayuse Indian War at the rank of First Sergeant. John and his wife, Mary had eight children. He died in Marion County, Oregon in 1870 of tuberculosis. He was 46 years old.

Beede Ann (Reeda) Keizur Ford was well known for her medical talent, although she had never had any formal medical training. Reeda's first born was the first child born on the trail to Oregon. He was named Tilman and became a well-respected lawyer. Tilman served two terms in the Oregon State Legislature.

Two of Reeda's daughters graduated from medical school and became distinguished early physicians in Oregon. Another daughter became a nurse. John and Reeda had nine children. Reeda died in Portland, Oregon in 1880 at the age of 55.

Pleasant Cicero Keizur served with the Oregon Rangers and was a Second Sergeant in the Cayuse Indian War. He and his wife Sarah had five children. He died in Salem, Oregon (before 1871) at about 43 years of age.

Francis Marion Keizur probably never married. He died some time after 1900.

Thomas Cullwell Keizur was a miner and a farmer. He and his wife Sarah had twelve children. He died near Cottage Grove, Oregon as the result of an accidental gunshot. He died in 1906 at the age of 73.

Elizabeth Jane Keizur Cornell and Hayden Cornell had five children. She died in Salem, Oregon in 1911 at the age of 76. She was the last of the emigrating family of Keizurs to pass away.

William Henry Harrison Keizur was only four years old when the family emigrated to Oregon. He and his wife, Mary, had two children. He died in Idaho.

DONATION LAND CLAIM ACT OF 1850

The Keizurs and most of the emigrants of 1843 left Independence, Missouri with the assurance that there would be "free" land in Oregon. They had reason to feel optimistic. Senator Linn, the powerful Senator from Missouri, had been successful in getting a Land Act through the Senate. The emigrants had every reason to believe that it would also pass the House of Representatives. While the Keizurs were on the trail to Oregon, and unbeknownst to them, the proposed law failed in the House. They did not hear of this turn of events until they reached Champoeg, nearly at the end of their journey.

The newly formed Provisional Government of Oregon passed their own Land Laws, also while the Keizurs were on the trail to Oregon. Things were spinning fast. The Provisional Government passed their own laws because they were not sure when or if Congress would finally pass a Land Act, and they wisely wanted to restrict land speculation, such as they experienced in Tennessee, Texas, Ohio, and about every place public land was opened up for settlers.

The Donation Land Claim Act, usually just called, the Donation Land Act, was finally passed, but not until 1850, seven years after the Keizurs had arrived in the Willamette Valley. The law was finally passed primarily due to the efforts of Samuel R. Thurston, the Oregon Territorial delegate to Congress. The Donation Land Act was signed into law by President Fillmore on September 29,1850. This was arguably, the most important action, of Fillmore's Administration.

The Donation Land Act was a historic law for many reasons. The purpose was intended to promote homestead settlement in the Oregon Territory (comprising of the present day states of Washington, Oregon, Idaho and part of Montana). The law makers wanted to reward the early emigrants that led the way, such as the Keizurs, and whom they felt put the "American boots on the ground" that helped resolve the question of sovereignty between England and America in the treaty of 1846. And at the same time they wanted more pioneers to be encouraged to take the gamble represented by the Oregon Trail.

The law "granted" 320 acres (free) to every unmarried white male citizen eighteen or older and 640 acres to every married couple, arriving in the Oregon Territory before December 1, 1850, but half that amount of land if the pioneer arrived after that date. Thus the Keizur family and all the emigrants in the "Great Migration" of 1843 were eligible for the greater amount of land. Another interesting aspect of this law was that in the case of a married couple, the wife owned half the claim in her own name. This law was one of the first to allow married women to own and hold property in the United States. Claimants were required to live on the land and cultivate it for four years to own it outright.

Several unintended consequences occurred. For example, girls twelve and thirteen, and even younger, were suddenly being proposed to and married. "Half-blood" native Americans were also eligible, which enabled the offspring of many French Canadians to claim land if they "declared for citizenship." Indian women marrying white men were eligible for half their husband's land, which meant that many Indian women owned land whereas male Indians could not.

A total of 7,437 claims were patented under the law until its expiration date on December 1, 1855. But the law was considered so successful in accomplishing its goals that the so called Homestead Act of 1862 was patterned somewhat after it for the purpose of settling the Great Plains states. The Homestead Act also applied to Oregon.

Order form for books
By Jerry McGee

Name_____

Address_____

Phone #_____

For:

Whiskey Riley $14.95
The Lewis River Highscalers and the Dam Kids $14.95
Follow the River $14.95
Lost and Found $14.95
It's a Long Way to Oregon $16.

Please include $2.50 per book for shipping and handling

Esjay Press
1030 Ridgepoint St. N.E.
Keizer, Oregon 97303-1774
Ph# 1-503-390-2519
e-mail address: mcgee_jerry @msn.com

Note: Please indicate if you want the books autographed
and to whom.